CLAIMING
GRACE

DISCOVER OTHER TITLES BY SUSAN STOKER

Ace Security Series

Claiming Grace

Claiming Alexis (July 2017)

Claiming Bailey (TBA)

Unsung Heroes: Delta Force

Rescuing Rayne

Assisting Aimee (novella) *losely tied to DF*

Rescuing Emily

Rescuing Harley

Marrying Emily

Rescuing Kassie (May 2017)

Rescuing Bryn (Nov 2017)

Rescuing Casey (TBA)

Rescuing Wendy (TBA)

Rescuing Mary (TBA)

Badge of Honor: Texas Heroes Series

Justice for Mackenzie

Justice for Mickie

Justice for Corrie

Justice for Laine (novella)

Shelter for Elizabeth

Justice for Boone

Shelter for Adeline

Shelter for Sophie (Aug 2017)

Justice for Erin (Oct 2017)

Justice for Milena (TBA)

Shelter for Blythe (TBA)

Justice for Hope (TBA)

Shelter for Quinn (TBA)

Shelter for Koren (TBA)

Shelter for Penelope (TBA)

SEAL of Protection Series:

Protecting Caroline

Protecting Alabama

Protecting Alabama's Kids (novella)

Protecting Fiona

Marrying Caroline (novella)

Protecting Summer

Protecting Cheyenne

Protecting Jessyka

Protecting Julie (novella)

Protecting Melody

Protecting the Future

Beyond Reality Series:

Outback Hearts

Flaming Hearts

Frozen Hearts

Stand-Alone Novels:

The Guardian Mist

Writing as Annie George:

Stepbrother Virgin (erotic novella)

CLAIMING GRACE

ACE SECURITY

BOOK 1

Susan Stoker

Published by Montlake Romance, Seattle

www.apub.com

Amazon, the Amazon logo, and Montlake Romance are trademarks of Amazon.com, Inc., or its affiliates.

ISBN-13: 9781503942431
ISBN-10: 1503942430

Cover design by Eileen Carey

Printed in the United States of America

Prologue

The three brothers gathered around the coffin, huddled into their jackets as the cold spring wind blew around them. A cemetery worker stood nearby, at a respectable distance, patiently waiting for the men to say their good-byes.

Logan Anderson shifted uncomfortably. It had been years since he'd seen his brothers, and standing at their father's grave wasn't exactly how he wanted to reconnect. It was difficult, if not impossible, to settle on one emotion. Anger at his mother, grief for the father he'd grown distant from, shame that he hadn't reached out to his brothers before now, and frustration at the entire situation sat heavily on his shoulders. He kept his hands in his pockets, hunched forward under the weight of his emotions and the chilly air.

"We should've been here," Logan declared in a low voice, his lips drawn down in a slight frown, his hands fisting inside his pockets.

"Don't do that," Blake warned his brother. "We didn't know she'd do this."

"Bullshit," Logan said. "We knew this might happen sooner or later. We wouldn't have left town the second we graduated from high school if we weren't afraid she might totally lose it one day." He continued, his voice tight and hard, cracking with his grief. "I didn't think it'd be Dad, though."

"There wasn't anything we could've done. If he didn't want to leave her, there's nothing we could've said to convince him otherwise," Nathan argued.

"Maybe. Maybe not. But what if there was?"

"What do you mean, Logan?"

Logan turned to his brothers, who he hadn't seen more than a handful of times since he'd joined the Army at eighteen. Too many painful memories of dodging their mother's fists, and the fear of all the negative emotions rushing back, had kept them from being close. But standing with them now, he regretted that. These were his brothers, his flesh and blood. Yes, they had bad memories, but they also had good ones. They'd always been "Those Anderson triplets." He wanted that back. They were fraternal triplets and had been born minutes apart, but they didn't look much like each other beyond a typical family resemblance.

They were all the same height and all had the same sandy-brown hair, but that's where the similarities ended. Nathan, the youngest, was tall and slender. He'd spent most of his time indoors behind a computer, which kept him out of their mother's crosshairs. He was a fast learner and sailed through school. Numbers were his passion, and he made no excuses for it. He went to college on an academic scholarship when he'd left town and eventually got a job as an accountant. Logan figured he probably preferred to use his brain instead of his brawn as a direct result of how they were brought up and because of his introverted nature. From what Logan had heard, Nathan was good at what he did, damn good.

Like Logan, Blake had joined the Army right out of high school, but he had done his four years and gotten out. He joined a private investigation company and worked security for large events and concerts on the side. He still had the muscles from his time in the service but not the super macho attitude his oldest brother sometimes displayed. Logan sensed that Blake had often felt lost growing up, as if he didn't have a place in his family. Nathan was the smart one, Logan was the tough one, Blake was just Blake. As a result, he often went out of his way to get attention, picking fights with his brothers. This meant his mother constantly attempted to discipline him, but Logan usually protected him from her wrath.

Logan was the oldest, and the one who looked like he'd cut your throat if you were caught with him in a dark alley. Tattoos, muscles, and an attitude that came across with only a look. No one messed with Logan. It had been that way ever since middle school. Any time anyone had threatened either of his brothers, Logan had been there to protect them. Whether it was a bully at school or their mom at home, Logan always had stood between his brothers and danger. As a result, both Blake and Nathan had looked up to him as a leader, depending on him to keep them safe from their mom's fists.

"Blake, if you'd known how bad things had gotten between our parents in the last few years, would you have done something about it?" Logan asked.

"Yes," Blake answered without hesitation.

"And Nathan, if Dad had called you and said that Mom was out of control, and he was scared she was going to do something crazy, would you have come home?"

"You know I would've," his brother answered, without even thinking about it.

"Me too. Why then do you think he *didn't* tell us?" Logan wasn't exactly asking. He was more musing about how unfair life was sometimes. "I only talked to him once every couple of months, but it was enough for him to say *something* about his situation. Every time we talked, he seemed so proud of me, of all of us. That we were out in the world making a difference. All it would've taken is one word, and any of us would've been there to get him out of the situation."

"He was embarrassed," Nathan concluded. "He was embarrassed that his wife was beating him up. Who would believe him? If he went to the police, they'd look at him as less of a man. He was probably afraid *we'd* look at him the same way. There aren't any men's shelters he could've gone to around here. He was stuck."

"Yeah. Exactly." Logan took his eyes away from his brothers to look at the coffin in front of them. "Not to mention he didn't want to suck us back into the life we'd left. But why *aren't* there any shelters? Why doesn't anyone think it's possible that a man could be abused?"

They looked at each other, but they were all at a loss for an answer.

"What if we do something about it?" Logan asked.

"Like what?" Blake asked, his head cocking to the side and his eyebrows going up. "What can we do?"

"How invested in your job are you?" Logan asked his younger brother instead of directly answering his question.

Blake shrugged. "I could take it or leave it."

"And you?" Blake turned to Nathan. "You like being a bean counter out there in Missouri?"

"Not particularly."

"I've got another two months, then I'm out of the Army," Logan told his brothers.

"What are you proposing?" Nathan asked, a glint in his eyes showing his interest.

"We've got skills," Logan proclaimed. "I've been in the Army for ten years. Done two tours over in the Middle East. I've been trained in close-quarters combat, and I've already got my concealed-handgun license. Blake, you were in for four years as an MP. Not only that, you got your associate's degree in computer science. You're a tech whiz and would be great at research. Nathan, you might not be the fighter we are, but your accounting skills are just what we need to get a business going and keep it running in the black.

"Mom killing herself after murdering Dad was cowardly, and I wouldn't have expected it of her, but she's gone, and so is our main reason for leaving our hometown in the first place." Logan's fists clenched at his side, and every muscle in his body tensed in frustration and anger. "I'm saying, let's move back here and start our own company. Ace Security. Named after Dad. We all know this isn't the first time a woman has killed her husband or boyfriend after abusing him for years. We can provide a safe, nonjudgmental place for men to go to get help when they're at the end of their ropes. Not a shelter, but a place where they can get nonjudgmental assistance and figure out what their next steps should be. We can do anything from providing them new identities to helping them start their lives over, to hooking them up with a lawyer. Restraining orders, finding them safe houses, even serving as bodyguards, if that's what's needed."

Logan paused and tried to gauge his brothers' reactions to his proposal. Nathan nodded immediately, the expression on his face eager. Blake, on the other hand, was closed off. His arms were crossed and not one emotion was showing on his face. Surprisingly, it seemed as though Blake was going to be a harder sell.

"You guys know it's not just the men who need help," Logan said. "What about the kids who are stuck in the same situation? You *know* how it was with us. If the men are afraid to speak up, how do you think the children feel? Getting knocked around every day and not being able to say anything about it for fear they'll be made fun of or make their home situation worse. We can do something about it. Mom might have kept us cowed and scared for most of our lives, but we can do our best to try to make sure that others don't get bullied and abused by the women in their lives . . . or by anyone for that matter."

The wind whistled in the trees over their heads. Logan stepped away from his brothers and put a hand on top of his dad's coffin.

"Dad didn't deserve this. *We* didn't deserve this." Logan's voice had dropped to merely a whisper as his head bowed. He croaked out, "I'm sorry we didn't come home sooner, Ace."

"I'm in." There was a thread of steel in Nathan's voice that Logan had never heard before. "You're right, Logan. I talked to Dad every couple of months too, and he never said anything. If he'd reached out, we would've done something. He suffered in silence, just like we used to do. Back then, we didn't say anything to anyone either, and maybe if we had, if there had been someone we could've gone to, things would've turned out differently. My job is crap. I hate St. Louis. It's dirty and dangerous. The summers are hell on earth, with floods and the humidity. I've got some money saved up. We can use it to get us started and help with getting a loan. I can do the legwork on that end."

"Thanks, Nate."

The two brothers looked toward Blake. Their middle brother had always been the more cautious among them. He was chewing his bottom lip and looking above their heads as if contemplating something.

"What are you worried about?" Logan asked, stepping forward and putting a hand on Blake's shoulder.

"This isn't going to be easy. It's not like men who have been abused for years are gonna want to reach out and get help. Everything you said earlier still stands. It's about the shame they feel, not necessarily about whether they'll be believed. How in the hell can we make this work, if we can't get any clients?"

"We'll make it work," Logan said confidently. "With you at the keyboard doing your thing, Nathan doing the paperwork, and me providing the bulk of the security, it'll work."

"I can help with the physical security stuff too," Blake grumbled. "It's not like I sit on my ass every day. I still have my certifications from when I was a police officer in the Army."

Logan grinned, knowing he'd gotten to his brother. "Then you're in?"

Blake sighed, but nodded. "Yeah, I'm in. Like I'd leave you two on your own. You'd probably be arrested within a month without me."

Everyone chuckled, knowing he was probably right.

The smile faded from Blake's face, and he took a deep breath. "For Dad," Blake stated firmly. "We'll do this for Dad."

"Ace Security. I like it," Nathan stated.

Logan put his hand back on the center of the mahogany coffin in front of them. "For Dad," he repeated.

"Ace." Blake echoed, placing his hand over his brother's.

"For abused families everywhere," Nathan vowed, adding his own hand to the stack.

The three brothers looked at each other for a long moment, seeing the shared pain of their adolescence, their resolve, and the determination to make their new venture a success.

Knowing they were on a path to a new life, a new purpose, the three men stepped away from their father's coffin. They turned as one and headed up the slight rise to Logan's pickup.

"I'll get the ball rolling on the finances and the legal paperwork to get the company started," Nathan told his brothers.

"I'll see if I can find an appropriate place for an office," Blake chimed in.

"And I'll find us places to live. This is gonna work," Logan vowed.

Blake and Nathan nodded their heads in agreement.

And with that, Ace Security was born. Logan might not have been able to save his father, but maybe he could save someone else.

Chapter One

Six Months Later

"What the hell happened between you two?"

Logan ignored his friend Cole as he concentrated on lifting the weight bar. He hadn't seen Cole in the ten years since he'd left town, but the moment he'd entered Rock Hard Gym, they'd reconnected as if no time had passed. Of course, Cole being Cole, he wouldn't let the current subject drop.

"You two were thick as thieves in high school. Everyone figured you and Grace would end up married or some shit. But she stayed here and you never came back. And now," Cole threw his hand up, indicating the attractive woman who walked by the gym on her way to the coffee shop across the street, "the two of you won't even look at each other. It doesn't make sense."

Logan huffed out an annoyed breath and put the weight bar back on the floor and faced his friend. "We grew up."

"Bullshit."

"Look, Cole, it doesn't matter. We're both older and wiser. What we had in high school was just teenage shit. She stayed here and I wanted out. End of story."

Cole eyeballed his friend shrewdly. "So you saying what *we* had was just teenage shit?"

"No, of course not."

"Then why are you dismissing what you had with *her*?"

Logan ran a frustrated hand through his sweaty hair and sighed. "I just am. Now, can you drop it?"

"You know Felicity and Grace are best friends, right?"

"So?"

"So Felicity is co-owner of this joint and a good friend of mine. Felicity told me that Grace was glad you were back in town, but because of the history between you two, she wasn't all that thrilled about talking to you. You guys have managed to avoid each other so far, but there'll come a time when you'll run into each other again. I just don't want it to be awkward."

"It won't be," Logan said firmly.

Cole didn't say anything for several moments, but eyed Logan with a piercing gaze. Finally, he confessed in a quiet voice, so none of the other patrons working out could hear, "She hasn't had an easy time since high school, she—"

"I don't want to hear it," Logan said resolutely, interrupting his friend. "It's not my problem."

Logan hated the disappointed look on his friend's face, but he had his reasons for staying away from Grace Mason.

"Her folks—"

"I said no," Logan repeated, deciding to cut his morning workout short. He had a ton of shit he had to get done, including escorting a man up in Denver to the home he'd shared with his wife so he could get his stuff out without being harassed.

In the two months since Ace Security had opened its doors, they'd had more business than they had expected. It turns out there were men *and* women everywhere who needed their services. Oh, they'd made it known that their target customer was male, but when push came to shove, none of them could deny that there were statistically more women than men who were getting the shit knocked out of them on a daily basis by a significant other. They could no sooner turn down a crying, scared woman who showed up on their doorstep begging for protection than they could turn a blind eye to a crime in progress, not if they could do something to stop it.

Seeing Cole frowning at him, Logan tried to backpedal. "I get it. She's got issues. We all do. But she's single, has a great job at her parents' architectural firm, and she's richer than I'd ever hope to be in my lifetime. She's practically Castle Rock royalty. She doesn't have anything to worry about. She can just go to Mommy and Daddy, and they'll fix whatever is bothering her, just like they always have."

Cole shook his head in disgust, turned on his heel, and walked away without another word.

Logan had expected some sort of comeback. Cole wasn't the kind of man to not speak his mind, but Logan was thankful for the reprieve. Discussing Grace Mason with anyone wasn't high on his list of things he wanted to do. Ever.

As if her name in his head conjured her up, Logan turned to watch her walk out of the coffee shop. She wasn't smiling. In fact, the few times he'd seen her since he and his brothers had been back in town, she'd never smiled. Logan remembered back when they were in high school, he'd thought she had the prettiest smile. She didn't have a toothy grin. It was a lot better than that. Whenever she saw him, her lips would curve up just enough and her face would light up. But that joy was missing now.

She turned toward the end of the street, where Mason Architectural Firm was, where she worked from eight to five every day, and walked away.

Grace forced herself to take a sip of the caramel macchiato she held in her hand as she walked down the sidewalk toward her parents'

architectural firm. She hated coffee. Loathed it. But she needed the caffeine to get her going in the morning. So she made sure to get the sweetest, weakest-tasting coffee as possible, just to make it palatable.

Aware that Logan Anderson was most likely in the gym near the coffee shop, she did her best not to look longingly at the large mirrored windows facing the street. She knew there was no chance in hell he was actually watching her. He'd made it abundantly clear, no matter what he'd said before he'd joined the Army, that he wanted nothing to do with her.

They'd met in the tenth grade when Grace had been asked to tutor Logan in history. They'd forged a bond over dead presidents and long-ago wars that she thought could never be broken. It wasn't long before their tutoring sessions became more like two friends hanging out. Grace wasn't popular, but she wasn't unpopular either. She was quiet and reserved, as her parents expected her to be, and spending time with Logan was exciting.

He'd been rough around the edges back then. He and his brothers were constantly getting in trouble for petty offenses such as vandalism, smoking pot, and the occasional trespassing complaint. Grace remembered the conversation they'd had one night about why he did what he did. His response surprised her.

He'd said, "It's what's expected of me."

She got it now.

Boy did she get it.

She'd been twenty-two and had graduated from college the year before with her office administration degree. Her parents had set her up to work at their company, and she'd decided she would start there, and once she'd learned the basics, would look for another position. After a year, Grace had tried to make it clear to her parents that she was an adult, they didn't need her helping out anymore, and she was going to look for a job up in Denver and get her own place in the city.

Her mother, Margaret, had lost it. First she'd cried and said that they couldn't get along without her, that they were getting older and she needed to be around to help take care of them. When that hadn't changed her mind, Grace had been forced to sit at the dining room table and listen to both her parents tell her how incompetent she was, and how she wasn't ready to live on her own. But when she didn't budge in her decision, her parents' tactics changed. Grace got up to walk out, and her father grabbed her arm, forced her to sit back down, and handcuffed her to the chair with her arms behind her.

They'd left her there all night. In the morning, she'd been allowed to use the restroom, but they'd cuffed her right back to the chair.

After seven days of verbal abuse, Grace had had enough. She gave in and agreed to stay in Castle Rock at Mason Architectural just to get her parents to shut up. But that had been the start of her internal rebellion. She could've taken their censure, she'd dealt with it her entire life, but that night something broke free inside her. Their escalation to physically restraining her had made her realize that she needed to get away from her parents for her own self-preservation.

She'd stayed in their home for another year, but after dropping enough hints that it looked odd for someone her age to still be at home, thus playing on their need to preserve their perfect image to the outside world, they'd allowed her to move into a small apartment between their home and the firm. It wasn't exactly what Grace had wanted, but she was grateful for any small piece of freedom.

But she wasn't completely free. Both her parents kept her on a short leash. They guilted her into helping with business parties at their home, and every time they had the sniffles, they acted like they were dying and persuaded her to spend the night and help around the house until they were feeling better.

Grace had tried to be strong in the face of their manipulation, but she caved every time. Every single time. Even though she had her own place, she spent almost as much time in her childhood home "assisting" her parents as she did in her own apartment.

So while she hadn't really understood Logan's answer about doing what was expected of him back then, she definitely did now.

It almost killed her to stay in town and do what her parents wanted. Margaret and Walter Mason owned her. They were her jailers even if she didn't officially live under their roof, and no one knew it. No one could understand it.

Grace sighed and unlocked the door to the office, closing it behind her and latching it securely again. They didn't open for another hour and a half, but she was always early. Always. The hour or so before anyone else got there was *her* time. She could be alone with her thoughts, and do what she wanted without fear of reprisal.

Grace didn't kid herself. She had no true friends, except for Felicity. Every single person employed by her parents spied on her. If she talked back to a customer, she heard about it. If she stayed out five minutes longer on her lunch break, she was reprimanded.

So the hour before work started was hers. Hers alone.

Grace turned on the computer at her desk, making sure to log into her company account. Her parents would see that she'd arrived at her usual time and would assume she was working. After making sure she logged into both her email and the company software program, Grace sat back in her chair and pulled out a cell phone that her parents didn't know she had.

Her paycheck was directly deposited into her account at the local bank . . . an account that was monitored carefully by her father. If she spent one dollar that he didn't approve first, she was grilled unmercifully and made to feel guilty for purchasing something for herself rather than helping her "elderly" parents.

Grace had learned to be sneaky. She had to. She was nearing thirty years old. She hated having to answer to her parents for every cent she spent. She was given an "allowance" every week. Money that her parents thought she was spending on lunches and proper clothes to wear to work, among other things. And she did spend money on those things, but she also hoarded some by opening an account in a large corporate bank up in Denver. She'd built up a good nest egg over the last five years or so. Money Walter and Margaret had no idea existed.

One of the first things Grace had done with her extra money was buy a cell phone. One that wasn't monitored or paid for by her parents. The bill went to Felicity's house, just in case Margaret stopped by her apartment and grabbed the mail just to be "helpful." She could talk freely, surf the Internet to her heart's content, and pretend she wasn't completely under the thumb of her controlling mother and father.

Lunch today?

Grace smiled at the short and sweet text. Felicity wasn't one to mince words.

If it hadn't been for her friend, Grace thought she would've probably killed herself by now. And that wasn't an exaggeration. Felicity knew how manipulative Grace's parents were, how stifled Grace's life was, but amazingly, it didn't seem to matter to the gregarious woman.

Grace and Felicity looked like complete opposites. While they were around the same height, Felicity looked like a bodybuilder. She had muscles upon muscles, skin that was covered in tattoos, and wore mostly gym clothes, seemingly unaware that anything called "fashion" even existed.

Grace, on the other hand, hadn't worked out a day in her life, and while she wasn't fat, she did carry extra pounds. Her skin was lily white, and she was always immaculate. Hair styled, fingernails polished, clothes ironed, high-heeled shoes on her feet at all times.

They'd met when Felicity and her business partner, Cole, had come into the firm to hire someone to draw up plans to make their vision for the run-down building down the street a reality. To this day, Felicity still bitched about giving Margaret and Walter a dime . . . even though the firm had done a beautiful job on the remodel.

Grace quickly typed out a response.

Yes. Same time, same place.

C U there.

Grace smiled, relieved she could talk to Felicity. As much as she hated being curious, she wanted to hear every bit of gossip that her friend had about the Anderson brothers. It had surprised the entire small town when they'd come back and started up their business after Ace Anderson had been killed by his wife. But they'd not only returned; their business seemed, so far, to be thriving.

She wanted to be jealous of the Anderson brothers breaking free of their tyrant of a mother, but she couldn't. She was proud of them.

Logan had changed. She'd seen him a few times since he'd been back in town. He was harder. She didn't see one ounce of the friendly boy she'd known when they were teenagers. The boy she'd foolishly thought would be her friend forever. The one who she'd secretly dreamed would come back after basic training and take her away from her life.

These days, he often wore a grim expression, he had tattoos peeking out the edges of his tank tops, he worked out every day at Felicity's gym, and he never, not once, gave her the secret chin lift he used to when he saw her outside of their tutoring sessions.

That boy was gone, and in his place was a man she didn't know.

Grace clicked on her Facebook page. The profile wasn't under her own name, because someone would've told her parents, so Grace didn't have many online friends, but it was nice to see what others outside her limited circle were doing. Ace Security's Facebook page was gaining more and more likes every day, and she'd saved the picture that had been posted of Logan, Blake, and Nathan in front of their office space. All three were standing with their arms crossed and stern looks on their faces. And while each of the brothers was hot, Grace had eyes only for Logan. It had always been that way.

Too bad he hated her.

Chapter Two

"Have you heard back about your application yet?" Felicity asked discreetly while they were having lunch in Subway later.

The sandwich chain was cheap, and every dollar saved was a dollar Grace could squirrel away in her hidden bank account for whatever her future might hold.

"No, but they said it would take a few weeks."

"And you're sure you want to major in marketing?"

"Yeah." Grace nodded her head. She caught the sad look on Felicity's face and felt as if she needed to reassure her. "I know I'll probably never get to do anything with a marketing degree, but for once, just once, I want to do something *I* want to do."

"I know."

Realizing she needed to change the subject before Felicity went off on how horrible Walter and Margaret were . . . again . . . Grace brought up a topic she knew her friend wouldn't be able to resist. "So, was Logan there again this morning?"

"Of course. And Cole tried to talk to him but—"

"He didn't say anything about . . . me . . . did he?"

Felicity shook her head. "No. But not for lack of trying. Logan refused to talk about you at all. Shut Cole down."

When Logan came back to town, Felicity had caught Grace moping and wouldn't let up until she'd spilled her guts. Grace had told Felicity all about her and Logan's history. "I don't know what I did, Leese. What could I have done that was so awful that he decided to never talk to me again? I don't get it."

"It's not you," Felicity soothed immediately, putting her hand on Grace's arm. "Whatever it was, it's on him, not you."

Grace shrugged. She didn't believe her friend. There was no way someone as honorable as Logan would just cut off a relationship—a friendship that had provided a refuge to them both— over nothing. Grace could remember the conversation they'd had before he'd gotten on the bus for the Army as if it were yesterday. She'd snuck out of her house to meet him at the bus station early one weekday morning.

They'd stood together, Logan holding both of her hands in his as they spoke.

"Don't be upset, Grace. I'll write as soon as I get to basic training. You'll get sick of hearing from me soon enough."

She shook her head. "No, I won't. I can't wait to hear all about it. You promise not to forget about me?"

"I'd never forget about you. Ever."

"Was your mom pissed that you and your brothers are leaving town?" Grace asked.

Logan shrugged. "No more than usual. She ranted and raved to get us to stay, but nothing she said could make us change our minds."

Grace reached up and brushed her thumb against the black eye that was forming on his face. "Ranted and raved, huh?"

Logan pulled his face away from her touch and leaned down, resting his forehead against hers. "It's nothing. I'm getting out of this town, Grace. I'm not coming back. I know you're going to college up in Denver. You going to live at home?"

"Yeah. My parents thought it'd be best."

"Maybe, when I get to my first duty station, you might consider visiting? Seeing if maybe we might be more than friends?"

"You mean it?"

"Yes. I definitely mean it. I like you. I haven't pushed because we both know a relationship between us wouldn't really work here because of our folks and you being rich and me being poor. But I really like you. A lot."

Grace blushed. "I like you too. And I'd like to come and see you after you've graduated and are a real soldier."

Logan had smiled then. A bright smile that Grace hadn't often seen. He didn't have the kind of home life that was conducive to smiling. "I'd like to see you too."

"I'll miss you. Be safe, okay?"

"I will. You too. Wait for me, Grace Mason."

All she could do was nod.

Logan had leaned down and kissed her briefly on the lips. The first time he'd ever touched her in more than a friendly way. With just his lips on hers, goose bumps had broken out over her arms and she felt a little breathless.

The last words she'd heard him speak to her were, "I'll be in touch," before he'd let go of her hands, grabbed his duffel bag from the ground, and climbed aboard the bus headed up to Denver.

But he hadn't been in touch.

Not one letter.

Not one phone call.

Nothing.

So much for the whole "more than friends" thing.

". . . this weekend. Cole invited a bunch of people to the gym for black-light dancing."

"Sorry, what?" Grace questioned, having missed most of Felicity's comment.

"Cole decided we needed to branch out and try some new things. So Saturday night we're gonna have a black-light party at the gym. Everyone is being asked to wear white . . . it's gonna be really cool. I want you to come."

"I don't know, Leese. Saturday night?"

"At least try," Felicity urged.

"Bradford is coming over for dinner tonight," Grace blurted.

Margaret had been trying to hook her up with Bradford Grant for a year and a half. Grace had nothing against Bradford, he was nice enough, good looking, and his family was rich as hell . . . but he wasn't what she was looking for.

Her mother had started inviting him over more frequently, though, and Grace knew that wasn't a good sign. Her mother didn't take *no* for an answer, and if she wanted Bradford and her daughter to be together, then by God, they'd be together.

It was just one more thing for Grace to worry about.

Grace had no idea what she was going to do if she was manipulated into marrying Bradford. Yes, she wanted a husband and a family, but not someone her mother picked out for her. She'd never get out from under her thumb if that happened. Never.

"Oh shit. Bradford Grant? That stick-up-his-butt architect?" Felicity asked, eyes wide in disbelief.

Grace nodded. "I don't think he's that bad. He's actually pretty nice. But I'm not attracted to him. At all."

"And let me guess, your mother invited him and told you she couldn't serve a simple dinner without your help?"

Grace nodded again and could see her friend's mind racing.

"That's not good. You know she's just manipulating you to get you to be there and to shove Bradford down your throat."

"I'll see what I can do about Saturday." Grace didn't bother responding to the *not good* or the rest of her comment. Grace was well aware of her mother's manipulation . . . even if she couldn't seem to let it stop affecting her.

"Let me know if you need a ride. I know your folks are going to somehow get you to stay over there this weekend."

Just because she got sucked into spending the night at their house instead of her apartment didn't mean that Felicity would let her off the hook. She and Felicity had worked out a system in which Grace would sneak out of the house after her parents had gone to bed and meet up at the end of the street. Luckily her bedroom was on the opposite side of the monstrous mansion from her parents' suite, and they had never caught her.

"I will. Thanks, Leese. I don't know what I'd do without you."

They were done with their meal, and both stood up. Felicity leaned over and engulfed Grace into her embrace. She then pulled back and looked at her friend seriously, holding her shoulders in a strong grip. "I love you, Grace. You're one of the most pure and honest people I've ever met in my life. I hate that you live like you do, under their thumb. I hate that you have to spend a minute longer in that house when you should be enjoying your freedom and living how you want. And I most especially hate that no one, other than me and Cole, knows the hell you go through every day of your life."

"It's okay."

"It's not. But I'm telling you, Grace. If you need me, all you need to do is call. Or text. Or email. And I'm there. Got it? No matter when. No matter what."

"Thanks. I . . . That means a lot."

"It means shit unless you agree."

Grace smiled at the fierceness of her best friend's words. "I will."

"Promise," Felicity ordered.

"I promise." Grace was lying, but if it made Felicity feel better to hear her promise, she would.

"Thank you. Now, come on. You have 4.2 minutes to get back to work before the spies report back that you're late."

Grace smiled, even though Felicity wasn't wrong. Sometimes it was worth being late. Sometimes.

Chapter Three

"I don't know why you're bothering to look for anything in that house," Logan told Blake as he walked into the office.

Blake was the brother who thrived on solving mysteries, on digging and digging and digging until he found answers. Even though the business had been open for only a couple of months, Blake had single-handedly found the information needed to wrap up several cases already, gaining Ace Security the respect of both local detectives and the Feds.

In one such case, a woman down in Colorado Springs had been harassing her ex-boyfriend and his new girlfriend for months. She'd started with small irritants, such as letting the air out of his tires, but had escalated to showing up in their house in the middle of the night, screaming obscenities at the couple until they'd been scared for their lives. Blake had actually established a link between the crazy ex and a case out in Washington, where a woman had broken into an ex-boyfriend's house and killed his new girlfriend. That woman had disappeared, but Blake discovered enough coincidences to alert the Colorado Springs Police Department and the FBI. The woman was now in custody and being extradited back to Washington to face murder charges.

Given his tenacity, the fact that Blake was riffling through the years and years of crap their parents had kept in their house wasn't too surprising. But Logan didn't give a shit. He'd spent the last ten years trying to forget his childhood and had no desire to delve back into it. Not even for his brother.

"Do you really think you're gonna find anything that will explain why Mom was such an abusive asshole?" Logan asked his brother.

"Don't know. But I won't find anything if I don't look," Blake responded.

"We got other shit to do," Logan told him in a hard voice. "We got two new cases yesterday."

"I know, and I'm on them. But aren't you just a little bit curious as to why Mom was the way she was?"

"No."

"Come on, Logan, you—"

"I said no."

"Fine. But I'm not going to stop."

"Whatever. Just don't bring it to work, okay?"

"No problem."

"You really want to live in that shit hole?" Logan asked the other thing that had been on his mind. When the three brothers had moved back to Castle Rock, Logan had rented an apartment, Nathan had bought a small house, but Blake had wanted to move into and remodel the house that had been left to them after the death of their parents.

"Yeah. It's a good house. And the area isn't as bad as it used to be when we were living there. I can fix it up and turn it into a great house."

"The memories don't bother you?" Logan asked, curious.

"Not really." Blake shook his head. "Mom was the hardest on you. I'm not saying she didn't knock me and Nathan around, but you were the one who got the worst of it. Maybe because you were always protecting us."

Logan refused to delve into it. He didn't want to be reminded about the hell of his childhood. Besides, he would've done anything to protect his brothers. The black ball of guilt about the times that he couldn't protect them threatened to explode out of his gut, but he held it back and tried to shrug nonchalantly. "Whatever. Just don't expect me and Nathan to hang out much over there."

"I wouldn't ask you to."

Needing the change in subject, Logan asked, "You going to Cole's party this weekend?"

Blake shrugged. "Hadn't thought about it much. Maybe. You?"

"Yeah. Might be a good place to hand out business cards."

Blake laughed. "You ever *not* work?"

"Nope."

"Then good luck. And if I don't show up, say hey to Cole for me."

"I will. Think there's any chance I can get Nathan to come with me?"

"Not a chance in hell. You know he hates that kind of thing."

"What, dancing?" Logan asked.

"Dancing. Talking with strangers. Crowds . . . you name it," Blake confirmed.

"It might be good for him."

"Maybe, but good luck getting him to agree."

Logan grumbled under his breath. If he didn't know for a fact Nathan was his brother, he might've thought the man was adopted. He was the exact opposite of him and Blake. He was introspective, soft-spoken, and rarely spoke up for himself . . . a lot like their father had been. But he wasn't a pushover. Logan had witnessed Nathan beating the hell out of a man who'd dared smack his kid in public. He had no problem sticking up for someone weaker, but didn't seem to give one shit if he himself was made fun of.

"Maybe he'll say yes this time," Logan countered, smirking.

"You're not gonna stop asking him to step outside his comfort zone, are you?"

"Nope."

"Good. He needs someone to shake him up. He spends too much time with his beloved numbers anyway," Blake commented.

"You'll let me know what you find out on the new cases?" Logan asked.

"Of course. You headed up to Denver?"

"Yeah. I have an interview with a potential client. His daughter is harassing him, contesting her mother's will, saying she was left out and the father owes her."

"How old is the father?"

"Eighty-three."

"Damn," Blake breathed. "Go. I'll hold down the fort here."

"Will do. See you later."

"Bye, Logan."

Logan left the office of Ace Security and headed for his motorcycle. He didn't drive it often, but it was a beautiful day and he needed the ride.

He saw Grace and Felicity eating lunch at the sub shop before he'd gone into the office. Grace had been laughing at something her friend had said. Her head was back and she looked more carefree than he'd seen her since he'd been back in town.

Logan thought back to the Grace he used to know. She had been friendly, happy, and would drop everything to talk to him when he needed her. She'd listened to him bitch about his mother for hours. When she noticed he had a black eye, she'd brought him a bag of ice from the nurse's office, with no questions asked.

He knew about her dreams of working in marketing for a big firm and how she wanted to travel. They'd discussed what the ocean would look like, and how the sand would feel under their feet more than once. Back then, Logan could see her hopes and dreams in her eyes and had no doubts she'd accomplish each and every one.

He'd been flummoxed when he'd moved back to Castle Rock a few months ago and had run into her for the first time. They'd been in the grocery store and he'd run his cart right into hers as he'd gone around the corner of an aisle. She'd looked up at him as if she wanted to say something, but after seeing it was him, merely bit her lip and turned in the other direction.

It wasn't the direct snub that had concerned Logan; it had been the look in her eyes. The Grace he'd known in high school was gone. There were no stars in her eyes anymore. No dreams. It was as if he'd run into a robot. There was no welcoming smile on her lips, only a blank stare. Logan had opened his mouth to say something, he wasn't sure what, but Grace disappeared down another aisle.

Every morning he watched as she came out of the coffee shop across from Rock Hard Gym and headed to work. As a security expert, he hated that her routine never varied, but as a man who'd once thought they might end up together, he loathed the fact that it seemed as if she wasn't living her life, was merely going through the motions.

And while she might be able to fool those around her, she couldn't fool him. Even though she'd ripped his heart out, he still cared about her. Way too much. He'd thought he was over her, but the second he'd seen her, the attraction came back with a vengeance.

Grace was as put together as she always had been in high school. Her shirts looked tailored and professional, she wore small heels that showcased the muscles in her calves that were exposed in the knee-length skirts she always wore. Her light brown hair was pulled back into its customary bun at the back of her neck, which made Logan want to unravel it and wrap it around his hand as he kissed her. She'd always been curvy, but she'd grown into her body over the years, her hips full, her ass swaying as she walked down the street.

But it wasn't only her looks that interested Logan. He'd been watching her from a distance for the few months he'd been back. She was considerate to just about everyone she met, stopping to talk to an old homeless man who was sitting outside the coffee shop one morning, even giving him her coffee. One morning, Grace even entertained a stressed-out woman's toddler while the woman searched her purse for her wallet.

Grace was reserved and quiet, but just as he remembered from spending so much time with her in high school, she genuinely cared about those around her. It was that trait that still tugged at him today.

He might've been able to blow her off if it wasn't for the fact that Felicity and Cole thought the world of her. Logan knew they were both hard to impress. Cole hadn't stopped trying to pry into what had happened between them, and Felicity wasn't much better.

But seeing Grace smiling and laughing with Felicity was a blow. Apparently she wasn't as dead inside as he'd thought. But it wasn't Logan who brought that joy out in her anymore. That hurt. More than he was willing to admit.

Logan mentally shrugged and grabbed the helmet off the handlebars of his Harley. He knew he would have it out with Grace at some point. He had to. If he wanted to move on with his life, or if they were even going to live in the same town together, he needed answers. But he wouldn't rush it. Eventually they'd get their chance. Until then, he had a job to do.

Logan revved the engine of the big motorcycle, loving the power of the machine under him. As he pulled onto Interstate 25 and headed north toward Denver, he forced his thoughts of Grace Mason to the back of his mind so he could concentrate on the upcoming interview.

Chapter Four

Grace sat ramrod straight in her chair at the dinner table that night listening to her mother and Bradford make small talk. She'd assisted in the kitchen, making sure the cook had Bradford's favorite drink ready to go, as well as setting the table, vacuuming the dining room, and dusting before the guests had arrived. Even though her parents had servants, they always had last-minute things they "needed" Grace to do.

"What are you working on next, Bradford?"

"Well, Mrs. Mason, I'm finalizing the blueprints for a new apartment complex up in Denver. It's a part of the beautification of the downtown area."

"Wow, that's impressive," Margaret gushed.

Bradford shrugged. "I wish I could say I had a hand in it, but I'd be lying. Most of the groundwork for the project was done by one of our executive assistants. She was like a bulldog, never quitting even when doors shut in her face."

"See, Grace? You need to be more like that," her father scolded. "If you tried a bit harder, you could get out of that front office and move up in the ranks."

Grace blushed but didn't defend herself. There wasn't a point; she'd learned that well over the years.

"Oh, I didn't mean—" Bradford started to say, but Margaret interrupted him.

"It's okay. Grace knows she has a ways to go before she's executive-assistant caliber. But I think with the right man by her side, she wouldn't have as many outside distractions."

Grace thought she was going to die. It was bad enough listening to her parents disparage her in front of others, but to practically throw her in Bradford's lap was a whole new kind of low.

"I'm sure she'll be fine," Bradford tried to soothe. "I've worked with her a few times and she's always been nothing but wonderful."

"Thanks," Grace said in a small voice. Bradford wasn't a bad person. He was pleasant and didn't go along with her parents when they belittled her. He always tried to either change the subject or praise her. But she felt nothing with him. No spark. No desire to hold his hand. No chemistry whatsoever. The thought of actually sleeping with him was abhorrent. It would be like sleeping with a brother or something. Grace had no idea how Bradford felt about her, but she guessed it was much the same.

The few times they'd been thrown together and had some privacy, he hadn't overstepped his bounds and or even tried to kiss her. They'd simply talked business and made small talk. They liked each other, and Grace considered Bradford a friend of sorts . . . even if they didn't hang out. She was comfortable with him and didn't really worry about him trying to kiss her or get in her pants. The fact that it was obvious her mother was trying to throw them together was becoming awkward for them both.

The rest of the dinner was painful, but finally the dessert had been eaten and Margaret pushed back from her chair.

"It's been lovely seeing you again, Bradford. Please tell your parents that I'll be calling them soon. It's been too long since we've chatted."

"I will, Mrs. Mason. Thank you for a lovely dinner."

"Call me Margaret. It's only appropriate, after all." Not giving them time to ponder her comment, she continued, "I'm feeling a bit tired.

We will leave you two to continue chatting. Grace can see you out after you're done visiting."

"Of course. Thank you."

Walter held out his hand as he stood up. "Thanks for coming over tonight, Bradford. It's always nice to spend time with an ambitious young person such as yourself. Grace could learn a lot from you."

Her father's subtle digs didn't even faze her anymore. Grace kept her spine straight and the smile on her face polite as her parents left the large dining room. She turned to Bradford. "I'm sorry about that. Seriously."

"It's fine, Grace. I don't want to embarrass you, but I feel like I should say something here. I like your parents, look up to them as a matter of fact. They've built an amazing company and are extremely successful. I know my folks wouldn't be where they are without their backing. I don't know how to say this, so I'm just going to come right out with it—I'm not interested in dating you."

"I know. And I like you too, but yeah, not like that," Grace agreed immediately.

"Whew!" Bradford breathed out, pantomiming wiping sweat away from his brow. "For a second I thought they were going to bring a preacher out from behind a curtain and insist that we get married right here and now."

Grace laughed weakly. "I feel like I have to warn you, Bradford, they aren't going to give up the idea of us being together easily."

"Please, call me Brad. Bradford sounds so stuffy. And I realize that. They wouldn't own one of the most successful architectural companies in Colorado if they gave up easily. Don't worry," he patted Grace's hand, "I'm sure they'll come around eventually. Walk me out?"

He pushed his chair back, putting his napkin on the table and pulling out her chair. She stood gracefully and walked behind Brad to the ornate doors that led into the house. Brad's Porsche was parked in the circle driveway and Grace followed him to the driver's side.

"Don't look so worried, Grace. Your parents are reasonable people. They'll figure out that we're nothing more than friends eventually."

Grace didn't respond, but merely nodded instead. She let Brad lean down and kiss her on the cheek briefly. She stood back and watched as he pulled away down their driveway, until he turned and she couldn't see the sleek black car anymore.

Knowing what was waiting, she trudged back inside the house.

"Grace Mason, you are a complete failure. You were supposed to bring Bradford into the sitting room. How do you expect him to get to know you if you don't spend time with him? And you stood in front of him out there like a frigid piece of wood. Next time he kisses you, you need to kiss him back. You'll never bring him to heel if you don't at least give him a taste of what he could have once you're married."

"But I don't want to marry him," Grace protested in a small voice, knowing it was useless, but needing to say it anyway.

Margaret Mason blew off her daughter's words with a wave of her heavily jeweled hand. "Nonsense. You have no idea what you want. You never have. You're a weak woman who can't make any decisions without a man by your side. Bradford is just what we need. His family is rich, and having our two companies connected by marriage will make us even stronger. You'll do as I say, or you'll regret it for the rest of your life."

When Grace didn't respond, Margaret came over to her daughter and gripped her chin, raising her head so she had to look her in the eyes. "Am I clear? You *will* be marrying Bradford Grant. It's the best thing that you could do for yourself, and us. The Grants have the money we'll need to help us keep up our standard of living after we retire. I know you don't want us to be embarrassed, right?"

"Of course not." Grace said the words her mother expected to hear.

"I hope you aren't thinking about driving home this late at night. Go to your room and get some sleep, Grace. You have huge bags under your eyes and I know you wouldn't want to be seen in public like that.

It would be mortifying. You've also been gaining weight. It's obvious to everyone, I've even had some comments from some of the clients about it. I've told the cook you don't need breakfast when you're here. You're overweight and becoming an embarrassment to us. I hope you're not stuffing your face with doughnuts when you're on your own. If you moved back in, I could help you take much better care of yourself. We need you to be healthy so you can take care of us when we need you. Did you know that I had chest pains the other day? It was awful, and I couldn't get ahold of you.

"Oh, and I wish you'd stop having lunch with that Felicity person. You know, the one covered in those awful tattoos. Why anyone would permanently mark their skin with that crap, I have no idea. She's beneath you, and now that you'll be married to Bradford, you can't associate yourself with anything that makes you look bad. People will start talking and take their business elsewhere. Then what would we do? The business could go under and we'd be penniless. Go on now. Get upstairs and get some sleep. I'm sure you'll feel better in the morning. Maybe we'll go shopping tomorrow, and I'll help you find some appropriate clothes to help you portray yourself in a more flattering light."

Grace didn't comment and calmly walked out of the room and headed for the stairs. She undressed and got ready for bed robotically. It was only eight thirty, but it didn't matter. Grace didn't feel like fighting with her mother tonight. The second she tried to show a backbone, Margaret slayed her with a guilt trip or viperous words that ate away at her soul.

She'd thought about taking the money she'd hidden away and just disappearing, heading to the coast to put her toes in the sand for the first time ever, but something always stopped her. It was as if Margaret knew when she'd pushed too hard and would suddenly become "mom of the year." Saying how proud she was of Grace and how grateful she was that her daughter was living in the same town and could help out her parents when they needed it. Grace lived for the words of praise she rarely heard from her mom. Even though she knew she was being manipulated, Grace couldn't stop it.

She knew Felicity didn't understand, and Grace wasn't sure she could even explain it to the other woman. She wanted to leave. *Wanted* to be out from under her parents' thumbs. But every time she got up the nerve to do it, her mom would need her desperately, and she'd stay.

She'd once been on the verge of leaving for good. She'd secretly packed a bag, hidden it in the trunk of her car, and had put a deposit down on an apartment in Denver. But the day before she was supposed to leave, the landlord called and told her the apartment wasn't available any longer.

That night at dinner, Margaret had asked how her day had been and then tsked at her. "Grace, I'm not sure what you were thinking. That apartment up in Denver wasn't good enough for you. Did you know there were three sex offenders living in the complex? It would be insane for you to live there. Besides which, the commute to your job here would be way too long, and there's no way you'd be able to get a job up there that was suitable. Walter and I discussed it, and we agree that you obviously aren't in your right mind. Therefore, you'll be spending the next month at West Springs Hospital."

West Springs Hospital was a mental health facility in Grand Junction. Her parents had bribed, blackmailed, threatened, or somehow persuaded a physician to admit her involuntarily with an M-1 hold. That allowed her to be held for only seventy-two hours, but Grace had been so scared of what her parents would do when she was released, she told the doctors that she wanted to stay thirty more days . . . just as she'd been told to do by her mother.

The month or so that she'd lived alongside mentally ill people, legitimately sick, not forced to be there like she was, had been horrendous. It'd been enough to show her that it was better to just go along with what her parents wanted. Not to mention the fact that when she got out, her father had gone to the emergency room because of severe abdominal pain—brought on, he'd claimed, by the stress of worrying about his daughter.

For the first time in a long time, Grace's thoughts turned to the black place they'd been before she'd met Felicity, when she'd been scared and alone in that mental hospital. Before the other woman had given her a glimpse of the person Grace had always wanted to be. She was going to have to give up Felicity. Their lunches. Her dream of working in the marketing field. All of it. She'd known it was a pipe dream, but had grasped hold nevertheless. Tonight had shown her that it wasn't to be.

Margaret Mason always got her way. Always.

Chapter Five

Wear your hair up tonight

Grace stared at the text. She was in the office, on a Saturday, because Margaret had decided that her daughter needed to show some initiative. She supposed she could always lie and *say* she worked on the weekend, but her mother would probably check the security cameras. It wasn't worth the grief. In Margaret's mind, if Grace worked on the weekend, that somehow was supposed to prove to Bradford's parents that she was "wife" material . . . even if she didn't *want* to be a wife to Brad.

After work, she was going back to her parents' house instead of her apartment. She'd wanted to eat ice cream and watch *Cinderella* for the millionth time. It was one of her favorite movies because she could totally relate to poor Ella. But her father wasn't feeling well and had asked if she could come and make him his favorite chicken noodle soup that he claimed only she could prepare correctly. She'd agreed, loving that he wanted something only she could provide.

She was the only one in the office, of course, and Grace had risked taking out her phone to see if Felicity had gotten ahold of her. She hadn't had lunch with her the rest of the week, scared of what her mother would say if she did, but had continued to talk with her via email and text.

Grace: I'm not sure I can go

Felicity: Bull. Ur coming

Grace: I can't

Felicity: U going to ur parents house?

Grace: Yes

Felicity: I'll be on your street to get u at eight

Grace: Leese, I can't

Felicity: If ur not there, I'll come up & knock on the door

Grace sighed. She would too. The fact that Felicity wouldn't take no for an answer was one of the reasons why Grace loved her.

Grace: Fine. Eight

Felicity: Wear your hair up

Grace: I can't

Felicity: U can. I want to see ur tattoo under the blk light. No one will be there who will tell the witch

Grace bit her lip. She loved her tattoo. She'd told Felicity one night that her tattoos were gorgeous and she wished she could get one. And that had been that. Felicity had pushed, cajoled, and literally browbeaten her into getting it done. They'd driven up to Denver on a Sunday— Grace told her mother that she was visiting Bradford—and the artist who'd done most of Felicity's ink had completed the small design within twenty minutes.

It was two sparrows in flight and located just below her hairline at the base of her neck. Margaret urged Grace to wear her hair in a low bun at all times, calling it refined and proper, so the tattoo was usually covered. Even if it wasn't, it didn't matter, because it was done in a special ink that could be seen only with a black light.

Margaret would have a fit if she knew about it. Literally, would probably have a heart attack if she had any clue her daughter had gotten a tattoo permanently inked on her skin. The small rebellion had made Grace smile for days. It wasn't so much that she had a tattoo, but more that she'd defied her mother and gotten away with it. It was a simple thing, as far as rebelling against her strict parents went, but it was something.

Her phone vibrated with another text from Felicity.

Felicity: Do it bitch :)

Grace quickly typed out a response, knowing Felicity would continue to badger her until she agreed.

Grace: Okay fine

Felicity: Don't b late. 8

Grace: I'll be there

Hearing an engine outside, Grace quickly shoved the illicit phone back into her purse and stood. She wandered over to the windows of the office and looked out.

Logan Anderson.

He'd pulled up on his motorcycle in front of his new office quite a few businesses down from the firm and Grace caught him just as he'd swung his leg over the seat of the bike.

Good Lord in heaven. He was fine.

Grace looked her fill, knowing he couldn't see her behind the tinted glass of Mason Architectural Firm. She checked him out at length for the first time since he'd been back in town.

He was wearing a black pair of jeans that molded to his legs. She couldn't see much of his thighs, but his butt was outlined clearly. He had the kind of ass that was just begging to be squeezed. He turned toward the machine and reached up to unbuckle his helmet.

The short-sleeved shirt on his frame did nothing to hide the muscles in his arms as he flexed and moved to hang the helmet on his handlebars. As Grace watched, he put both hands on top of his head and stretched, obviously working out the kinks from riding the bike.

He leaned backward, then side to side, his shirt sliding up, giving Grace a glimpse of a tattoo on his side. Then he turned and leaned his hands on the curved seat of the motorcycle and bent over. Grace's mouth watered and she gulped.

Again, his shirt rode up, exposing the strong muscles of his lower back, but it was his butt that drew her attention once more. She wanted to shove her hand down the back of his jeans and cup it. To tease him into growling and shoving her back on his motorcycle and throwing up the skirt she was wearing, pulling down her panties and . . .

Grace took a deep breath as Logan turned and headed for the front door of Ace Security. She stumbled backward until the back of her thighs hit the edge of her desk. God. She had no business drooling over Logan Anderson. He'd left her all those years ago and had never looked back. It didn't matter what pretty words he'd told her before getting on the bus. But it didn't stop her from wanting him with a kind of need she'd never felt before.

Grace had had sex a few times. Her mother didn't know, wanting her to stay the same lily-white virgin she'd been the day she was born, but it had been one more way for Grace to defy her. She'd gone out with a man she'd met at work, the son of the president of a rival architectural firm up in Denver. He'd come into the firm with his father for a meeting. They'd chatted, Grace had had dinner with him, and had gone back to his place afterward. The sex wasn't very good, and Grace had gone back to her apartment with extremely mixed emotions. Satisfied that she'd finally lost her virginity, happy that she'd managed to defy her mother's wishes, but guilty about it all the same. Regardless of how her mother treated her, Grace loved her and wanted to please her so she'd love her back.

Grace had managed to have sex twice more, with two different men, and had had the same lackluster results. It wasn't that she hated sex, exactly, but the men she'd been with were more concerned about getting themselves off than worrying about her and her pleasure. None of her sexual experiences had been remotely satisfying, but Grace some-how knew to the marrow of her bones that Logan wouldn't be like that. She just *knew* when he took a woman to bed, she'd leave exhausted and sated.

Fingering the tattoo at the base of her skull, Grace closed her eyes and sighed. She wasn't going to think of Logan and bed. Wasn't going to think about how much she wanted to have just one night with him. Wasn't even going to go there. Nope. No way, no how.

The first day she'd met Logan Anderson, sitting across from her try-ing to be so tough as she attempted to tutor him in history, she'd been hooked. He'd acted like he couldn't care less about his grades, but with the way he'd listened to her and worked really hard to grasp the concepts she was teaching him, it was more than obvious he *did* care. As she got to know him, and saw him stand up for, and protect, his brothers, she felt a bone-deep yearning to have someone like that in her own life.

But he'd never given her any indication that he wanted to be any-thing other than friends, and Grace hadn't pushed it. When her mother learned who she was tutoring, she warned Grace about spending too much time with "that white-trash Anderson boy." She said he'd only bring her down, and it would look bad for a Mason to be seen with someone of Logan's ilk.

At first, Grace resisted. Logan was a good person. Funny. Kind. Protective. It was one of the first times she defied her mother. But when her mother told her that her father could make a call and cause Logan's dad to lose his job if she continued to spend too much time with him, Grace relented and cut the time she tutored Logan in half.

But she couldn't stay away from him. Grace knew she was confusing him. Hell, she was confusing herself, but every time she told Logan she couldn't tutor him anymore, he'd tease and cajole and generally be sweet and funny with her until she agreed to meet him again . . . and the cycle would continue. This happened all throughout their last two years of school, with the last threat by her mother to jeopardize Logan's enlistment in the Army, the one that made her tell him once and for all that she couldn't tutor him anymore.

Logan and his brothers hadn't had an easy life. He'd come to school all the time with bruises and cuts. Each time, Grace knew his mom had smacked him around, but she'd never brought it up, just as she never brought up how her own mother was disappointed in the woman Grace was becoming. They'd only had one conversation about his home life. Just one.

He'd come to school with a black eye that was almost swelled shut. Grace had heard through school gossip that he'd told people he got into a fight with some guys up in Denver, but Grace couldn't help asking him about it when they settled into their quiet corner in the library.

They spent their entire forty minutes of tutor time talking. Logan told her how horrible his mother was to his father. How he and his brothers always walked on eggshells around her, not knowing what would set her off. He told her that he'd gotten the black eye protecting Nathan and Blake from his mom's wrath. His brothers had apparently not cleaned their rooms to her expectations, and she'd lit into them. Logan had stepped into the fray and goaded his mom enough that she'd turned her attentions to him rather than his brothers. Logan looked

Grace right in the eye after he told her the story and admitted that as soon as he graduated, he was leaving town and never returning.

Grace tried to comfort him, thinking that out of all the people in the school, she was the one person who truly understood what he was going through. Oh, her parents didn't hit her, but they certainly knew how to slice her to ribbons with their words. It was usually her fault, though. If she were a better daughter, then they wouldn't have to keep bringing up all the ways she embarrassed them. Not to mention locking her in her room when she displeased them so they didn't have to look at her.

The best, and worst, day of Grace's life was the day Logan Anderson left Castle Rock. She knew she'd miss him terribly and couldn't believe she wouldn't see him every day. But he'd told her he'd keep in touch. That he wanted her with him. And finally, the one thing she'd wanted for three years of high school looked like it would happen.

Until it didn't.

His words had stuck with her for years . . . until finally she had to admit that he'd changed his mind. That he'd realized she wasn't worth the effort. Her parents had been right, she was a disappointment to everyone around her, and she had to work harder to be the kind of person they would be proud of.

Grace scooted around the desk and settled into her chair once more, trying to concentrate on the emails she needed to send.

The thought had been niggling at the back of her mind for months now. She wanted to know. Wanted to confront Logan and ask him why. Why he'd said he would write, and then didn't. She wanted answers, but was more afraid of what those answers would be.

A small rebellious side of her said that she deserved to know why he'd so cruelly dismissed her. The same side that allowed Felicity to talk her into getting a secret tattoo. The side that said yes to a virtual stranger's offer of dinner and then a nightcap in his apartment. The side that snuck out of a house to hang out with her one and only friend when she was supposed to be at home taking care of her aging parents, making them proud.

Gritting her teeth, Grace made a split-second decision.

Tonight. If Logan was at the party at the gym, she'd ask. She wanted to know. Before she had to marry Bradford. Before her parents had her completely under their thumb. She *needed* to know.

Chapter Six

Logan stood at the back of the gym, enjoying the ambiance. Felicity and Cole had outdone themselves. Castle Rock wasn't exactly the hub that Colorado Springs or Denver was, but this was a first for the small town.

The disco ball whirled and spun over their heads, spotlighted by a few bright white lights. The fluorescent lights overhead had all been replaced by black lights. The result was a disorienting blend of purple light and spinning circles. Felicity had actually made sure no one had epilepsy before they walked into the gym, for obvious reasons.

Everyone was also wearing white. If they weren't when they arrived, Cole and Felicity had provided either plain white T-shirts for the men, or a white scarf for the women. The result was an amazing visual that outdid any of the clubs Logan had been to.

There weren't a ton of people at the party, but surprisingly, Nathan had decided to show up with Blake, as had most of the gym regulars. Cole had brought a cooler filled with ice and beer, and Felicity had supplied other bottled drinks, including soft drinks and water for those who were either driving or trying to watch their caloric intake. The gym didn't exactly have a liquor license, but as long as no one got out of control, Felicity and Cole figured they could get away with "throwing a party."

Nursing the Lone Star beer in his hand, Logan watched as the newcomers smiled and gawked when they first entered the gym, then wandered around greeting their friends. The music was loud, but not obnoxiously so. So far, not many people were dancing, but Logan figured it was only a matter of time.

Logan was extremely aware of Grace Mason standing on the other side of the room. She'd arrived with Felicity and was wearing a white tank top and a pair of jeans. He could count on one hand the number of times he'd seen her look so casual. Even in high school, Grace typically wore slacks and shirts. Her hair was always styled and perfect. Her clothes pressed, her classy one-inch heels always present.

But tonight she looked . . . amazing. More down to earth, more approachable. Logan shifted where he stood, frustrated that the woman still had any kind of power over him. He still wanted her. The attraction they'd flirted with all those years ago was still there. But even more so on his part now. Grace Mason had grown up. She was no longer a girl, she was a woman, and his palms almost itched to touch her. But it wasn't only that. Every time he'd seen her talking with another man, he'd wanted to rush over and punch the other guy for being too close to what he wanted for himself. It was irrational as hell.

There hadn't been a day since he'd left when he didn't think about Grace. Where she was. What she was doing. Who she was with. At least for the first few years.

With time, came distance. He stopped seeing her every time he caught a glimpse of a pretty brunette. Eventually, he stopped hoping there would be a letter from her when he went to the mailbox. And he only occasionally wondered "what if" anymore.

But tonight, she looked phenomenal. Her hair was pulled up in a simple ponytail that sat high on her head and gave him glimpses of her slender neck, which made him want to suck on it and place a hickey there for everyone to see and know she was taken. Her tank was tucked into her jeans and she was wearing a black belt with a huge buckle. Her jeans tapered down her legs to a pair of flip-flops. The outfit wasn't sexy. She wasn't trying to attract attention to herself . . . but she was nonetheless.

Logan couldn't stop looking at her feet. He'd never, not once, seen her wearing flip-flops. Even though he was on the other side of the room, he could still see her sexy little toes. Grace laughed at something Felicity said, and her white teeth shone clearly in the black lights in the room.

"Why don't you just go over there and talk to her?"

The question startled Logan out of his introspection. He turned to see Cole standing next to him.

"I don't want to."

Cole laughed as if Logan had just told a hilarious joke. "Oh, that's such bullshit. You're dying to talk to her. Any moron can see it."

Logan scowled and crossed his arms over his chest and glared at Grace and Felicity across the room. "Why are you harping on this, Cole? Haven't we had this conversation already? Just let it go."

Instead of answering, Cole leaned against the wall, mirroring Logan's stance, and motioned at the two women with his head. "Felicity picked her up tonight. She parked down the street and waited for Grace to sneak out of the damn mansion she spends more time at than her own apartment. She climbed out her window and met Felicity on the street."

"Doesn't want her parents to know she's slumming?" Logan sneered. He didn't know why he was being such a dick. He *did* want to go and talk to Grace, get to know her again, see if the connection they'd once had was still there, but he was afraid that if he did, he'd hear her say she didn't want anything to do with him. It was insane. He was a badass former soldier. He shouldn't be such a pussy about talking to her.

For the first time, Cole looked pissed. "Dammit. Listen to me," he demanded, standing up straight and glaring at Logan. "Felicity keeps clothes in her car for Grace to change into, because if Margaret Mason found a pair of flip-flops or jeans in her daughter's closet, or found them on one of the many surprise visits she pays to Grace's apartment, she would lose her shit. I know you think you're smart, and you have Grace all figured out, but I'm standing here telling you, you don't know dick. I've never seen a woman so lost in all my life."

Logan gestured toward Grace, who was giggling and laughing with Felicity. "Really? Because she doesn't look all that lost to me."

"Then you're not looking hard enough," Cole returned immediately and with force, smacking the wall next to his friend to emphasize his point. "Rumor has it that she's practically engaged to Bradford Grant."

Logan looked sharply at his friend then. "Bradford?"

"Mommy and Daddy want it to happen. So it'll happen."

Looking back across the room at Grace, Logan muttered, "Makes sense. He's loaded. She's loaded. They'll make a good couple . . . ouch!"

Logan took a step away from his friend and rubbed the back of his head where Cole had smacked him. "What the hell?"

"You aren't *listening* to me," Cole said easily.

"I *am* listening, but you're talking in some damn code. Just fucking spell it out." Logan was pissed. He hated games. He was a black-and-white kind of guy. Not to mention the thought of Bradford Grant and Grace together made him want to go and find the man and beat the shit out of him for taking what was his. The thought startled him, but he didn't have time to reflect on it.

"Grace Mason is so far under her parents' thumbs, she can't breathe. She's drowning, and every day that goes by, she goes farther and farther under. She wants their approval more than she wants to live her own life. They've manipulated her since the day she was born and have used emotional blackmail to get her to do whatever they want. Grace doesn't own a pair of *jeans*, Logan, because her parents have told her that she looks like a slut when she wears them.

"Her parents own her lock, stock, and barrel. And if you don't get your head out of your ass, she's going to be married to Bradford Grant by the end of the year. Then she'll be lost to you, and Felicity, forever.

47

And the shit of it is, she knows it. She's laughing now, sure, but if you look closer, you'll see it's all on the surface."

Logan narrowed his eyes at his friend for a beat before turning to look at Grace again. He tried to put aside his insane anger at the thought of Grace with someone else, and look at her as a private investigator would. What was Cole seeing that he'd missed because of his own feelings and memories?

There were only about thirty feet between where he and Cole were and where Grace stood with Felicity. Her back was to the wall and her feet were crossed as she leaned against it. Now that he was really concentrating on Grace's body language, Logan could see what Cole meant. One hand held a sugary-sweet alcoholic drink, but the other was constantly fiddling with herself nervously. She rubbed the back of her neck, she fingered the belt buckle around her waist, she wiped her hand on the side of her jeans. Grace's eyes constantly roamed the room, as if looking for someone . . . or waiting for someone to show up. She laughed and smiled, but also bit her lip nervously. Her shoulders were hunched over, as if she were uncomfortable in her own skin and wanted to be anywhere but where she was.

"What's really up with her?" Logan asked Cole, feeling the protectiveness he'd thought long gone well up inside of him again as if it were a wave crashing over his head. He'd promised himself that he wouldn't go there again, but seeing Grace, *really* seeing her for the first time since he'd been back in town, made his promise dissipate into a thousand tiny grains of sand. "She's got more money than she could ever spend in this lifetime. She's pretty. She has a good job, but you're right, something's wrong. I should've seen it before now."

"I don't know. Not really. I have my suspicions, as do all of us who know her, but nothing concrete."

"What does Felicity say?"

Cole shrugged. "Nothing. Not to me. She wouldn't break Grace's confidence. She's only hinted to me that Grace's parents aren't June and Ward Cleaver. But that wasn't exactly a revelation."

"She doesn't *look* like she's being abused," Logan noted, seeing no signs of bruises on her arms or face. "Is she? The light in here is shit and I can't tell."

"Physically? I don't think so. Emotionally? That's a whole 'nother thing," Cole responded.

Logan waved his hand. "Emotional abuse doesn't really exist. It's just a thing made up by psychologists to give weak people a reason for not being mentally strong enough to break free of an unwanted relationship."

"Wow, man. That was harsh."

Logan looked up at Cole in confusion. "What?"

"You can't really believe that."

"What? That emotional abuse doesn't exist? Yeah, I do. Look, you know what a bitch my mother was. *That's* abuse. Spending every day wondering if she was going to beat the shit out of me, my brothers, or my dad. Wondering if she was going to get the cane out of the closet or if she would use a belt. Trying to figure out how to hide another bruise. Making up stories so the authorities didn't separate Blake, Nathan, and me. *That's* abuse. Grace is an adult. She can just leave if she doesn't like spending so much time at home. She has her own apartment; she doesn't have to stay over there. It's called free will."

Cole looked at Logan for a moment, a look of such disgust on his face, Logan took a step back.

"If that's really what you think, and you're not just talking out your ass because you're pissed about something else, then stay the hell away from her. I mean it, Logan. I know we're friends, and I'm happy as I could be you're back in town, but that woman doesn't need another person fucking with her head. I know the two of you have a history, but just because you can't see what's right in front of your face doesn't mean it's not there. Yeah, you had a shit childhood. Your mom hurt you, your brothers, and your dad. A lot. If you haven't figured out that sometimes words can hurt a whole hell of a lot more than fists, then you're not half the man I thought you were."

With that parting shot, Cole turned and headed across the gym to the woman they'd been discussing.

Logan watched as Cole put one hand on Grace's shoulder and leaned down and kissed her lightly on the cheek. He put his arm around her shoulder and pulled her into a half hug. She smiled up at him and said something back to him. Logan clenched his teeth.

He didn't need this. Not now. He and his brothers were getting their business up and running . . . and it was working. They were busy, and word was obviously getting around. He didn't have time to ponder Grace Mason and what her situation might be.

But that didn't stop his mind from turning over what Cole had told him and wondering if everything he'd thought his entire life about abuse was wrong.

It didn't stop his feet from moving in Grace's direction.

It didn't stop his long-buried attraction from rising up from the depths of his soul.

His. Grace Mason was his, dammit.

If she was in trouble, he wanted to be there for her.

Needed to be there for her.

Their new relationship was starting today.

Right now.

Chapter Seven

Grace tried to concentrate on what Felicity was saying, but it was hard. She was on edge. First, she thought for sure she'd been caught sneaking out of the house earlier that evening. She'd had one foot outside her windowsill and heard creaking outside her bedroom door. She'd frozen in fear for at least five minutes, not moving a muscle, but when neither her mother nor father came bursting into her room, she'd finally shimmied the rest of the way out her window.

Over the last few years, she'd gotten good at sneaking out of the house. It was ridiculous, really. She was well over the age where she should *need* to creep out of her parents' house, and she didn't even live there full time, but it was what it was.

She'd changed into the jeans and tank top her friend had brought for her as they drove back into Castle Rock. Felicity hadn't commented on the ponytail Grace had put her hair in, but she'd seen her eyes go to it and the small smile creep over her lips. Pleasing Felicity meant almost as much to Grace as pleasing her parents sometimes.

As if worrying someone would notice her and word would get back to her parents wasn't enough, Logan Anderson had taken up position across the gym and had been staring at her for most of the night. She'd said hello to his brothers, and they'd stopped to chat for a bit, but had quickly moved on. Even though there was a strong family resemblance among the Anderson brothers—they were fraternal triplets, after all—in Grace's eyes, Logan had always been the best looking.

And tonight was no exception. He was still wearing the black jeans he'd had on earlier, but now he was wearing a white T-shirt, as were most of the men. But somehow it seemed so much sexier on him than anyone else. Logan was taller than her five feet eight by a couple of inches, and looked like he could bench-press a car. He obviously spent a lot of time in the gym, and it showed. She couldn't see his tattoos from across the room, but she knew they were there.

". . . don't you think?"

Grace turned her attention back to Felicity. "I'm sorry, what?"

Felicity laughed, but luckily didn't embarrass her by pointing out what had obviously made her mind wander. "I said, I think we should do this more often. Yeah?"

"Sure. It looks like you have a pretty good turnout for the first time. And you didn't really advertise, except for signs around the gym. If you had more time, you could've put an ad in the paper, and even maybe paired up with some of the gym owners up in Denver that you know. You might need to apply for a liquor license, though, if you want to keep serving beer and cocktails. Maybe you could do some sort of reciprocal gym exchange thing or something. Or let their customers use your equipment for free, and the people here could go up to Denver sometimes and work out. It would be a good marketing tool for you both and—"

"Whoa, hang on there!" Felicity exclaimed. "I didn't mean for you to go into work mode on me, I only wanted to get your preliminary thoughts. Although, none of those are bad ideas, actually."

Grace blushed, glad for the low light. "Sorry."

"No, it's great. Speaking of which . . . have you heard back from the college yet?"

Grace looked around, happy to see that no one seemed interested in their conversation. "Yeah, I got the acceptance email this week. It said a packet should be in the mail, so you should receive something for me soon."

Felicity screeched and pulled Grace into a big hug. "That's great! I'm so happy for you!"

Grace hugged Felicity back and then pulled away. "Thanks. It's not a huge deal. It's only an online program. It's not like I got into Harvard or anything."

"Yeah, but since you already have one undergrad degree, you've got all of the basic education classes already done. You just need to take the marketing ones now. You'll have that second degree done in no time."

"Yeah," Grace agreed with no enthusiasm. It wasn't as if she would ever get to *use* a marketing degree. Once she was married to Bradford, she'd be stuck being a secretary for the rest of her life; at least until she started having kids. Then she'd have to stay home with them, host tea parties, be taught how to be a better mother by Margaret Mason, and probably die a slow, lonely death.

Felicity held up her beer bottle. "Cheers. To great things ahead."

"Cheers," Grace mumbled, and took a small sip of the screwdriver in her hand, not really tasting the sweet drink.

"Hey, what are we toasting?" a deep voice asked next to them.

Grace looked up to see Cole standing near them. He leaned in and kissed her on the cheek, then threw his arm over her shoulder. Cole was big. He was around six-four and towered over most people. He and Felicity were close friends, but Felicity told her time and time again that they thought of each other like brother and sister. Grace hadn't believed it at first. Cole was hot and Felicity was beautiful, but the more she hung out with the two of them, the more she believed it. She hadn't gotten any sense that the two were holding a torch for each other.

"Hey, Cole," Felicity answered. "We're just toasting to a successful night."

Grace breathed out a sigh of relief at the wink Felicity threw her way. It wasn't that she thought the other woman would spill the beans about her starting college classes again, but with Felicity, she could never be sure what would come out of her mouth. Unlike her, she didn't seem to worry about pleasing anyone else or following social norms.

"Hi, Cole," Grace said looking up at the big man. "Great turnout tonight."

"Yeah. I think we definitely need to do this more often," he agreed. "Hey, Leese, you got a second?"

"Sure, what's up?"

"I had an inquiry today that I want to talk to you about."

"Right now?" Felicity asked, her brows scrunched up in confusion.

"Yeah."

"All right then. I'll be right back. You'll be okay?" Felicity asked Grace.

"Of course. Go. I'll be fine."

Grace didn't see the glance Cole shot over her head before he walked away with her best friend.

"Hey, Grace."

She startled so bad, she almost dropped the glass in her hand. Turning, she saw the man she couldn't get out of her head standing next to her. He'd obviously come up right before Cole and Felicity had left, and she hadn't heard him over the music.

"Sorry, I didn't mean to scare you."

"Uh, hi, Logan."

"You look good."

"Thanks. You too." Ugh. This conversation was *not* going well.

"Got a second to talk?"

Grace looked around, wishing the ground would open up and swallow her whole. She'd told herself earlier that she wanted to talk to Logan once and for all, clear the air, find out what she'd done to make him lie to her face before walking away, but having him standing in front of her, looking so . . . masculine . . . she suddenly changed her mind. She never wanted to talk to him again. Never wanted to know what she'd done wrong to make him dump her as he had. Gah, she was so weak. "Uh, now? The music is kinda loud."

"Yeah, now. And Cole and Felicity won't mind if we use one of their offices."

Grace's breath got stuck in her throat. Before she could answer, Logan held out his hand as if he knew she wanted to bolt. "Please?"

It was the *please* that did it. Without thought, Grace put her hand in his. The warmth of his skin and the feel of his calloused palm against hers, made tears spring to her eyes. His hand closed around hers and he said, "Come on."

As she followed behind him, letting him lead her out of the gym and into the quiet hallway, Grace let the experience soak into her soul. It had been so long since she'd felt like this. The last time she'd held *his* hand, as a matter of fact. They'd been at a football game at the high school, and someone standing behind her had spilled their entire soda down the back of her shirt. She'd looked down at herself in disbelief, knowing her mother was going to blame her for ruining the designer blouse. Logan had seen what had happened from a few rows behind her, elbowed his way to her row, chewed out the boy behind her, taken her hand, and led her down the bleachers.

He'd taken care of her then, and she had the same feeling back then as she did now. As if as long as Logan Anderson held her hand, she could take on the world.

Chapter Eight

Logan didn't say a word as he headed for Cole's office. The feel of Grace's hand in his reminded him of high school. He hadn't held her hand often, only a few times that he could remember, but feeling her warm palm in his after all the years that had gone by made him recall one time in particular.

They'd been at a football game and some douche had spilled his drink down her shirt. He'd seen it happen from a few rows behind her, where he'd been watching her as usual, and had moved before he knew what he was doing. He'd grabbed hold of her hand, just as he was doing now, and towed her out of the bleachers to the concession stand. He'd grabbed a ton of napkins and taken her to the parking lot, near his truck.

He'd helped her try to dry off, which hadn't worked very well. Finally, realizing she'd be extremely uncomfortable if she didn't change shirts, he'd grabbed an extra T-shirt he'd had in his truck. He'd turned his back while she'd put it on. The thing had dwarfed her, it was so big. They'd laughed, and he'd helped her tie the extra material in a knot at her stomach.

The feeling he'd had seeing her wearing his shirt, smiling up at him, when his fingers had brushed against the warm skin of her belly, had stuck with him for years. He'd realized at that moment that his feelings toward his history tutor had definitely switched from tolerance, to respect, and finally to protectiveness and affection.

Back then he didn't think he had anything to offer her. She lived on the other side of the city, the side with the large houses and the parents who had more money than they knew what to do with. But he was a different person now. Successful, more sure of himself . . . and he still wanted her.

Logan twisted the doorknob of Cole's office and led them inside, shutting the door behind them. He looked around. Typical of Cole, it was a mess. There were papers stacked everywhere. The bookcase against one wall was chock-full of books, and there wasn't an ounce of empty space on his desk.

Luckily, the love seat was relatively clear. He figured Cole must take catnaps there, and Logan steered Grace over to it. "Sit."

She did as he asked, but wouldn't meet his eyes. He settled in next to her and sighed.

Grace was sitting ramrod straight with her hands clenched together in her lap. She was looking down at her fingers as if they held the answer to the meaning of life.

"Look at me, Grace."

She didn't move.

"Please."

At that, her eyes came up to his, reluctantly.

"It's time to clear the air," Logan told her. "I'm back in town for good, and I don't want either of us to feel weird being around each other. I admit I've been avoiding you, and that's on me, but I'm done with that. Cole is one of my good friends, and I know you and Felicity are close. I don't want things to be uncomfortable with us anymore."

Grace nodded, but didn't say anything.

"I meant every word I told you that morning ten years ago. I know we were young, but I had every intention of moving you to whatever base I was stationed at." He hadn't really planned to start out their conversation that way, but once he thought about confronting her and finding out what happened, he couldn't *not* bring it up first thing. Logan winced when Grace's eyes widened and she looked as though he'd hit her.

"I . . . I don't think I want to do this," she murmured and started to stand up.

Logan put his hand on her leg, halting her flight. "Please, Grace. We need to. I think we both have questions we need answered." He knew he was being a bit heavy-handed, but he really wanted to talk to her. She settled back on the couch and nodded. It was a reluctant nod, but he'd take it.

"I was never so glad to leave a place as I was here," he told her. "This town held nothing but horrible memories for me and I wanted out more than I wanted my next breath. Yeah, I could've simply moved out of my house and gotten my own place, but I'd still have to see my mom. Still would've seen my dad being knocked around by my bitch of a mother. I didn't want to witness it anymore. Didn't want to have to look the other way and pretend it wasn't happening as I'd done my entire life. Joining the Army was my way out."

Grace's eyes were wide and her cheeks were flushed, as if what he was saying was affecting her emotionally. Her hands gripped tightly together, enough so that her knuckles showed white. But she nodded as if she understood perfectly.

"You were my safe harbor, Grace," Logan told her honestly. "When I was with you, I felt like the man my mother never let me be. I felt as though you liked me for who I was. That night at the football game, when you wore my shirt, it felt good. I realized that I liked being around you. I liked looking after you. I liked protecting you."

"I liked it too." Her words were soft and Logan breathed out a sigh of relief. He knew he was bungling this, and he probably sounded like a pussy, but he shouldn't have worried. The Grace he knew wouldn't make fun of him or make him feel bad about his feelings. He went on.

"So, when I left that morning, I was being completely serious about wanting you to move in with me once I got settled. I thought you felt the same way, but when you didn't answer my letters, I figured you'd changed your mind. Or found someone else to be with." Logan shrugged, trying to be nonchalant about the explanation. The words seemed too inadequate to explain the hell he'd gone through at the time.

"Wait, what?"

"It's okay," Logan hurried to reassure her. "Again, we were young. I never really told you how I felt, other than that morning at the bus station. That's on me. After a while, when I didn't hear from you, other than getting my letters sent back, I figured it was selfish of me to ask you to be an Army girlfriend. I moved every two years. You would have had to quit your job if you came with me with every change of station. Not to mention the deployments and long hours. I also figured you'd moved on from this town to follow your dreams and probably found the man of your dreams to share it with."

Logan stopped talking when Grace put her hand on his arm and dug her fingernails into it. He had no idea if she knew what she was doing or not, but her words caught him by surprise.

"You didn't write."

He looked at her in confusion. "I did," he insisted. "Every week when I was in Basic, and then every so often after that. For almost an entire year."

"No, you didn't," she insisted.

Logan was getting angry now. "Grace. I *did*. I should know, I was the one who wrote the letters. Handwrote them, by the way, not typed. I was the one who waited every day for you to write me back, to acknowledge me. But you sent them all back, except for the last one. Unopened. The last few you even wrote, 'I'm dating someone. Leave me alone,' on the back."

Grace didn't respond, but leaned over her knees and started to hyperventilate.

"Grace! Shit. What's wrong? Are you okay? You need to slow your breathing down or you'll pass out. Come on, Smarty, breathe." The nickname he'd given her when they were kids popped out without thought. "You're scaring me, Grace. Take a deep breath. Good. Another. Keep doing that. Yeah, that's it."

Finally, when her breathing had slowed down and gotten close to normal, Grace turned her head to look at him. She hadn't bothered to sit up, just stayed huddled over her knees.

"I didn't get any letters."

He barely heard the whispered words. Logan didn't believe her. "It's fine, Grace. I'm over it. It was a long time ago."

"I. Didn't. Get. Any. Letters," she enunciated slowly, then closed her eyes and put her forehead back on her knees. Her voice was muffled, but Logan heard every word as if they were knives plunging into his heart.

"I waited. Every day after my college classes I rushed home to check the mail. And every day, there wasn't anything from you. At first I told myself you were just busy. I can imagine how Basic Training is. You were probably really tired, and didn't have time to write me. It was fine. After eight weeks went by, I thought for sure you'd start writing. But every day I was told there was nothing. I was writing *you*, though. I must've written at least fifty letters. I figured I'd save them and send them all at the same time, as soon as I got your address. But you never wrote. So I figured you were just being nice that morning at the bus station." Grace's voice trailed off, and she didn't look up.

Logan was frozen in disbelief. Suddenly he sprang up and paced in front of her. Neither of them said anything for a few moments. Finally, Logan stopped in front of Grace and put both hands in his hair, holding onto his temper by a thread. "Grace, I swear to you, I wrote. I poured my heart into those letters. I made it through the eight weeks of hell that was Basic because I thought you were waiting for me. I couldn't wait to see you again."

His words seemed to break through some barrier with Grace, because she suddenly stood up and stalked over to Cole's desk, bent over, and swiped every piece of paper and knickknack onto the floor. "No! No, no, no, *no!*" She turned to him then, face red, breathing so hard Logan could see her chest rising and falling in her agitation. "I didn't get them, Logan. *None* of them. Not one letter! I waited. Every night, I'd cry myself to sleep telling myself that tomorrow would be the day I'd hear from you. Tomorrow I'd be able to send you the letters I'd written to *you.*" Her anger drained out of her as if it'd never been there, and her shoulders slumped. She continued, but this time her voice was defeated. "They kept them from me. They knew. Of *course* they knew."

Logan didn't know who "they" were. He had a good idea, but at the moment it didn't matter. He felt the ice around his heart melt away as if it'd never been there. For the first time in ten years, he felt hope. He strode toward Grace with a determined stride. Without a word, he wrapped his arms around her and pulled her into his embrace.

"Every time I struggled with a test, I thought about what my tutor taught me. How to relax and let the information come to me. You always told me I was smart, and I never believed you. But you were with me on every single road march, every deployment, every test I took. I heard you cheering me on. Even when I was pissed. Even when I thought you'd blown me off, I couldn't stop thinking about you."

"I didn't get your letters, Logan," she mumbled into his neck.

"Yeah, I think I got that, Smarty. I still have them if you want to read them."

Grace looked up at him then. Her eyes wide and sparkling with tears. "What?"

"The letters I wrote. I still have them. They were all returned but one. I wouldn't want you to see that one anyway, but I kept them. Guess I'm a glutton for punishment."

Grace bit her lip. "I'm sorry, Logan. I'm so sorry. I thought you were kidding. I thought you left and didn't care."

"I care." Logan knew he was using the present tense, but it seemed right. He didn't really know Grace Mason anymore. But if the spark in his gut was anything to go by, he knew he'd only be fooling himself if he pretended he wasn't still attracted to the woman in his arms. "I still care about you, Grace."

"What time is it?"

The question seemed incongruent to their current conversation, but Logan glanced at his wrist. "Ten thirty."

"I have to go."

"Stay. I want to know what you've been doing all these years. I want to know about your job. Gossip about people we know from high school. I don't want to let you go yet."

Grace lowered her head and snuggled it back into the side of his neck. Logan felt her warm breath brush over his skin, her hands resting lightly on his sides, and tightened his arms around her waist.

"I can't. I have to go."

"You're an adult, Grace. You can stay out past midnight. It's okay."

His words seemed to break whatever spell she'd been under, because she stood up straight and took a step away from him. She looked around in dismay at the mess of Cole's office. "Will you apologize to Cole for me? I don't know what came over me."

"Of course, but Grace—"

"I'll stay for a bit, but not too long."

Logan breathed out a sigh of relief. He'd missed her. Missed her smile. Missed the feeling he had when he was around her. Like he could stand between her and anything that might hurt her.

"Come on," he held out his hand. "We'll go and hang out in the gym for a bit. Is that okay?"

"Okay."

Her one-word answer sounded unsure, but her fingers closed around his tightly, as if she was holding on for dear life. They left Cole's office, hand in hand, just like they'd arrived. Even though they hadn't worked through everything, Logan felt good. He wasn't happy about the fact that she'd never received his letters all those years ago, but he felt as if he had a second chance.

They went back into the gym, wincing at the volume of the music. It seemed extra loud after the silence of the back office.

"Want another drink?" he asked Grace.

"Can I have a water?"

"Of course. I'll be right back," Logan told her, letting go of her hand reluctantly. He headed over to the coolers and grabbed an ice-cold water and immediately turned back to where he'd left Grace. She was still standing against the wall, but he could see her looking around the room, as if searching for someone.

"Who are you looking for?" he asked as he walked up behind her.

Grace shrugged. "No one, really."

"If you're waiting for someone, I could—"

"No!" Grace interjected. "I just . . . I wondered who was here, that's all."

Feeling pleased that she wasn't trying to find another man, Logan cracked open the top on the bottle of water and handed it to her. "One water, for the lady."

She smiled, and Logan felt the room shift under his feet. It was as if the years hadn't passed. He eyed the woman in front of him with the eyes of a fully grown man instead of a boy on the cusp of manhood. And he liked what he saw. Grace had the same curvy frame as she had in high school. The tank top she was wearing didn't hide her voluptuous chest at all. Her hips flared out in the jeans she was wearing, and he remembered the pink polish on her toenails. She was a couple inches shorter than his six-foot frame. Remembering the feel of her in his arms in the office, Logan smiled, realizing how well they fit together.

She stared up at him, the bottle of water halfway to her mouth. So much for him being discreet in his perusal of her. Suddenly, what he'd seen as he walked up to her clicked in his mind. He leaned to the side and got another glimpse of her neck. Bringing a hand up to her nape, he brushed her ponytail out of the way and leaned down, turning her body so the lighting fell over them fully.

Logan ran a thumb over the small glowing tattoo at the base of her neck and felt Grace shiver under his touch. He did it again, and got the same reaction. The tattoo wasn't anything out of the ordinary . . . two birds in flight, but it was the fact that it was done in a special ink that only glowed under the black fluorescent lights that fascinated him.

The tattoo was like Grace. It was there, clear as day, for anyone who bothered to take the time and a second look, but most people wouldn't bother. Suddenly Logan felt sick inside. Even knowing Grace back when he left, knowing she was sweet and honest, he'd believed the worst of her.

Logan leaned down, keeping his thumb brushing over her nape, loving her involuntary reaction to his touch. "I like it, Smarty. It fits you. Birds?"

He could barely hear her over the sound of the music, so he took a step closer and wrapped an arm around her waist tugging her back into him until he could feel her heat all along his chest. All he had to do was move his hand from her nape and pull her the remaining couple of inches and she'd feel how he really felt about her. He didn't move.

"I like birds. They're free."

Free. He got it. After their little chat tonight, and hearing about what her parents had done, he got it.

"And the special ink?" Logan thought he knew, but didn't ever want to presume anything when it came to Grace again.

"I . . . I didn't want anyone to know. It's mine."

Logan knew exactly who she didn't want to know about it. He let it go. "It's beautiful, Smarty. I adore it. I'd love to use that ink on my own skin, if you'll tell me who did it."

"Thanks and uh, Felicity can tell you where we went to get it. It was somewhere up in Denver. I'm not sure exactly where."

Logan brushed his thumb over the two birds one more time, then reluctantly brought his hand down to her hip. He wanted to lick the tattoo. Wanted to suck her skin into his mouth and worship the courage it took to put the ink on her body, but he didn't, it was too soon. He needed to move slowly. Grace had just found out he wasn't the asshole she'd thought for the last decade. But that didn't mean he couldn't let her know what he wanted.

Leaning against the wall, Logan turned Grace and pulled her into him, until she was resting against him. They were face to face now, and there was no way she couldn't feel his erection against her stomach. He took the water bottle out of her hand and bent, putting it on the floor next to them, then stood and hooked his fingers together at the small of her back, once more holding her against him. Trying to ignore the aroused state of his body and enjoy the feel of Grace in his arms, Logan apologized for his behavior since he'd been back in Castle Rock, "I'm sorry it took me so long to get up the nerve to talk to you."

She shook her head. "No, I should've—"

"No, don't take this on yourself. I was purposely avoiding you, Grace. I was hurt because I thought you'd been playing with me when I left."

Grace shook her head and said sadly, "I hate that you thought that."

"I know you do. But I shouldn't have let it go this long."

She bit her lip. "I did too. I should've said something the first time I saw you back in town."

"But it happened. Neither of us wanted it to, but it did. But we're moving on. Tonight is the start of our new and improved relationship.

I want to get to know the Grace Mason that is standing in front of me today. Not the person I remembered from all those years ago."

"Why?"

"Why?" Logan repeated in confusion. "Why do I want to know about you?"

"Uh huh. I'm just me." Grace shrugged awkwardly in his embrace. "I'm no one special. I'm a secretary at my parent's architectural firm. That's all."

Logan chuckled. "That might be the Grace that the world sees, but I know there's a lot more to you than that. I've seen signs of her in there, and I'm intrigued as hell."

"Logan, I don't think—"

"Don't think, Smarty," he interrupted gently. "Even though we shared our first and last kiss at the bus station that morning long ago, I've thought about it, and more, a lot since then. I liked the person you were back then enough to want you to move out to be with me. I've seen nothing since I've been back in town that has changed my mind. That's part of the reason it took me so long to get up the nerve to talk to you. You were this perfect woman in my mind, I was scared to shatter that illusion if I talked to you. But, Grace, it hasn't been shattered at all. You've changed, but so have I. And I want to get to know you again. Get to know the new you. See if the woman you are today is someone I'm as attracted to as the girl back then. And I have to tell you . . . so far, you are exceeding my expectations in a big way."

Grace looked up at him with huge eyes. Opened her mouth to say something, then shut it again.

"Will you let me take you out? Do you think you might want to get to know me, the man I am today, as well?"

She immediately nodded. "Yes. I definitely want to get to know you again."

Logan smiled. "Good. Want to get a late-night snack with me?"

"Now?"

"Yeah, now. No time like the present to get reacquainted."

Grace looked around the gym as if just now remembering where they were, then stepped away from him, putting a good half a foot between them. The look of longing in her eyes contradicted the words that came out of her mouth. "I can't. I'm sorry, Logan, but I need to go. I'm glad we cleared the air. I do want to get to know you, but I just don't know if it's going to work out. I know that I said I would, but I just—"

Logan grabbed her hand and pulled her back into his chest. "What are you afraid of, Smarty?"

"I'm not afraid of anything." Grace's eyes were wide and communicated her lie loud and clear even as she tried to sound tough.

"Grace—"

"I need to go."

She began to struggle in his arms, and Logan let her go. He'd never forced a woman to do anything before, and he wasn't about to start now. Especially not with Grace.

"Okay, easy, Grace. Let me take you home then."

"No." Her answer was immediate. "Felicity needs to take me. My stuff is in her car."

"I can get your things. Don't you trust me?"

"No. Yes. It's not that," Grace stammered, backing toward the door. "I just . . . I need to go."

Logan could see Grace was on the verge of panicking again. And he hated it. The last thing he wanted was for her to feel afraid of him. He held up his arms in capitulation, giving her the space she needed. "Okay, okay. No problem. I'll help you find Felicity."

"It's okay. I can find her on my own." Grace had reached the gym doors and looked up at Logan. He couldn't quite read the look in her eyes. "Thanks, Logan. I'm glad we could talk. I'll see you around. Take care."

"You too, Smarty."

At his words, she turned and all but fled out of the gym.

"And I'll take care of you too," Logan said softly as he followed her at a more sedate pace. Something was wrong. Seriously wrong. And he hadn't spent the last ten years learning all he could about investigations to let this go. Knowing that Grace had somehow not seen even one of his letters all those years ago, and had apparently been as desperate to hear from him as he'd been to hear from her changed everything.

Everything.

Chapter Nine

Grace sat huddled in the front seat of Felicity's PT Cruiser with her arms around her waist. She'd changed back into the black slacks and Louis Vuitton blouse she'd worn at the beginning of the night. On her feet were the two-inch heels her mother insisted she always wear. Her armor was back in place, but she felt more vulnerable than ever.

"Please tell me what's wrong, Grace," Felicity begged. "You're really worrying me."

"He wrote," Grace told her friend in a toneless voice.

"What? Who wrote what?"

"Logan. He said that he wrote me after he left. I never got any of his letters."

She'd never told Felicity about the letters. She hadn't told anyone. The hurt Logan had caused her had cut too deep for her to share it with anyone. Even her best friend. But somehow tonight he'd managed to lance that sore . . . make it not hurt so badly. Enough so she *could* share with Felicity what had happened.

"He wrote you a letter?"

"Dozens, apparently."

"And your asshole parents hid them from you, didn't they?" Felicity's voice rose in the small interior of her car.

"Returned to sender, unopened."

"Mother*fucker.* Those assholes. Seriously. Who does that? You need to get them out of your life once and for all, Grace. Seriously. That is *not* okay."

"I was only eighteen. I'm sure they thought they were doing what was right for me."

"No. Don't do that. They've kept you under their thumb your entire life. You're twenty-eight. An adult. You don't need their approval anymore."

"They're my parents."

"Yeah, they are. But they've done nothing but make you feel like shit your entire life. Parents are supposed to love their kids without strings. Yours dangle their approval in front of you like bait."

Grace twisted in her seat and gave her complete attention to Felicity. "You're right. I'm twenty-eight and have nothing of my own. My mother has bought every stitch of clothing I own. They pay my salary, which pays for my apartment and the food I eat. My car. But they need me. They're getting older and if I'm not here to help them, what will they do?"

Felicity laughed, but it wasn't humorous. "Grace. They're not *that* old. They're using you."

"I want them to love me. I've always been a disappointment to them."

"Oh, Grace. You're not a disappointment. You're an amazingly smart woman who has the world ahead of her, if only you'd reach out and grab it."

"I'm afraid if I don't help them when they ask, or if I quit, they'll force me to stay."

"You're being paranoid, Grace. Cut it out. Your parents don't have that sort of power. All you have to do is stand up to them and say *no.*"

"It's not that easy. Believe me, I've learned that lesson."

Felicity's face fell in concern, and Grace hurried on and changed the subject. "I got the impression tonight that Logan wants to go out with me."

"That's great!" Felicity gushed, then sobered. "Why aren't you happy about it?"

"I *am*. I've pretty much loved him my entire life. But my parents don't like him. I'm afraid they'll do something to hurt his new business."

Felicity laughed. "Logan Anderson? You have got to be kidding me. That man can take care of himself."

"I can't take the chance. Hiding letters back then was nothing compared to what they could do today."

"Not if he's aware of it and is prepared for whatever they might try."

"I love you, Felicity," Grace told her friend seriously, ignoring her last comment. "I don't know what I would've done the last few years if you hadn't been there for me."

"Don't."

"Don't what?"

"Don't act like this is good-bye. Just because you learned, once again, what assholes your parents are, doesn't mean that you'll never see me again."

Grace sighed. "I'm just . . . this is hard."

"*Life* is hard," Felicity retorted somewhat harshly. "Really hard, sometimes. You know that I know it as well as you. You know what happened to me, Grace. But you gotta push through the hard times. Get pissed. You didn't ask for asshole parents. You didn't ask to be in the situation you're in. But if you continue to let Margaret and Walter run your life, and choose your friends and boyfriends, you'll *never* get out of it. Fight, Grace. Fight for what *you* want for once. I don't think your parents will ever be happy with anything in their lives, but that's on *them*, not you. Let me help you. And Cole. And even Logan. I have a feeling he'd do anything you asked, and even things you don't ask for. Maybe him coming back to town is a sign. He runs a business that helps people in situations like yours."

"I'm not like his clients," Grace protested immediately.

"Not exactly, no, but close."

Grace shook her head but smiled at Felicity in capitulation. "You're right, in a way. Hearing that Logan *did* write me all those years ago, shook me. It hurts. I don't know if things would've worked out between us back then, but we didn't even get a chance to try. I like him. Well, I liked the boy he was, and from what I've seen and heard about since he's been back, I like who he is today too. I want to see if what we had back then was real. If it can maybe work with us again. I think it's time."

"Time for what?"

"For me to stand up to my parents."

"Hell to the yeah!" Felicity said with a huge smile on her face.

"I don't know if I can, though. You'll help me?"

"Of course," Felicity answered immediately.

"I know I should be stronger, but I'm really weak when it comes to them."

"You are not. You're one of the strongest women I know," Felicity told her. When Grace shook her head, Felicity continued, "You *are*. You have the kind of inner strength I've rarely seen in women in your situation."

"But I do everything they want me to."

"Usually, but it hasn't broken you. *That's* the strength I see in you."

"I *feel* broken."

"But you're not." Felicity insisted. "And you don't have to do it alone anymore. I'm here. Cole too. And I bet Logan and his brothers will be as well. Use the strength you have inside of you to reach out to us."

"I don't know what they'll do."

"Are you scared of them?"

"Yeah. But they won't hurt me, well, not so much I can't handle it. They've never hit me before. Never *truly* abused me, just disciplined me."

"There's abuse, then there's abuse," Felicity said in a dry voice.

Grace waved off her friend's concerns and said in a voice that was meant to be stern but came out a bit uncertain instead. "You're right, though. It's time I stood up for myself. I've let them push me around for too long. There are things that I haven't told you about, but they are in the past. I realize now that I need to be careful in my interactions with them and don't need their approval for every single thing I do in my life. It'll be fine. We have some things to talk about. I'll simply sit them down and let them know that it's time I got the job I really want. I'll continue to work at the firm until I get my marketing degree. I'll give them plenty of time to hire my replacement."

"I'm proud of you." Felicity leaned over and hugged her friend. They'd pulled over near Grace's house several minutes ago while they chatted.

"I'm proud of me too," Grace said. "Thank you."

"You're welcome. Now scoot. I'll text you tomorrow. Lunch?"

"Better not. I'm supposed to help schmooze a client. Baby steps."

Felicity laughed. "Fine. But shoot me a note to let me know you're okay. I want to hear all about your chat once it's over."

"Will do. Thanks for making me go out tonight. I had a good time."

"You're welcome. And I won't even gloat over the fact that it was me that got you and Logan back together."

Grace rolled her eyes at her friend and got out of the car. She headed toward the large house she'd grown up in, waving one more time at Felicity and the PT Cruiser as she disappeared around a corner. She wanted to go home to her little apartment. To her couch and brainless movies. The large house her parents lived in didn't hold a lot of good memories, but the thought that she'd be able to break free, to start a new life doing what she wanted for a change, put a spring in her step.

She wanted to be the kind of woman Logan wanted to be with. And she knew, without a doubt, a weak woman who wouldn't fight for the man she wanted, wasn't Logan's kind of woman.

Grace had no idea if she and Logan would ever get back to where they'd been all those years ago, but knowing he hadn't forgotten about her the second he left town went a long way toward patching the raw wounds that had festered in her soul over the years. Wounds her mother had picked at until they bled. Grace hadn't missed the erection Logan had been trying so hard to keep from her as they'd talked against the wall of the gym. He apparently liked what he'd seen of her. He liked her tattoo, and seemed to appreciate her ample curves, which her parents had always hated.

And she wanted Logan Anderson with a bone-deep desire that flowed through her veins like a stream bubbling over the rocks underneath it. She wanted him. Wanted him to be hers and wanted to be his in return.

In order to get that, she had to stand up to her parents once and for all.

Chapter Ten

"What's up with you today?" Nathan asked his brother. They were all at Ace Security, following up on the last week's activities. Because they were scattered around the state most weekdays, each doing different jobs, they'd made it a habit of coming into the office to exchange notes, discuss cases they should or shouldn't take, and getting an update on the status of their bank account from Nathan.

Blake and Nathan had been happily contributing to the conversation while Logan brooded.

"Nothing."

"Bullshit. What is it? One of the cases getting to you?" Blake asked.

"No," Logan reassured his brothers. "Nothing like that."

"Grace Mason then?"

Logan looked up sharply at his obviously observant brother. "What do you know about her?"

Blake laughed and held up his hands. "Whoa there. Nothing really. Just that you guys disappeared last night for a long while, you came back and huddled against the wall of the gym, then she left not long after."

Logan ran his hand though his hair and sighed. "Yeah. I can't wrap my head around it. You know how I told you guys that she blew me off when I joined up?" Not waiting for their affirmation, he went on.

"Turns out she never got any of the letters I sent her. She thought I had dissed *her*."

"What the fuck?" Blake breathed.

"Wow, that sucks," Nathan agreed.

"And the hell of it is that her parents kept the letters from her. Had them all returned."

"I'm never getting involved with a chick with money," Blake said resolutely. "Seriously. None of them are normal. They either are all into themselves and only want to shop, or their parents are totally wacko."

"What rich girls do you know?" Nathan asked in confusion. "I didn't realize you came across that many in the Army or at the community college."

"Fuck off," Blake told his younger brother with no heat. "I know what I'm talking about. Trust me, if you ever come across one, run like hell."

"I can't say anything about Grace's need or desire to shop, but I would agree with the wacko parents thing," Logan said dryly.

"What can we do?"

He smiled at Nathan. He might be the youngest, if only by a few minutes, but he was the first to stick his neck out for them, and for any underdog. "I don't know yet. I'm taking things one day at a time. I told her I wanted to date her, get to know her again, and I'm pretty sure she feels the same way about me. But something's wrong with the entire relationship with her parents. I didn't want to rush her last night, but knowing she felt the same way about me as I did about her back then, and the fact that she's still unattached, gives me hope that maybe we can make a fresh start. Get to know each other again and see what happens."

"You really like her," Blake drawled, somewhat surprised.

"I really like her," Logan agreed.

"If she means that much to you, she means that much to us. Let us know if you need anything," Nathan told his brother.

Logan sighed in relief. His feelings for Grace were a jumbled-up mess in his head, but he couldn't deny the pull to her was there. He'd thought he was in love with her when he'd left, and those feelings were obviously still buried deep within him, even after ten years. One look had been all it had taken for the feelings to come back with a vengeance. "I will. We about done here? I want to see if I can catch Felicity at the gym. She took Grace home last night, and I want to make sure she was okay when Felicity dropped her off."

"Go, we got this," Blake reassured Logan. "We were almost done anyway. You still good for that escort job down in Colorado Springs tomorrow?"

"The one where the woman needs to come out of hiding to show up at the court hearing against her asshole ex?"

"Yeah, that's the one."

"Wouldn't miss it," Logan reassured Blake.

The three men smiled at each other. There was nothing they liked more than showing bullies that the person they'd harassed for so long was no longer alone. That they had the support of someone bigger and meaner than they were. It didn't matter much anymore if the bully was a man or a woman. It was a heady feeling.

"Talk to you tomorrow when you get back then," Blake said, standing up and thumping Logan on the back.

He returned the brotherly gesture and gave Nathan a chin lift. "Later."

"Bye."

"See ya."

Logan left Ace Security and looked across the square at Mason Architectural Firm. If it was Monday, rather than a Sunday, he could've gone over and asked Grace to lunch. So they could talk some more, but knew he needed to give her space to think everything through. His own head was still reeling after finding out they'd been purposely kept apart by her parents, so he knew Grace's would be too. He'd talk to Felicity and see what she could tell him before he approached Grace again. He wanted to have as much information as possible before he made his next move, so he didn't inadvertently screw things up between him and Grace before they even got started.

Logan entered Rock Hard Gym, which surprisingly was just as busy on a Sunday as it was the rest of the week, and sighed in relief at seeing Felicity at the front desk.

"Hey. Got a minute?"

"Figured you'd be by sooner or later. Yeah, let me get Josh up here," Felicity said, indicating a high school kid who'd been working at the gym for a few weeks.

Logan waited as Felicity went into a back room and came back out with the tall, gangly teenager. She gestured for Logan to follow her to her office. As soon as the door shut behind them, Logan asked impatiently, "She get home okay?"

Knowing he was talking about Grace, Felicity nodded and said, "Yeah. I haven't heard from her this morning yet, but I'm not surprised. You know she has a secret cell phone, right?"

"What? No. Why the fuck does she need a secret phone?"

Felicity shrugged and sat in her chair behind her desk. "Her parents pay for the phone she uses for work stuff and scrutinize each and every number she calls. They have it tracked as well, and Grace is convinced they can read every text and email she sends. She has an alternate email address that we use to talk to each other. I also keep some clothes in her size at my place and in my car, so when we go out, she can dress in something comfortable and appropriate. Hell, I think I have just as many outfits for her in my closet as I do of my own."

Logan thought his head was going to explode. When he came back to town, he'd bought into Grace's outward appearance . . . and was ashamed of himself. He'd thought she was stuck up, cold, and too good to talk to someone like him. The more he learned about her, the more he questioned everything he'd thought before.

"She has her own place, right? Why does she still spend so much time over at her parents' house?"

Felicity eyed Logan carefully. "I wasn't around when you were growing up, but I've talked a bit to Cole."

Logan didn't like the fact that his friend had been gossiping about him, but gave Felicity the "go on" motion with his hand.

"You and your brothers went through a lot. And this is going to sound wrong, but hear me out. Your mom hit you, right?"

"Yeah."

"She threw things at you. Left marks on your body."

"You have a point?" Logan bit out.

"I do. Were you afraid of your mom?"

Logan ground his teeth together. It somehow felt as if he was sitting in front of a shrink, and he didn't like it. "Of course."

"No," Felicity shook her head. "I mean, I know you hated when she smacked you around, but when you weren't around her . . . were you scared of what she could do to you?"

Logan thought about it for a long moment before answering. "Not really. Not being around her was a relief. That didn't mean that I wasn't scared of what would happen when I got home, but school felt safe. She couldn't reach me there. I liked it, it was an escape from her."

"And you left town as soon as you could to get away from her."

It hadn't been a question, but Logan treated it as if it was anyway. "Yeah. All three of us did."

Felicity nodded. "And once you left, her control over you was over. But what if you *couldn't* get away from her? What if you had no idea if you turned a corner she'd be there? What if you didn't *have* a safe place?"

"Grace's parents don't hit her," Logan stated, seeing where Felicity was going with her comments.

"You're right. They don't," she agreed immediately. "But they control her nevertheless. They have spies all over this town. Grace works at their company. She has her own place, but they manipulate her with lies about their health and how "old" they are to get her to spend most weekends at their house so they can keep some control over her. They pay her bills. Her mother takes her shopping and tells her she can't be trusted to pick out clothes she actually looks good in. Grace literally can't do anything without them finding out about it. The fact that I can convince her to sneak out of their house and come to a party like the one last night is a miracle. The fact that she defies them to have lunch with me, when we both know her parents can't stand me, is a miracle. The fact that she applied to go back to school to get a degree that she actually wants so she can do something she's always wanted to do rather than being a damn secretary slaving for her parents' company is a miracle."

"Felicity—"

"I'm not done," she scolded, shifting forward in her seat and piercing Logan with her intent gaze.

"Sorry. Continue."

"Grace told me about the letters last night. It was the first I'd heard about them. She never got them, Logan. She wouldn't lie about that. If you wrote her, she didn't get any of them."

"I wrote her," Logan stated in a flat voice.

"I believe you did. And as I told her last night, there's abuse, then there's abuse. Make no mistake, Grace is one of the strongest women I've ever known in my life. It might not look like it at first glance. You might think she's meek and docile and a total doormat, but she's got a will of iron. If someone were hitting her, causing her to bruise, she'd have sympathy from everyone in town, and her parents know it. But they're sneaky. They have her so scared to defy them, she can only manage to rebel every now and then, and only in small, safe ways, like the tattoo on the back of her neck. She wants their love and approval so badly, but they hold it out of her reach, dangling it like a damn carrot. But last night she made a decision. I thought at first she was giving up. She was this close, Logan." Felicity held her hand up, her thumb and index finger almost touching.

"I honestly thought she was telling me good-bye forever. That she was going to do something stupid to herself. But she made a decision *not* to give up. At least I'm pretty sure she did. She's determined to break free of them once and for all. To do what she wants to do with her life, no matter if they approve or not. And that's Grace's strength that most people never see. And I have you to thank for her sudden need for independence. I've begged until I'm blue in the face, but she never listened to me. She never had the yearning to put aside what Margaret and Walter Mason thought of her . . . until now. Until you told her that you wrote her and said whatever you said to her when you came back to the gym."

Logan clenched his jaw. He should've seen the signs. He'd observed enough abused women to recognize it for what it was. He'd been an idiot. Letting his own experiences blind him to Grace's plight.

"What can I do?"

"Don't give up on her," Felicity answered immediately. "She said she was going to talk to her parents. I have no idea how that will go. She might backpedal and chicken out. It could take awhile for her to really break the strings that are holding her there. They've manipulated her her entire life, so they'll certainly try to continue to do so, no matter what she says. I think Grace is scared to death of her parents, even though she'd deny it and say that they're only doing what they do to make her a better person. She hinted that they'd done more than merely humiliate her, but she wouldn't talk about it. But, unfortunately, unlike you, she doesn't have a safe place to get away from them. They show up at her apartment unannounced all the time. She's never free of their watch over her."

"Fuck," Logan swore.

"Yeah," Felicity agreed.

"I'll make sure she always has somewhere to go, somewhere safe to be, if her parents take it badly that she wants to do her own thing," Logan declared.

Felicity chuckled, but it held no humor. "I told her the same thing. Believe it or not, she's just as scared of what her parents could do to *other* people as she is about what they could do to her."

"What *could* they do?"

"Look what her mother did to you and her with the letters," Felicity told him without humor. "That was child's play compared to some of the rumors I've heard about them. They have ways of getting to people. I don't know how many others in this town they've coerced into doing what they want, but I can guarantee Grace isn't the only person's head they've fucked with. Besides that, money talks. Grace was worried the gym could go under with enough pressure from them."

"Fuck that. This isn't 1822. Castle Rock is small, yeah, but Margaret and Walter can't control everyone in Denver or Colorado Springs. It's insane."

"Give her some time, Logan. For what it's worth, I'm on your side. If anyone can convince her to break free from them, I think it's you."

"Thanks. I'm not sure I'm worthy of that support, but I appreciate it all the same. I should've done more back then, and even right when I got back to town. I shouldn't have just let it go."

"Maybe. Maybe not. But what's done is done. You can't go back," Felicity told him.

"I can't. But I can do now what I should've done back then."

"Yeah. You can."

"Thanks, Felicity. I appreciate it."

"You're welcome. But if you hurt her—"

"I won't." The two words held all the conviction Logan could muster. Hearing from Felicity what Grace had been through, *was* going through, made him want her for himself all the more. He wanted to be her safe place. He needed to be that for her.

Felicity eyed Logan for a long moment before standing up. "Good. Maybe between the two of us, we can convince her that her parents can't hurt her once she gets out from under their thumb. I know she wants their love, but I don't think at this point she's ever gonna get it."

"My brothers will help too."

"I figured."

"You'll let me know when you hear from her?"

"I will."

Logan reached out a hand, and when Felicity shook it, he hauled her into a hug. "I know we don't know each other that well, but fuck it. Any friend of Grace's is a friend of mine. Thank you."

Felicity laughed and hugged Logan back. "Ditto. Now, get out of here. I have a business to run." She shoved him gently out of her arms and toward the door.

"I have a job down in the Springs tomorrow, so I won't be around, but if you need anything, Nathan and Blake will be here," Logan told her.

"Got it. Be safe."

"Piece of cake," Logan told her as they walked out of her office.

He waved as he left the building and thought over everything Felicity had said. Had he missed any clues back in high school about Grace's home life? He wasn't sure. He'd been so concerned about his own mother hurting him that it hadn't even occurred to him that Grace's home life was anything but idyllic.

Hell, it hadn't occurred to him in the ten years that had followed that maybe there was a reason she'd returned his letters. He'd just assumed she hadn't wanted to talk to him anymore.

He had a lot to learn, and a lot to make up for. Grace Mason had no clue how her life was about to change.

Chapter Eleven

"Mother. Father. Can we talk?"

Margaret sighed as if her daughter wanting to talk to her in the morning was a cardinal sin. She put down her knife and fork and turned to Grace. "It can't wait until tonight? You know I don't do well with stress before I've had my breakfast."

Grace swallowed and pushed on. "I'm sorry, Mother, but I wanted to talk to you both before you got too busy."

"Spit it out then," Walter growled, obviously annoyed that his habit of reading the paper at breakfast, and ignoring both his child and wife, was interrupted.

Deciding it would be better to get it over with quickly, like taking off a Band-Aid, Grace said, "I'm going to be starting on my second degree soon. It's in marketing. I never wanted to major in office administration and have always loved advertising and the psychology behind it. Not only that, but it's time I got out of your hair. I'll always be around when you need me, but I can't keep staying here every weekend."

Not one muscle moved on her mother's face. There was silence in the dining room for a moment, then Margaret asked in a monotone voice, "Is that it?"

"Um . . . yeah."

"No."

Grace watched in disbelief as her mother picked up her fork and continued eating her scrambled eggs as if her daughter hadn't spoken.

She tried again. "I know this is a surprise, and I'm sorry. But I'm twenty-eight. I have my own apartment, and you guys need to be on your own as much as I do. I'll still be nearby, but this way we all get some privacy."

"Grace, your mother said no. We need your help around here. We aren't as young as we used to be, and you need to show some respect for us. This conversation is over."

Grace flushed at the reprimand from her father. She'd known the talk most likely wouldn't go well, but this was ridiculous. She tried to put some steel in her voice. "You guys are fine. There are lots of servants here who can help you. I'll come over every now and then, but my spending the night here is over."

Margaret sighed. A huge heaving sigh as if Grace were a toddler throwing a tantrum and her mother was tired of hearing it. Her mother very carefully put down her fork again and wiped her mouth with the white linen napkin, pressed into crisp points. She folded it and put it down on the table and stood.

"Walter."

She didn't say anything other than her husband's name, but it was obviously enough for him to understand what she wanted because he got up and left the room.

"Mother, I know this is a surprise, but—"

"Come with me, Grace."

"Can we discuss this a bit more?" Grace was even more nervous now. She didn't like the look in her mother's eyes. Even though she hadn't raised her voice, Grace knew she was pissed. She'd seen that look only a couple times in her life, and each time had not gone well for her.

"No. Now, come on."

Grace reluctantly stood and gasped when Margaret grasped her upper arm and tugged her toward her bedroom. Grace knew she could've pulled away, her mother wasn't that strong, but was reluctant to show such blatant defiance after her bold announcement.

She followed along behind her mother docilely, hoping she'd have a chance to convince her that her moving on and breaking the tight ties was really the best decision for all of them.

Thoughts of being able to eat what she wanted, wear what she wanted, do what she wanted for a living, and spend time with whoever she wanted dangled before her like a steak hung in front of a starving lion. Grace suddenly wanted that independence more than she'd wanted anything in her entire life. Even more than she wanted appreciation and approval from her parents.

Margaret tugged her into the bedroom she'd slept in all her life and pointed to the bed. "Sit."

"Mother, can we—"

"All your life you've been a disappointment," Margaret said in a monotone voice, crossing her arms in front of her chest as if she were addressing a child rather than a grown woman. "From the moment you came out of my womb, you were a failure. You were supposed to be a boy. The only reason I married Walter was to get a son. After you, I couldn't have any more children because you ruined my womb."

Grace sat stock-still on the bed. She knew her parents had wanted a son, of course she did, but the venom in her mother's voice was something new.

"We tried to bring you up right. If we couldn't have a son, then at least we could mold you into the kind of woman we could rely on. But you just wouldn't cooperate. We gave you blocks to play with, and you only wanted to read. We gave you Legos, an Erector set, and even bought an expensive computer program you could use to build simulated buildings and towns. And what did you do? Ignored them in favor of dolls, playing teacher, and watching childish movies on the laptop we got you."

Margaret wasn't pacing. She didn't even look all that agitated, but Grace knew she was seething. She stood there, her arms crossed, spitting the words out as if they were repugnant and would tarnish her soul just for having come from her lips.

"So with you being an architect out of the running, we decided the only thing you'd be good for was being a secretary in our company, taking care of us, and giving us a grandson we can mold into what we've always wanted."

Grace gasped and stared at her mother in horror. What was she talking about? A grandson?

Walter came into the room carrying something in his arms that Grace couldn't see. What in the hell was going on?

Margaret continued. "You've become more and more willful as the years have gone by, and it's time it stopped. Picking the wrong friends, sneaking out of the house when we needed you here, signing up to take marketing classes behind our back . . . oh yes, you think we didn't know about that? Poor Grace, so naïve thinking you can keep anything from us," she tsked. "Hold out your hand."

"Mother, can we—"

"Hold. Out. Your. Hand."

Grace's hand shot out immediately. Her mother was scaring the shit out of her. How she'd found out about her applying to take more college classes, Grace had no idea, but it just reaffirmed her belief that Margaret Mason had spies everywhere. She'd known she was a disappointment to her mother, but had no idea the depth of the woman's hatred for her.

Her father grabbed her wrist and wrapped something around it. It was a cuff of some sort. It was lined with lambs' wool and was soft against her skin. He clipped the leather together and tightened it until it felt like it was cutting off her circulation. She watched dumbfounded as he did the same to her other wrist, locking them onto her.

"I didn't want it to come to this, you know," her mother went on, as if she wasn't watching her husband handcuff her daughter. "I could tolerate you sneaking out of the house every now and then. Your little mutinies were expected. But it comes to an end now. Hear this, Grace. You belong to us. You will do what we want, when we want, and with who we want."

"And what *do* you want?" Grace found the nerve to ask. She was still scared, but seeing her mother with absolutely no humanity in her eyes had broken the last string of affection she'd been hanging onto for so long. She'd never gain Margaret's approval. Never. No matter what she did. The thought gave her the ability to speak out. Finally.

"You will seduce Bradford Grant. Your only job is to get pregnant. You'll lie and say you're on birth control. He and his parents won't be able to stop a wedding once you're carrying his child. Of course you'll have to quit your job and spend the days here with us, where we can watch over you, make sure you're not pushing yourself too hard. Once you have our grandson, we'll have you declared unfit to raise him and we'll finally have the son we always wanted. If you don't want to be a loving daughter and help out your parents in their golden years, being a brood mare is all you're good for anyway."

Grace stared at her mother with her mouth open. She was looney tunes, batshit, off her rocker, daft.

Feeling a tug on her wrist, Grace looked over at her father. She'd been so distracted by the crazy coming out of her mother's mouth that she hadn't realized that her father had attached a chain to the headboard of her bed. He'd grabbed her wrist and locked it to the chain.

Grace pulled hard on her hand and cried out in pain. She looked in horror at her mother. "What? You're going to keep me chained to the bed until I agree?"

"No. I'm going to keep you chained to this bed until you realize that I can do whatever I want. You only have your own apartment because I allow it. You eat lunch with your tattooed friend because I let you. And if you defy me now, it'll just get worse for you . . . and those people you think are your friends."

Her father grabbed her other hand and connected it to another long chain attached to the opposite side of the bed. Grace had plenty of room to move. She could stand, lie down on the bed, but she couldn't reach the door, window, or even the bathroom. She wondered exactly how long they'd been planning this.

Margaret leaned down until her face was only inches from Grace's. "And make no mistake. I *will* win. You've always had a defiant streak. It's why I haven't been able to love you. If you'd been more . . . just more . . . you could've been a person I wanted to be around, to love. But this is the last straw. You will eat what I tell you to eat. You will say what I want you to say. You will do what I want you to do. Period."

"And if I don't?" Grace managed to ask.

Margaret stood up and laughed. And it froze Grace's bones.

"If you don't, I'll ruin Felicity. And her little gym."

"You can't," Grace cried desperately.

"Stupid. You've always been so stupid. I can. And you know what else? I know you've been drooling over that Anderson boy again. How lucky for you that he and his white-trash brothers came back into town, huh? You've wanted in his pants ever since high school. Thank God you didn't get pregnant with *his* offspring as a teenager. You would've had an abortion if you had. I want a son, but not one with a speck of DNA from that disgusting Anderson family. I'd rather you had a child by *anyone* than one of them. Did you take him down your throat when you had your little talk at that revolting party last night?"

Grace gasped. How in the world did her mom *know* any of what went on last night? Now she was just pissed. It was one thing to talk shit about her, but bad-mouthing Logan and Felicity was a whole other thing. She took the bull by the horns. "Why did you hide his letters from me?"

"Seriously? Did you not hear me earlier?" Margaret sneered, not even denying she'd hidden the letters he'd written her. "He wasn't good enough for the Mason name. And I was right. His mother murdered his father. That's about as low as it could get. White trash to the core. Besides, there was no way I was letting you get away from me, *daughter*. I knew Logan was infatuated with you back then, and that his feelings were returned. It was never going to happen. No way in hell. I needed you here. With me. Doing what I wanted you to do. And it worked perfectly. I have the last letter that boy sent, if you want to see it. I kept that one, didn't return it. He'd written "last chance" on the back and I knew it was going be the last one he ever wrote to you, thank God. I have to hand it to him, though, he wrote for longer than I expected him to. I figured one day you might find out what I did to protect you from becoming a tramp, and you'd want to know how he really felt after you returned all his letters."

Grace tried not to hyperventilate. How was she even related to this monster? Why had she spent her entire life trying to gain her approval? Her love? It was hopeless, it had always been hopeless. Margaret had hated her from the moment she found out she didn't have a penis. She turned to her father, hoping to get some support from him. "Father?"

"You brought this on yourself. If you'd only been a better daughter, this all could've been avoided," Walter said, not even looking at her.

Even after everything he'd done to her tonight, his words still held the power to hurt Grace. So much for him helping her.

"I don't need to show it to you," her mother told her with no inflection in her voice. "I remember every word of it. It was short and to the point. You want to hear what he said?"

Grace didn't. She really, really didn't. She merely glared at the woman who'd given birth to her but had never loved her, not showing any outward sign of how badly she was hurting.

"Dear Grace," her mother recited as if reading the long-ago-sent letter. *"You win. I get it. This will be my last letter to you. But you fucked up. I would've given you the world. Treated you like a princess. If you didn't want to go slumming with me, you should've just told me and saved us both*

the time and effort. Well, fuck you. You're a stone-cold bitch. I wish I never met you."

Margaret smiled evilly when she was done. "He hates you. I have no idea what nonsense he's told you now, but he's obviously only pretending to like you to get back at you. To get you to lower your guard and trust him, so he can drop you, just like you did him. It's revenge, daughter. Plain and simple. He doesn't care about you, not after you returned all his letters."

Grace gritted her teeth and willed the tears not to fall from her eyes. She didn't believe a word her mother was telling her. Not now. Twenty minutes ago, if Margaret had shown her the letter at breakfast, she might've. She might have thought that Logan really was just trying to get back at her. But chained to her bed, after hearing the plans her parents had for her life? No.

Logan probably had written that letter. Grace wouldn't blame him, especially after getting all of the letters he'd sent to her returned. But there was no *way* he talked to her as he had last night only to play some juvenile game of revenge. There was no way the passion in his eyes and body was a lie. No way he would've tenderly swiped his thumb over her tattoo over and over if he hated her. Grace might be naïve and stupid for thinking she'd be able to get out from under her parents' yoke, but she knew to the marrow of her bones, Logan was a good person. That he hadn't said the things he'd said to get back at her.

Grace kept her mouth shut, refusing to give her mother the satisfaction of thinking she'd gotten to her.

It worked. Margaret Mason was pissed.

"I'll let them know tomorrow at work that, unfortunately, you're under the weather and won't be in today. Or the next day. Maybe not even this entire week," her mother spat, her arms crossed over her chest. "Think about it, Grace. I'll keep you chained to your bed as long as I have to until you realize that you're ours to do with as we want. Free will doesn't exist in this household. Never has. Never will."

"If you piss in your bed, you'll sleep in it," Walter said with no emotion in his voice from the other side of her mattress.

Grace looked over and saw he was holding a bucket.

"Just pretend that it's the 1800s and this is your chamber pot." He laughed without humor as he dropped it. Grace flinched at the hollow sound the bucket made as it hit the floor.

Margaret took a step back and tugged on the bottom of her blouse, straightening out the non-existent wrinkles. "Do have a good day, daughter. I hope you don't get too hungry. Think of this as a new diet plan. We'll see you later." With that parting shot, she turned and waltzed out of the room, her husband following close behind her.

Grace tugged hard on her wrists, wincing at the clanging of the heavy chains. She snorted in amazement. It looked like they'd bought some sort of bondage cuffs for her. God forbid her mother bruise her skin in any way and make visible the pain she'd been causing her daughter for years. The cuffs were soft on the inside, but absolutely impossible to get off.

She was stuck.

A prisoner.

Her parents were evil.

She'd known they weren't the nicest people on the block but had never thought they'd go this far.

Grace lay back on the bed in defeat. She could defy them. And she would. But Grace knew she'd give in eventually. She had no choice unless she wanted to live the rest of her life chained to her bed.

Marrying Bradford wouldn't be too bad. But she'd never give up her son to Margaret and Walter. Never.

Chapter Twelve

"You haven't heard from her?" Logan asked Felicity in disbelief the day after he'd gotten back from the escort job in Colorado Springs. It had gone off without a hitch, the asshole who'd taken his ex-girlfriend to court over some petty bullshit hadn't said a word to her before or after the hearing, which was the goal of the escort in the first place. Logan knew the woman would still probably have to deal with the man at some point, but he'd told her that if she needed more assistance, not to hesitate to contact Ace Security.

He'd gotten home late last night and as much as he wanted to call Felicity to check on Grace, he knew it was too late. So he'd slept like crap, tossing and turning, worrying, and had gotten to the gym half an hour before his usual time.

Felicity had shown up after he'd showered. Logan had been waiting impatiently in the lobby, shooting the shit with Cole. The other man knew most of what had been happening, but didn't know anything new about Grace.

"No," Felicity said in a worried tone. "I've texted and emailed, but she hasn't answered. I even bit the bullet and went to her office yesterday, but there was a temp sitting at her desk who said that Grace was sick, and she didn't know when she'd be back."

"Fuck," Logan swore. "She's in trouble."

"You don't know that," Felicity told him, although she didn't sound convinced. "She was really stressed the other night. It could've gotten to her. After learning that you didn't dump her, making the decision to break some of the ties with her parents . . . it was a lot."

"Or maybe they did something to her," Logan said, gritting his teeth in frustration.

"Now just wait a minute," Cole held up his hands in capitulation. "Do you really think the Masons, who have lived here their entire lives, who own one of the most successful businesses in the city, offed their daughter because she said she wanted a second degree and didn't want to sleep over at their house anymore?"

It did sound ridiculous, but the hair on the back of Logan's neck was sticking up, and he wasn't going to put anything past Grace's parents. Not after what they'd done to sabotage his relationship with their daughter. He ran his hand through his hair in agitation. "I didn't necessarily mean that they'd *kill* her, but they're extremely controlling. You said it yourself, Felicity, and who knows how far they'd push that?"

"They're a bit stiff, but I can't see them doing anything crazy," Felicity said firmly. "Why don't you just go over there and see her? I'm sure she's probably just sick."

Logan ran the suggestion over in his head. He wasn't sure he could be polite to Grace's parents after what they'd done to the both of them, but if it meant seeing firsthand that Grace was all right, he'd do it. "Okay, I will."

"You can't just bust in there all Logan-like and demand to see her," Felicity warned.

"Logan-like? What the hell does that even mean?" he demanded.

"Look, you have to play their game. If you go in there acting like the former Army soldier you are, they'll shut down. Believe me, I've known people like this. Go home. Change. Put on a pair of slacks and a collared shirt. Ring the doorbell civilly instead of pounding on the door with your fist. Greet them politely, ask if Grace is home. Tell them you heard she was sick and you were concerned about her health. Shoot the shit about the weather. Whatever it takes. Play. Their. Game. If you don't, you won't get to see her."

Logan ground his teeth together. He knew Felicity was right, but it still pissed him off. "Fine."

"And call me right after."

Logan rolled his eyes. Sometimes Felicity was a badass business owner who took no crap from anyone, and other times she was like a fifteen-year-old.

"You want backup?" Cole asked Logan.

"Yeah, but I don't think it would help Grace," he told his friend honestly. "I appreciate it, though."

"You gonna tell your brothers?"

"Of course. But I need to know what I'm dealing with, if anything, first. I don't want to start something if there's nothing going on."

Cole nodded. "Get the lay of the land. Recon."

"Exactly. I'll be in touch as soon as I have a better idea of what's happening."

"I'll be waiting," Cole grunted.

"*We'll* be waiting," Felicity corrected with a huff.

Logan nodded absently, already running different scenarios over in his head about how his visit to the Masons could go as he headed out the door to his motorcycle. He wanted to ignore Felicity's advice, but knew he couldn't. She was right. He needed to change, get cleaned up, look respectable . . . even if it was a façade. He'd never been respectable, and putting on nice clothes wouldn't make it so, but he'd do it. For Grace.

An hour later, Logan rang the doorbell at the Masons' house. He'd forgone his motorcycle and instead drove his truck. It probably wasn't the kind of car the Masons would respect, but it was a lot better than his bike. He resisted the urge to shift in discomfort. He was wearing a gray suit Nathan had insisted he purchase when they started the business, and it felt awkward as hell. He'd forgone the tie, but had put on a white button-up shirt and a pair of his brother's black dress shoes.

There was a security camera pointed right at him. He'd noticed it as soon as he'd walked up to the large porch in front of the house. Logan stood ramrod straight with his hands folded in front of him, waiting to see if the door would even open. He had his doubts.

Finally, after what seemed like forever, but was probably only about thirty seconds, the door creaked open and Logan came face-to-face with a man who had to be a butler. He was around seventy or so and his deep frown paired with the permanent wrinkles on his withered face made him look meaner than a snake.

"Yes. Can I help you?"

"My name is Logan Anderson. I'm a friend of Grace's. I heard she's been sick and I came to check on her. See how she is. See if I can do anything for her."

"Miss Grace has been feeling under the weather, but I believe her parents are providing all the assistance she needs."

The man went to shut the door, but Logan was faster. He put his foot in the doorway and his hand on the door. "Please. She has a lot of people who are worried about her. I know everyone would feel better if I could just see her for a moment. I don't want to bother her, or her parents, and I certainly don't want to make her feel worse, but I feel as if I wouldn't be a good ambassador for her friends if I didn't at least give her our best wishes in person."

Logan hoped the old man would hear the idle threat in his words. He did.

He took a step back from the door and gestured for Logan to come inside. "If you would kindly follow me, I will notify Mrs. Mason that you are here to inquire about Miss Grace. If she thinks it is in her daughter's best interest to get out of bed and meet with you, they will be down shortly."

The man's words were completely polite, but it was the tone that got to Logan. The butler was irritated that he'd had to let Logan inside, but he didn't give a shit. He was going to see and talk to Grace no matter what. An old man wasn't going to stop him.

He followed the butler down a hallway filled with portraits of unsmiling men on the walls, into a dark room that looked like it was seldom used. There was an uncomfortable looking antique couch against one wall. The floor was a dark wood, and the curtains on the large window were a heavy red velvet. Two chairs, a bookcase filled with books on one wall, and a side table furnished the rest of the room.

"Make yourself comfortable. It might be awhile. If Miss Grace is healthy enough to come out of her room, she will need to make herself presentable." The man bowed his head, then left Logan in the room, closing the door behind him.

Logan eyed the room, finding what he'd been expecting. In the corner, high on the ceiling, was a security camera. Knowing he was being watched, Logan wandered the room, acting nonchalant. He checked out the titles of the books on the shelves, mostly nonfiction, looked out the window at the immaculate grounds outside, and paced.

In the three years he'd known Grace in high school, Logan had never been to her parents' house. They'd always met in the library at the high school for his tutoring sessions, or had seen each other at whatever sporting event was going on. He'd thought he'd known all there was to know about Grace, but he'd been so wrong. He knew she lived in the huge house on the outskirts of Castle Rock and had money, but he didn't know exactly how rich her family was. Logan would bet everything he owned that there were maids, a cook, and probably even a few drivers residing in the house somewhere.

Logan regretted not getting to know more about her back then. He'd been all about himself, drinking up her sympathy and attention, and not bothering to try to find out anything about Grace herself. Not once did she ever tell him she was unhappy. And Logan suddenly realized that it wasn't her style. She spent their time together trying to make him smile, trying to make sure *he* was all right. It was just one of the things he liked about her. Then and now.

He tried to look calm on the outside as he waited for Grace to appear, but on the inside he was seething. He simply couldn't picture her living here. She was so fresh, so unassuming. She'd given him no indication when they were teenagers that she cared about the money her folks had. Yes, she was always wearing designer clothes, and she had a nice BMW back then, but she didn't act like she was better than him, or anyone else at the school.

Without judging him, she'd listened to him go on and on about how horrible his mother was and how much he hated being at home. She'd commiserated with him when he'd told her that his mom sometimes bought booze instead of food. She'd even encouraged him to join the Army when he graduated, if only to get away from his home life.

Not once had Logan guessed that she lived in such a stifled environment. That she was desperate for her parents' love. She was too . . . vibrant to live in a tomb like this one.

The door behind him creaked as it opened, and Logan spun around.

Margaret Mason stood at the door, her arms folded in front of her demurely.

"Good afternoon, Logan. It is pleasant to see you after all these years. I am sorry about your parents' passing."

The words were polite and modulated, but Logan couldn't hear any sort of emotion behind them. There wasn't sympathy. No sincerity. It was obvious she frankly didn't give one whit that his parents were dead.

"Thank you, Mrs. Mason. It's been a difficult time for sure."

"You and your brothers are back in town for good then?"

"Yes, ma'am." Logan didn't elaborate.

"Mmmm. Grace will be down in a bit. As you know, she's not been feeling well and needs to change into more appropriate clothing to greet visitors. She was in bed sleeping, of course."

"I understand. I appreciate your allowing her to visit with me." Logan hated the words, but knew they had to be said. It was more than obvious that this woman ruled the house. If she didn't want Grace to talk to him, then she wouldn't. It was that simple. He was very aware of how she'd kept his letters from Grace all those years ago, and he wanted to rail at her for it, but he held his tongue. For the first time, he realized how Grace might feel. She probably wanted to defy her mother, but knew the power the woman had over her. It was definitely eye-opening, and suddenly, Logan was actually thankful for the first time in his life that his mother only physically abused him instead of manipulating and emotionally blackmailing him and his brothers. He knew what he'd gone through was easier to deal with in some ways than what Grace had been, and still was, experiencing.

"I'd offer you some refreshments, but with the way Grace is feeling, I know the smell of tea and scones would only make her nauseous. You understand, I'm sure."

Logan gritted his teeth. "Of course. I won't keep her too long. Her friends and I are just concerned about her well-being."

Margaret tittered. "I'm not sure what you think is going on here, young man. Grace's father and I aren't keeping her prisoner. She's simply not feeling well. Luckily, she was visiting us when she fell ill and wasn't alone at her apartment."

"Good to hear. I'm looking forward to talking with her."

After another ten minutes, which seemed like ten hours as Logan tried to make small talk with Margaret Mason, the door slid open another few inches, and Grace stepped into the room.

Logan's first thought was that she, indeed, didn't look well. Her face was pale and she had dark circles under her eyes. Her hair was back in its customary bun, although Logan much preferred the more relaxed ponytail she was wearing the last time she saw him. She was wearing a pair of black slacks, her usual heels, and a green silky blouse that buttoned up the front.

He eyed her critically. All in all she looked normal. Put together. Polished. Other than the circles under her eyes, her face didn't show any evidence that she'd been beaten. The skin around her neck was blemish free. Of course, bruises could be hidden under her clothes, but she walked toward him without a limp, showing him that her legs and hips were just fine. Overall, she looked like a young woman who'd simply been under the weather for the last few days . . . just as her mother had said.

She walked straight up to him and stopped, looking up with wide eyes. "Hello, Logan. It's nice of you to stop by."

Her words were polite, and emotionless. It was as if Logan were looking at a Stepford Grace instead of the vibrant young woman he remembered from a few nights ago.

"Hi, Grace. How are you?"

"I've been better."

"Let's sit," Logan told her, taking her hands in his own. They were ice cold. He frowned as he led her to the antique couch, the only place in the room he could sit next to her.

Margaret Mason moved to settle on one of the chairs next to the couch, well within hearing distance.

"Can you give us a moment?" Logan asked politely, even though he really wanted to tell her to give them some space.

"Oh, just ignore me. I just want to make sure that Grace doesn't overdo it. You know how she is . . . always thinking she can push herself. I don't want her to have a relapse."

Again, the words sounded concerned and polite, but there was an ugly undertone that Logan didn't understand. He wanted to talk to Grace without her mother around, but unless he wanted to bodily pick up Mrs. Mason and throw her out of the room, something that wouldn't help him actually get to *talk* to Grace, he needed to play it cool. That pissed him off. He hated being manipulated by the other woman.

Logan sat on the couch and angled his body toward Grace. He'd purposely seated her so her back was to her mother, sitting nearby. Margaret could see *his* face easily, but not Grace's.

"You have the flu?"

Grace shrugged. "I'm not sure. It's probably a virus of some kind."

"Have you seen a doctor?"

"Of course. Mother called the family physician. He examined me and said that whatever it was should run its course in a week or so."

"Hmmmm. Felicity stopped by your office and was surprised to hear you were sick."

Logan watched Grace carefully, studying her body language. Her hands were in her lap, clutching each other. She didn't fidget, she didn't shift at all. She looked composed and in control . . . except for her hands. Her knuckles were white with the strength she was using to hold onto herself. And the pulse in her neck was beating so hard, Logan could clearly see it. Those were the only outward signs that something wasn't right. But they were like huge blinking banners for him. She was practically screaming at him to help her, but he couldn't. Not when he didn't know what was wrong.

"I appreciate that. Please thank her for me," Grace told Logan without changing her facial expression.

"Is there anything we can do for you?"

"No, thank you. My parents are taking care of me, just as they always have. How are your brothers doing?"

Logan wasn't sure why she was asking, but he knew the more time he spent with Grace, the more clues he might get as to what was really going on. He felt in his gut that everything wasn't as it seemed. "They're good. I was in Colorado Springs yesterday on a job, and Nathan drove me crazy with his constant texts. I swear the man is connected to his cell. He wouldn't know what to do without his gadgets."

"I hope everything is all right."

"All right? Oh, with the job?" He waited for her to nod, then reassured her. "Yeah. The client merely needed an escort to a court appearance. Her ex was bullying her and she just needed to show him that she had someone on her side. It works most of the time with bullies. Once they see that the person they've had under their thumb for so long isn't afraid of them, and has someone to stand next to them, to fight for them, they slink away."

It was ballsy of him, but Logan couldn't have stopped the words if his life depended on it. He wanted Mrs. Mason to know that he had Grace's back.

"I admire what you do, Mr. Anderson," Margaret interjected, disapproval ringing clear in her words. "But if the young woman didn't make the wrong decision to be with an inappropriate young man in the first place, she wouldn't be in her current position. Correct?"

Logan tore his eyes away from Grace and turned to look at her mother. She had balls, he had to give her that. "Maybe, maybe not. The man could've acted one way toward her at the beginning of their relationship, but changed once he had her under his thumb. But regardless of how it happened and whose fault it might've been, it's never okay for one human being to bully another. Period."

Margaret didn't say anything, merely shrugged and gave him a fake half smile. Logan turned back to Grace, and noticed, in the short time he'd been talking to her mother, she'd moved. Only slightly, and if he hadn't been examining her so carefully earlier, he wouldn't have noticed.

Her hands were still clasped together in her lap, but she'd shifted so that one of her sleeves was pushed back a couple of inches.

"What are your symptoms? Have you been able to eat anything?" Logan didn't really care about Grace's answer, but wanted to keep her talking while he observed her.

She answered him in the same soft monotone voice, but he ignored it, trying to understand what Grace was obviously trying to tell him with her actions. There was some redness on the wrist she'd exposed, but no bruising. There was a line of what looked like a rug burn over the top of her hand, and another line right below her wrist. That was it. No finger marks, nothing that would scream to him that she was being held against her will.

". . . appreciate it."

"I'm sorry, what?" Logan asked, having missed what she was saying.

She smiled at him then. A polite vacant smile that she might've bestowed on any stranger she met on the street. "I said, thanks for coming by. I appreciate it."

Mrs. Mason stood up, and Grace followed her lead, leaving Logan no choice but to stand as well. "Thank you for caring about our daughter enough to stop by, Mr. Anderson. It means a lot to us that she has such *caring* friends."

"Grace has a lot of people who worry about her. I'm just glad it's nothing more serious. You'll get in touch with Felicity, won't you, Grace? I'll tell her that I saw you today, but you really should talk to her yourself."

"I will. When I'm feeling up to it."

Logan couldn't stand it anymore. He leaned forward and took Grace into his arms in what he hoped looked to her mother merely like a friendly hug. He wanted to whisper in her ear that she wasn't alone, that he'd figure out whatever was going on, but he couldn't. Not while her mother hovered nearby. Instead he pressed the fingers of one hand into the small of her back and wrapped the other around the nape of her neck, making sure his thumb brushed against her invisible tattoo just as he'd done the other night at the gym.

"Take care of yourself, Smarty. I wouldn't want anything to happen to you. You'd be missed," Logan told her earnestly.

"Thank you." The two words were a breath of sound next to his ear rather than actually sounds spoken out loud, but Logan heard them loud and clear.

He pulled back and put his hands on her shoulders. The pulse in her neck was still beating incredibly hard, and Logan felt her clutch his sides for a moment before her hands dropped and she stepped away from him.

"Feel better soon," he said lamely.

"I'm sure I will."

"Come on, Grace. It's time you got back to bed," Margaret said in a no-nonsense tone. "I don't want you to have a relapse. Your father is waiting for you. He'll help you back upstairs and get you comfortable again."

Grace swallowed once, then dropped her gaze to the floor before walking toward the door. She looked back once, and the hair on the back of Logan's neck stood up once more. It was the look of a woman who wanted to hope for the best, but was expecting nothing but the worst.

Remembering the silly thing he used to do when they were in high school that always made her smile, Logan looked her in the eyes and gave her a small chin lift. She didn't smile, but bit her lip, even as her eyes filled with tears, and returned his gesture with a similar one before turning around and exiting the room.

When Grace had left, Logan reluctantly turned to Mrs. Mason. He had to play this out. "Thank you for letting me see your daughter. She means a lot to me and her friends."

"Of course. As I already stated, she's not a prisoner. I am merely concerned about her health. That's all. Maybe you should call before you come over next time. I know it took a lot out of Grace to change so she could look presentable."

"I'll do that. Thank you again. I can see myself out."

"Nonsense. James will do that."

Logan wanted to roll his eyes. Of course the butler's name was James. He merely nodded and followed Mrs. Mason out of the room. The old man was waiting for them, and Logan thanked Grace's mother once more before following James to the front door.

He wanted to tear out of the driveway as if the hounds of hell were after him, but forced himself to drive sedately. As soon as he turned onto the street in front of the house, he picked up his phone and dialed.

"How'd it go?" Nathan asked, not bothering to say hello.

"She's in trouble."

"Why, what happened?"

"I'll tell you all about it when I get to the office. Call Cole. And Felicity."

"Will do. Did you see her?"

"Yeah."

"And? Give me something, man," Nathan said testily.

"I don't know. She said all the right words, but she was terrified," Logan told his brother.

"Of what? You?"

"Not exactly. *For* me, maybe. Of her mother, definitely. Give me forty minutes or so. I need to shower. Get the stink of that house and that woman off me."

"That bad?" Nathan asked, sympathy easy to hear in his voice.

"That bad," Logan confirmed.

"No problem. Blake is on his way in anyway, and I'll get Cole and Felicity. Anyone else we need to pull in?"

"Not right now. I don't have anything concrete, only my hunch. And that's not enough for anything official. But I'll tell you something, bro. She's getting out of that fucking house. One way or another."

"Anything you need, you've got it."

"Appreciated. See you in a bit."

"Bye."

Logan clicked off his phone and wondered what the hell had just happened.

~

Grace didn't say a word, but followed her father meekly up the stairs to her room. She'd so badly wanted to blurt out everything to Logan, but with her mother sitting at her back, she knew she couldn't. Her parents were batshit crazy. There was no telling what they'd do to Logan if she had. Probably lock them both in a secret hidden dungeon under the house.

She would bide her time. Grace had had a lot of time to think while she'd been chained to her bed. She couldn't win against her parents. Not right now. But she was done doing what her parents wanted her to do. *Done.*

She'd play the helpless victim, and the first chance she had, she was out of there. Out of the house. Out of Castle Rock. Out of Colorado. She'd start over somewhere. She'd waitress, clean houses, be a maid in a motel . . . it didn't matter. As long as she was away from Margaret and Walter Mason, and her friends were safe, nothing else mattered.

Grace didn't say a word as her father muttered under his breath, ranted against nosy men, and complained about chest pains. She changed back into the large T-shirt and sweat pants she'd been allowed to wear, not even caring that her father was in the room watching her change. She lay down on the bed and allowed him to snap the leather cuffs back on her wrists. They'd chafed her skin, enough to leave faint marks. Grace had no idea if Logan had seen them or not or even understood what he was looking at. It was the only physical sign she had of her captivity. The only clue she'd had to show him.

The chains rattled over her head as her father clicked the lock shut. He didn't say a word to her afterward, just left her lying captive in her bed. Grace would've killed for something to eat, but her mother was limiting her to a mere five hundred calories a day. She'd laughed and said it was a crash diet of sorts.

Grace hated her parents.

Hated them.

For so long she'd done everything she could to get them to love her. To appreciate her. To be proud of her. But all along, she'd been fighting a losing battle. They'd never love her. And with that realization, any love she'd held her in heart for the people who'd raised her died.

Grace understood Logan's desire to leave town the second he'd graduated even more now.

She should've gone with him back then. Bought a ticket and climbed onto that bus with him.

Shoulda, coulda, woulda. It was all a moot point.

But the second she was able, this time, she was gone.

Chapter Thirteen

Logan sat around a big circular table at Ace Security with his brothers, Felicity, and Cole. He'd gone over every word Grace had said and still wasn't exactly sure what she was trying to tell him. On the surface, everything seemed fine, but Logan knew it wasn't.

"She said her parents were taking care of her just like they always did?" Felicity asked incredulously.

"Yeah. Those were her exact words," Logan confirmed.

"They haven't taken care of her since she learned how to walk," Felicity groused. "Not really. I know I only met her a few years ago, but seriously. They are the coldest people I've ever had the misfortune to meet."

"And you said there were cameras?" Nathan asked.

"Yeah. I noticed them as I drove up, and they were even inside the house too."

"Blake, can you get into them?" Nathan inquired.

"What? No. I'm not a hacker."

"But you love computers," Logan argued.

"Yeah. I do. But that doesn't mean I can hack into any ol' system I want to. I can analyze video that someone gives me, I can research like nobody's business, and if I've got the hard drive of a computer, I can search it and pull up browsing history, see what websites someone's been to and things like that, but I'm no hacker."

"Shit, man. You were in the Army. Don't you have any contacts?" Logan complained.

"You were too. Don't *you* have any contacts?" Blake retorted.

"Fuck." Logan rubbed his temple. "I thought all you computer geeks knew each other. In the movies, there's always that one guy who seems to know everyone and can get information with the tap of a keyboard."

Nathan snorted. "Those people don't really exist. It only happens in the movies and maybe novels. Not in real life. Believe me, I wish I did know someone like that. He'd be a godsend in our line of work. Besides being illegal, someone would have to be really good, or *really* lucky to hack into cameras, satellites, and government databases on an ongoing basis."

"Dammit. We need to know what's going on inside that house," Blake complained.

Felicity said, "Grace put me down on her bank account, just in case. I can check it to see if she's withdrawn any money."

"Good idea," Logan told her. "What about her other phone? Can you contact her on that?"

"I've been trying. She hasn't answered. I don't know if her parents found it, or she can't get to it, or if she's just lying low."

The room was silent for a moment, then Cole asked, "So she had a mark on the back of her hand. Do you think it meant anything?"

Logan shrugged. "I thought so at first, but now I don't know. It didn't look like a handcuff mark. I've seen enough of those to know what they look like. This didn't look like anything other than a rug-burn mark.

"Where was it again?" Nathan asked, his teeth clenched in agitation at the suggestion Grace had been abused.

"There was a slight pink mark here and here." Logan held up his hand and drew an imaginary line above his wrist on the back of his hand, and about four inches below that.

"Too big for cuffs for sure," Cole agreed.

"But they could still be restraints of some sort," Nathan argued.

"Yeah," Felicity agreed. "If they want to make sure she isn't marked at all, they could've wrapped something around her wrists so they wouldn't bruise. Grace is smart. Why else would she purposely lift up the sleeve of her blouse?"

Logan gritted his teeth, but couldn't hold back his reaction. He stood up so suddenly the chair he'd been sitting in was knocked backward and fell to the floor with a loud bang. He smacked the table with his open palm, then turned to the wall and smacked it as well. He then braced both hands on it and leaned over, breathing hard. Pissed off.

The room was silent for a moment, before Felicity had the nerve to break it. "Why do you care so much, Logan?"

Logan whipped around and, between his clenched teeth, he ground out, "What?"

Felicity held up her hands in capitulation. "Don't get all pissy. I'm just saying, you've been back in town for a couple of months. You really only talked to her once in all that time. Granted, your conversation was intense, you both learned her parents fucked you both over, but still. Did you guys get engaged at the gym party the other night and not tell us or something? Is there more you want to tell us? Don't get me wrong, I'm happy that you care, because Grace needs a badass like you to give a shit what happens to her, but I'm honestly confused."

Logan wanted to chew Felicity out, but realized she was right. He wasn't even sure himself why he cared so much, he only knew he did. He paced as he spoke, his words coming out haltingly, then faster and faster as the emotion he was feeling poured out.

"I like her. A lot. Always have. Even though we've only kissed once, right before I blew out of town, it's still the most memorable kiss I've ever shared with a woman. And all we did was touch lips. When I thought she'd dumped me, it stung. I went a bit crazy, fucking a few women who offered, getting in fights just to fight. After a while I tried to date. I found a couple very nice women who would make excellent wives and mothers. No go. I didn't feel half the spark I felt when I was around Grace.

"When I got back in town I stayed away from her. I didn't want the fantasy I had in my head of who she was to get tarnished. Even though I thought she deliberately hurt and misled me, I couldn't get her out of my head."

Logan took a deep breath and looked at his friends. They weren't looking at him in pity, but with compassion and empathy. He continued.

"All it took was five minutes in her company, and all the feelings I'd had when I was eighteen came rushing back . . . tenfold. She was exactly as I remembered . . . and more so. So, yeah, Felicity, I care about her. A lot. Maybe she doesn't want anything to do with me. Maybe she just wants to be friends. But I don't think so."

"I don't think so either," Felicity agreed. "I've never seen her so . . . giddy as she was that last night I saw her. If I had my way, I'd lock the two of you in a room and leave you there for a week."

"I'm not sure that would get her out of my system," Logan said dryly.

"I hope not. I'd do it so you could both get under each other's skin so far you wouldn't be able to live without the other. But, I have to say it. Don't hurt her, Logan. I'll cut off your balls if you do."

"I won't." Logan managed to not even flinch at her choice of words.

"Good. So what's the plan?"

Logan's lips quirked and he looked over at his brother. "Blake? You're the best at this kind of thing." Logan wanted nothing else than to barge into the house on the hill and steal Grace away, but he knew he had to be smart. The last thing he needed was to be thrown in jail on kidnapping charges and to have Ace Security shut down. They had to be careful. And if that meant letting his brothers take control, he'd do it.

"We'll take turns watching the house, out of range of their cameras. We'll take pictures and see if we can't get a glimpse of Grace through the windows. Take note of who is coming and going and see if we can't get any information out of any of them once they've left the Mason house. Delivery drivers, visitors, employees. We'll get as much from them as possible, then decide on our next move."

"How long?" Logan asked. "If Grace is being hurt, we can't wait. Talking to everyone who visits the house will take too long."

"I'm not sure. I don't want her in that house any longer than she has to be either, but we have to play this smart," Blake said evenly.

"Fine. But if we get any indication that she's being hurt, we'll make a move."

"I swear, Logan. Now, let's make up a schedule as to who is doing what, when," Blake said, shuffling some papers in front of him.

The group huddled over the table discussing the best vantage points to the Mason mansion and who would take first watch.

The four men and one woman had made an unofficial pact to get to the bottom of what was going on inside the walls of Grace's prison. One way or another.

Chapter Fourteen

Grace sat with her eyes downcast and fiddled with a thread at the hem of her shirt as her mother spoke with Bradford's parents. It had been three days since she'd been allowed downstairs to speak with Logan. Three long days of silence interspersed with lectures and threats from both her mother and father.

She'd heard over and over how Logan and his brothers would be ruined if she so much as spoke one word about what was happening to her. Felicity and Cole's gym would burn to the ground if Grace dared speak of the long days of food and water deprivation.

That afternoon, Margaret had informed Grace that Bradford and his parents were coming over for supper so the seed could be planted about a "relationship" between Bradford and Grace.

Grace liked Brad's parents. She'd met them only a handful of times, but they seemed way more down to earth than her own parents. Bradford had a sister that Grace had never met, but the few times Brad talked about her, she seemed to be the kind of person Grace would like to get to know. Alexis was a few years younger than her, but from what Brad had said, she was extremely mature for her age. Even though the Grants had money, they hadn't let it strip away their souls as Margaret and Walter apparently had.

To ensure her cooperation that evening at dinner, Walter had told Grace exactly what would happen to Betty and Brian Grant if she didn't keep her mouth shut. He'd told her how they knew someone who could easily cut their brake lines, sending the couple to their deaths on the back mountain roads of Colorado as they made their way to their house in the mountains west of Denver one night.

Grace had a lot of time to think up in that room, and she realized that over the last year or two her parents had become even more harsh with their words and actions. Did she want to believe her parents were capable of murder? No. But their threats, combined with holding her against her will, told her that something had pushed them over the edge and they'd come unhinged.

So she'd nodded meekly at her father's threat.

And planned her escape.

Logan swore long and hard in his head as he watched the Mercedes SUV pull up to the Masons' house. He'd insisted on taking the night watches for the last few days, leaving Nathan and Blake to take turns during the day. For some reason, he had the feeling that Grace was more vulnerable at night, and even though he had no idea what was really going on inside the house, it made him feel closer to her to keep watch in the nighttime hours.

The last few nights, nothing untoward had happened as far as he could tell. Logan used his binoculars and the long lens on his camera to keep watch over the occupants of the house through the windows. Unfortunately, he couldn't ascertain much from his vantage points around the property. He'd seen Walter and Margaret eating dinner in the large impersonal dining room, and various house help wandering around with their eyes downcast, but no sign of Grace.

No matter where he moved around the property, he'd never glimpsed her. Not once. The curtains in the room that Felicity said was Grace's bedroom were drawn tightly over the window. There was a slight glow from the room that went off each evening, so Logan was pretty sure she was in there, but he hadn't even seen so much as her shadow walking around the room, which bothered him.

Bringing the binoculars to his eyes, Logan watched as Betty and Brian Grant got out of the Mercedes, followed by their children, Bradford and Alexis. Felicity had told Logan and his brothers that Grace's mother wanted Grace and Bradford to marry. Logan made a mental note to have Blake research the entire Grant family. If they had anything to do with whatever was going on with Grace, they'd pay. She wasn't a pawn to be moved around a chessboard, even if that's what she'd been in the past.

Brian Grant rang the doorbell and the butler opened it. The old man still didn't look happy, but he backed up, allowing the group to enter the large house without any hassle. For the thousandth time, Logan wished they had a hacker to help them. He'd give anything, absolutely anything, to hear what was going on inside the house at that very moment.

Logan pulled the hood of his black sweatshirt more securely over his forehead and shifted position. He made sure to stay out of range of the motion detectors he was sure existed, moving slowly enough so as not to raise or to attract attention to himself to anyone who might review surveillance videos later. Finally finding his usual observation spot where he could see inside the dining room, Logan settled in.

For the first time in three days, Logan caught a glimpse of Grace. At first glance, she looked fine. Her hair was in her customary bun. She was wearing a long-sleeve gray shirt, with some sort of scarf around her neck. Her slacks were black, and hugged her hips as she walked. She was smiling politely at the Grants, and shook all of their hands, before sitting down.

Luckily, she was sitting facing the large window so Logan could see her clearly from his vantage point. Her parents were sitting on either side of her, Bradford across the table from her between his own parents, and Alexis was seated at the end of one side of the table.

All in all, it seemed to be a strange seating arrangement to Logan, but what did he know about the proper way to seat guests for a formal dinner?

The longer Logan watched the group eat, the more concerned he got for Grace. She rarely spoke and ate little. There were a few times when he caught her biting her lip and could tell she was grinding her teeth together. Her jaw flexed with the movements.

Logan couldn't read lips, but the nonverbal cues were speaking volumes. Margaret Mason vacillated between pleasure, disapproval, and if he wasn't mistaken, triumph. Whatever direction the conversation was taking, it seemed to be mostly going her way.

The two-hour dinner looked extremely awkward, and Logan could tell Grace was close to her breaking point at the end of it. Margaret had waved off dessert when the servant offered it to Grace and laughed after saying something. Grace didn't respond and looked down at her lap.

After the meal was over, everyone stood up and headed out of the dining room. Logan imagined they were entering into the stuffy sitting room where he'd visited with Grace. He stealthily moved around the expansive lawn again, thankful once more that the curtains were pulled back. He watched the group through his binoculars, grinding his teeth at the urgency that beat through him with each passing minute.

The group sat and talked for another thirty minutes or so after the meal, again displaying many of the same mannerisms as they had at dinner. This time, however, Logan had a better visual on Betty and Brian Grant. They exchanged several worried glances, and there were a lot of hand gestures.

Whatever the conversation, it didn't look like it was going well. Finally, it seemed that the discussion was over, and James reappeared in the doorway. He escorted the Grants out of the house, and this time, they weren't smiling. Alexis looked confused and worried. Bradford looked incredulous, and their parents looked straight-out pissed.

As they drove away, Logan made a mental note to have Blake contact Alexis. He wasn't quite sure he could trust Bradford or the Grants, in general. Logan wasn't sure how they figured into Margaret Mason's plans, but the sister seemed to be a wildcard. Blake could talk to her, feel her out, try to see what she knew. She might talk to him, or she might not . . . but it was worth a shot.

At the moment, however, Logan was more concerned about Grace. She and her parents were still in the sitting room having what looked like an intense conversation. Well, Margaret and Walter were. Grace was sitting with her head down, not speaking at all.

Whatever they were saying didn't seem to be having much of an effect on Grace, but remembering what Felicity had told him, Logan was finally understanding that whatever her mother was saying to her probably hurt just as much as his own mother's fists had.

His thoughts were proven true when Margaret reached down and grasped Grace's chin in her hand and forced it upward. Through the lenses of Logan's binoculars, he could see the skin on her face turn white with the pressure from her mother's fingers. Logan's rage almost got the better of him before he tamped it down and controlled it.

The last time Logan was this angry was in the Army when a terrorist pushed a small child, around five years old, out of a car toward a checkpoint. The little girl had an adult-size backpack on her back, and she staggered under its weight.

All of the soldiers knew immediately what was happening but couldn't stop what was inevitable. The child didn't comprehend English, didn't understand the soldiers around her yelling at her to stop. To not take another step. But she obviously *did* comprehend what her father would do to her if she disobeyed him. She kept walking.

Logan hadn't been the one to take the shot that day, but he remembered the rage he felt toward the man who'd brainwashed her and made that little girl so terrified of him that she'd allowed herself to become a walking bomb.

Felicity had been right. Margaret might not have been physically abusing Grace, but she was slaying her with words. Probably had been for Grace's entire life. Hiding his letters was just a drop in the bucket of abuse Grace had most likely faced since she'd been a kid. It was a miracle that she was as strong as she was. Most people would've been beaten down and cowering.

Even though Grace looked uncomfortable, and there was fear on her face, Logan also recognized her determination. He vowed then and there, sitting in the dark outside her house, watching her quiet strength, that she wouldn't spend another twenty-four hours under her parents' thumb.

As Margaret continued to harangue Grace, Walter Mason wandered to the window and stared out into his yard for a long moment. Logan knew he was well hidden, but he found himself holding his breath and tightening every muscle in his body. With a quick flick of his wrist, Walter pulled a cord to the right of where he was standing and dark, thick blinds fell from the top of the window to block Grace and whatever was happening to her from his gaze.

Swearing, Logan reluctantly put down the binoculars and backed away from his hiding spot behind a cluster of trees. They'd done more than enough recon. It was time to act. He needed to meet with his brothers and get Grace the fuck out of that house once and for all.

Grace's mind swam with all that had gone on in the last few hours. Margaret was putting her plan in motion, and Grace had been appalled by her behavior. At first glance, Brian and Betty Grant seemed like the kind of people who would bow to pressure and cower under the might of Margaret Mason. But thankfully, they weren't.

They'd obviously been as surprised at her mother's plans as Bradford had been. They'd politely protested and said that they would not interfere with their children's love lives, but Margaret had continued to push, throwing Grace under the bus as usual, telling the Grants that Grace had had a crush on Bradford for ages, and how she was looking forward to getting to know him more intimately. The night had gone downhill after that, with everyone feeling awkward and anxious. The Grants had left soon after.

But it was the confused and angry look on Alexis's face that had hurt Grace the most. The other woman thought she was in on her parents' plan and seemed to hate her because of it. Any thoughts that they might someday be friends had just been obliterated by the actions of her parents.

Grace ground her teeth together as her mother continued to rage at her after the Grants left. She ignored the accusations and the threats and retreated into her head, plotting how she was going to get away from her insane parents. Her father hadn't said much, but he hadn't disagreed with his wife either.

She was jerked back to the present when her mother grabbed her chin and forced her head up, chewing her out so violently that spittle came out of her mouth, landing on Grace's face. She didn't move to wipe it away but just stared blankly up at her mother.

Finally, Margaret spat, "I don't need your cooperation anyway. I'll get what I want, one way or another. I always do," and thrust her head away from her in disgust. "Take her back to her room, Walter. Another few days without eating will make her come around, I'm sure."

Walter took her upper arm in his and yanked her upright. Grace stumbled alongside her father as they made their way down the long hallway to her room. Once again, she changed into a T-shirt and sweats and didn't make a sound as her father chained her back up. Surprisingly, the older man didn't say a word either, and soon Grace was alone in her jail cell once more.

She just had to wait them out. Margaret would get sick of her game sooner or later, and Grace would be ready to act. All she needed was five minutes, and she could make her escape.

Five frickin' minutes.

That's all.

When her chance came, she was taking it.

Chapter Fifteen

Logan and Blake crouched behind a bank of bushes alongside the Mason property. They'd plotted and planned for hours after Logan had returned from surveilling the family the night before. They had a plan, it wasn't exactly legal, but Logan didn't care. He'd seen enough to know that something was terribly wrong in the Mason household, and he wasn't going to wait any longer to get Grace out.

So the plan was to kidnap her.

It wasn't exactly the best plan, but it was the most expedient way to get her out of the house. There were a lot of unknowns, but they'd worked through as many of them as they could. Cameras, the Masons themselves, Grace's mental state, the servants whose whereabouts couldn't be accounted for . . . it was time.

Logan gestured at Blake after Nathan rang the doorbell to distract Walter and Margaret. They moved as one toward Grace's window. The curtain was closed tightly, as it had been all week, but there was a light on in the room. They'd spray-painted the lenses of the cameras at the side of the house to buy them some extra time and to make it harder for anyone to identify them. Both men wore all black, complete with gloves. Blake tried the window. Locked. They'd expected it. Logan pulled a glass cutter from his pocket and quickly and silently carved a hole into the glass big enough for his hand to slip through and unlock the window. He held his breath as Blake eased the glass up, relaxing as no alarms went off. Using Blake's hands as a step stool, Logan crawled into the room.

The object of their mission was asleep on her bed. Logan took a moment to drink her in. Grace was on her side, both hands under her pillow. She looked peaceful, which was a nice change after what he'd witnessed the night before.

The light next to the bed was on, and Logan ran his eyes over Grace, looking for signs of abuse. Her cheeks were flushed and her breathing came out slow and even. She was wearing a T-shirt and her arms had no bruises on them. The sheet had been pushed down to her hips and Logan could see her chest rising and falling rhythmically.

He breathed out a relieved sigh that, from what he could see, she looked to be unhurt. Silent as a ghost, he strode across the room, keeping his head down, and put one hand on Grace's shoulder and as he rolled her to her back, putting the other over her mouth to muffle any startled sound she made.

She came awake with a jerk, staring up at him in the low light.

"It's Logan. You're safe." He kept his voice low, so it wouldn't be picked up by any cameras in the room. "Don't make a sound. Understand?"

She nodded under his hand.

"I'm going to take my hand away. Please. Not a word. I'll explain."

Grace nodded again, faster this time.

Logan eased his gloved hand off her mouth and opened his to tell her what the hell he was doing in her bedroom, when she beat him to the punch.

"Get me out of here."

Logan had a million questions for her, but those five words answered the most pressing. "We don't have a lot of time. Grab only what you have to have." Logan turned to eyeball the room, scoping it out.

"Can you get these off?"

He turned back to Grace, not understanding the question, but tensing when he saw what she was talking about.

She was holding up her hands, which had been hidden under her pillow, showcasing the wide cuffs on her wrists with the chain attached to both snaking up to the headboard of her bed.

"Son of a bitch," Logan swore, narrowing his eyes on the padlocks keeping her prisoner. Her parents had locked her up as if she were an animal. Chained their daughter to her bed as if she were a mental patient. Logan wanted to kick himself for waiting as long as he did to come and get her out.

"They keep the key on them. I've tried to slip my hands out of the cuffs, but they're too tight. All I did was hurt myself," Grace whispered.

Logan sized up the situation quickly. "I don't have anything to cut them off with," he apologized, moving toward the headboard to examine it.

"Oh, I understand. Will you come back with something?"

Logan looked sharply at Grace. "I'm not fucking leaving you here, Grace."

"But—"

"Those assholes aren't as smart as they think they are. Stand up." Logan was beyond pissed. Pissed at her parents. Pissed that Grace thought he'd leave her there. Just pissed in general. He helped her stand next to her bed, getting angry all over again when Grace swayed on her feet. She was wearing a pair of gray sweatpants, which she held onto with one hand. The white T-shirt she had on hung on her frame.

Shifting her to the side, Logan leaned down and affirmed what he'd suspected. He turned back to Grace and said urgently, "Things are gonna go quick here in a second. I'm going to make a shitload of noise and we'll have to move. What do you need me to get before we go?"

She shifted in front of him, biting her lip and refusing to meet his gaze.

"What, Grace? Hurry. We don't have a lot of time."

She looked up at him then. "There's a stack of letters under my mattress. I'm sure my parents know about them, but for some reason they let me keep them. Probably because they thought it would hurt me to have them." She shrugged. "I didn't take them when I moved into my apartment because I was trying to move on."

Logan immediately bent to the bed and lifted the top mattress and pulled out the letters. They were tied together with a pink ribbon. He held them out to her. "These?" He tried not to feel a stab of pain at the thought of her receiving letters from someone else . . . and having them be so important she kept them under her bed.

"Yeah. They're um . . ." she wouldn't meet his eyes again. "I wrote you. All the time. I didn't know where to send them, but I thought I'd send them when I heard from you. Even when I didn't get anything from you, writing to you became a habit. I'd tell you everything that was going on here." Grace looked up at him then, self-conscious and defiant at the same time.

"Those are letters you wrote to *me*?" Logan asked, flabbergasted.

"Yeah."

"Fuck," he breathed, pulling her to him, crushing the letters between them. "Fuck," he repeated, not able to get anything else out. Finally, knowing he had to get this show on the road, he cleared his throat and pulled away from her. "Anything else?"

"No. Everything here was bought by my parents. I don't want anything from them."

"Your IDs and stuff?"

She winced and shrugged. "I'm assuming my mother has it all."

Logan nodded. It would be tough to deal with, but not impossible. Blake could help them replace the missing IDs.

"Do you have any sneakers?"

She shook her head. "No. Those letters are the only thing I want to take with me."

Logan's heart swelled in his chest. He'd once been a part of a rescue mission for a group of men over in the Middle East who'd been held captive. They'd had the same look in their eyes as Grace did. The only thing they'd wanted to do was get out of the building they'd been held in, and get the hell out of the city. The fact that he saw that same desperation in Grace's eyes now spoke volumes.

"Okay, time to go. Gather up the chains, but don't wrap them around your wrists," Logan ordered, nodding in approval as she did as he'd asked. "I can't break them, but I can destroy the headboard. See these slats?" He pointed at the thin spindles of her headboard. "I'm going to kick them out and since the chain isn't attached to anything else, as soon as they're broken you'll be free of the bed. We'll just take the chain with us and take care of it later. As I said earlier, it's gonna make some noise, so we need to move the moment you're free. Okay?"

"Yes."

"Blake is waiting outside the window. I know it'll be hard to move carrying those chains, but I'll help, and he'll make sure you don't trip." He eyed the armful of chains and the precious letters she held to her chest. "Do you want me to carry those? I promise I'll keep them safe."

Grace hesitated, and he saw her swallow and blush before holding out the bundle to him. "Yeah. Thanks. They're yours anyway."

He tucked the letters inside the pocket of his sweatshirt, not missing the look of relief on Grace's face. Logan climbed up on her bed, feeling the warmth of her body still on the sheets beneath him. If he'd been anywhere else doing anything else, he probably would've taken the time to enjoy being in her bed, but at the moment, he was just too pissed off and anxious to get out of the house.

"You ready?"

"More than."

"Step away as far as you can toward the window and turn around. I don't want you to get hurt when the wood goes flying."

"It wouldn't matter," Grace told him as she followed his orders. "If it gets me out of here, I don't care if I get hurt."

"*I* care," Logan told her, returning his attention to the headboard. He heard her indrawn breath, but ignored it. "On the count of three. One. Two. *Three*." His foot came down hard on the two spindles next to one of the chains. They split easily, with a loud crack. Logan quickly shifted and aimed his foot at the other two spindles holding Grace hostage. Using all the rage built up inside him, those two broke as well.

He hopped off the bed and put one arm around Grace's waist, pulling her toward the window as she frantically gathered up the loose chain. They clanged as she moved, and she winced.

"Sorry. Shit, I'm being too loud. I'm sorry."

"It's fine, Grace. You're doing just fine. Come on." Logan helped gather up the chain as they stepped up to the window. He threw back the curtains and saw Blake's anxious face.

"Jesus, bro. You made enough noise to wake the dead. I think our timetable just shifted."

Logan watched as the reason for all the noise became clear to his brother.

"Motherfucker. Really? They chained her like a dog?"

"I prefer to say like a pissed-off wild boar," Grace told Blake with a serious look on her face.

Blake managed a short chuckle. "Come on, honey, let's blow this Popsicle stand." He held up his arms to help Grace step out of the window.

She awkwardly held the heavy chains in one hand and reached out for Blake with the other. With his help, and Logan's behind her, she was soon standing on the ground. Logan appeared at her side within seconds.

"Shit," Logan swore, looking at her bare feet. "I forgot."

"It's fine, let's just go," Grace told him, obviously not wanting to wait another moment.

"Hold onto me," Logan ordered, bending over and picking her up. She squeaked, but didn't cry out as she was lifted into his arms.

She lifted one hand over his head, careful not to bash him with the chain still attached to her wrist.

Without a word, the trio made their way quickly and silently through the trees on the property until they reached Nathan's car.

"Hurry up!" the youngest Anderson barked. "They heard whatever it was that you did, and the shit hit the fan. I showed myself out and hightailed it back here. The element of surprise is obviously shot to hell. What the hell did you—"

Nathan's voice trailed off when he got a good look at Grace, then said to her grumpily, "Please tell me you're into kinky sex."

"Um, no," Grace said, slightly embarrassed.

"Damn. Didn't think so."

Blake got into the front seat of the older-model Ford, which most of the time sounded like it was on its last leg, and Logan climbed awkwardly into the back with Grace. As soon as the door shut behind them, Nathan floored it and started down the long driveway.

"What are we gonna say when the cops come to question us in the morning?" Nathan fretted as he drove.

"The cops aren't going to come," Grace said calmly.

"How can you say that?" Nathan barked. "Two men, dressed all in black, just unchained you from wherever you were being kept and stole you out of the house. And let me say, your parents are *pissed*, Grace."

"I bet they are," she agreed. "But think about what you just said. Two men unchained me from the bed and took me. *Unchained. Me.* My parents aren't going to want to draw attention to that."

"Damn," Nathan breathed, looking slightly relieved at her words.

"Are you all right?" Logan asked from beside her. Grace didn't look all right to him. She sounded fine, but he could feel her trembling and saw that she was clenching her hands together, like she had when he'd come to see her a few days ago.

"I'm fine. Thank you for coming to—"

"Don't bullshit me, Grace."

"Logan," Blake warned from the front seat, obviously not liking his brother's tone.

"No. She's not fine. She's shaking like a leaf and she's got fucking cuffs around her wrists. When's the last time you ate?"

Grace looked down at her wrist by rote, forgetting she wasn't wearing a watch. "Um, what time is it?"

"Fuck. Never mind. I don't want to know. It'll just piss me off more, which is saying something."

"Want me to stop?" Nathan asked.

"No. I'll feed her when we get home."

Grace put a hand on Logan's arm and looked up at him. "I'm okay, Logan, really. I'm sure Felicity will have something I can snack on when we get there."

"You're not going to her house," Logan informed her, putting his hand over hers on his arm.

"I'm not?"

"No."

When he didn't elaborate, Grace asked, "Why not?"

"Because I can keep you safe from your asshole parents better than she can."

Grace bit her lip and looked up at him for a long moment. The silence in the car was thick. Finally, she said, "They've threatened you, I don't want you, *any* of you, to get hurt because of me."

Logan couldn't stand the sadness in Grace's words. He brought a hand up and put it against her neck. "We can take care of ourselves, Grace. For now, I'm taking you to my house. You'll be safe there. I'll feed you, you can shower and try to relax, and know that you won't ever have to deal with those assholes again. Then tomorrow, everyone who cares about you will come over, and you can tell us everything that's happened, and we'll figure out where to go from there. Okay?"

"I'd kill for some cheese fries," Grace told him, staring in his eyes.

Logan smiled at her response. Without breaking eye contact, Logan said, "Swing by Outback, Nathan. They should still be open. Grace needs a large order of their cheese, ranch, bacon fries. To go."

Without waiting for an answer, Logan told Grace quietly, "I'm not eighteen anymore, Smarty. I'm a man who knows what he wants and won't let anyone get in his way anymore."

"They aren't going to let this go," Grace fretted.

"I didn't think they would," Logan said calmly, patting her leg to reassure her.

"I don't know how it got to this," she said sadly, picking at one of the cuffs. "All I ever wanted to do was make them happy."

"They knew it, and used your good nature against you."

"I'm scared," Grace admitted, tears sparkling in her eyes.

"I know. And I hate that. But this is gonna work out."

"I have money. I can pay—"

"No. Fuck no. This isn't about money. This is about you and me, Grace. About the connection we made when we were just kids that we weren't allowed to act on," Logan told her firmly.

"But I know Ace Security isn't cheap."

"We're not," Logan agreed, putting a finger under her chin so she had no choice but to look at him as he reiterated his point. "This isn't about our company. Didn't you hear me? It's about you and me."

"We wouldn't take your money anyway, honey," Blake piped in cheerfully from the front seat.

"Yeah, like we'd make you pay," Nathan agreed with a laugh, as if the thought of her paying them a dime was absolutely ridiculous.

"Answer me this one question, Grace," Logan ordered. "If things had gone the way we had thought they would back then, would you have sent me the letters that are sitting in my pocket right now?"

Grace nodded.

"Right. We can't change the past, but we can make sure from this point on, we're making decisions for ourselves and not letting someone else make them for us. No more talk about money. Okay?"

"Okay."

Logan tipped her chin up even farther and put his other hand on the side of Grace's neck. Leaning down, he'd done what he'd dreamed of doing for more years than he'd ever admit. He took Grace's mouth as if he'd done it a thousand times. As if he'd die if he didn't taste her right that moment. She gasped, and he took advantage, surging into her mouth.

Thankfully, Grace reciprocated immediately, tilting her head so he had a better angle, letting her tongue dance with his. Logan didn't close his eyes, not for a second, wanting to memorize every second of his first *real* kiss with Grace Mason. Her eyes had shut the second his lips met hers, and he watched as her eyes fluttered under her lids. Groaning low in his throat, Logan reluctantly pulled away. He licked his lips, tasting Grace on them, and waited for her to open her eyes and look at him.

The second she did, he leaned into her and put his lips right next to her ear and whispered, "Your parents might have kept you from me ten years ago, but that ends now. Got it?"

Her eyes got wide as she turned to him, and he could see her pupils dilate in the dim light from the streetlights in response to his words.

"Yeah, I got it," she whispered as she clutched his shirt at his waist. He could feel her shaking against him. "And you should know, I'd already made plans to find you whenever they let me go and tell you the exact same thing."

He smiled tenderly down at her. "Good. I know the location's not ideal, but I couldn't wait one more second to taste you."

Logan brushed his thumb over her bottom lip, wiping away the moisture left behind by his mouth and leaned down, kissing her once more. A swift, hard kiss that was more reassuring and affectionate than the passionate one they'd just shared.

Nathan and Blake gave no indication they knew what was happening in the backseat, but he didn't care if they knew or not. He was done pretending Grace didn't mean something to him.

They stopped at the restaurant and Nathan ran in and picked up the french fries, which Grace tore into right there in the car. Logan was pissed at the enthusiastic, if not desperate way she gobbled up the greasy snack. Not at Grace, but once more at her parents, who'd obviously not been taking care of their daughter. He'd hear the whole story the next day, but for now, he just wanted to revel in the fact that Grace was safe. Was with him. And was where she'd hopefully be for a long time to come.

By the time Nathan pulled up to Logan's apartment, Grace was sound asleep. She'd managed to make a good dent in the fries, but had petered out not too long after she'd started eating. Logan figured it was the fact that her belly was full and she felt safe.

"Want us to come up? Help with those locks?" Blake asked in a low voice so as not to wake Grace.

"No, I got it. I've got a pair of bolt cutters in my car. Thanks, though."

"What time you want us to come over tomorrow?"

"There's that escort job up in Denver in the morning. You know, the one where we're making sure the woman's ex doesn't harass her while she's collecting her stuff from their apartment. You can take it for me, right?"

"Of course," Blake told his brother. "Already planned on it. You didn't even have to ask."

"Come over at one. That'll give you time to get that done, get back here, collect Cole and maybe Felicity," Logan commented.

"You don't want to meet at the office?" Nathan asked, also in a quiet voice.

"No, I'd prefer to keep her at my place for now. Make sure she's safe."

"Makes sense," Blake agreed. "We'll meet here whenever we need to in the foreseeable future then. Anything else?"

"Can you please call Felicity and let her know Grace is safe? I know she's been really worried about her."

"Of course," Blake agreed. He paused as if unsure, then continued. "You positive about this?"

Logan knew exactly what his brother meant. "Absolutely. I don't know what it is about her, but my gut is screaming at me to keep her close. I thought we'd end up together when I was eighteen. Apparently my feelings haven't changed."

"What if she doesn't reciprocate?" Nathan asked.

"When I asked if she wanted to take anything with her before we left, the only thing she wanted was a stack of letters hidden under her mattress. Letters she'd written to me that she never got to send. She'd been waiting for me to write her to get my address. She's kept them all these years."

"Damn," Nathan breathed, understanding that the letters were answer enough to his question. "Anything you need, you got it. You know we'll protect her with our lives. If she's that important to you, she's that important to us."

"Thank you." Logan knew the words didn't begin to say what he wanted, but they were what he had at the moment.

"Go on. Get those fucking things off her wrists. I'll call Felicity, make sure she knows we're on this. See if she can't go to her apartment and gather some of her things to bring over. We'll see you tomorrow."

Logan nodded at his brothers and scooted carefully out of the car. Grace woke up enough to hold onto him as he climbed out.

"My letters?" she mumbled in concern. "You've still got them?"

"Yeah, Smarty. I've got them. You have no idea how much it means to me that you wrote, and that you still have these. I have a stack remarkably similar to this one back at my place. We can trade, yeah?"

"You kept them, even though they were returned?" Grace said, tightening her grip around his neck in reaction.

"Yeah." He met her eyes and said with open honesty, "I couldn't make myself get rid of them. They were my only connection to you."

They shared a look. One of understanding, longing, and frustration of all that had been kept from them.

"I'd like to read your letters, Logan," Grace whispered, laying her head back on his chest.

"Then you will," he reassured her.

Logan heard Nathan's car drive off as he strode toward his apartment, and he reflected on the woman once more dozing in his arms. Every word he'd told his brothers had been from the heart. He'd do whatever it took to make sure Grace was safe, to make sure she knew she belonged to him.

Just as she had back then.

Nothing would keep him from her now.

Not her fears.

Not her doubts.

And certainly not her parents.

Chapter Sixteen

Grace roused when she felt herself being lowered. She opened her eyes and saw Logan hovering over her after placing her on a couch.

"Hey," she said nervously.

"Hey. You awake?"

"Yeah, sort of. We're at your place?"

"Yeah. It's not the Ritz, but you'll be safe here," Logan told her with a small grin.

"I know I will. You're here. Thank you," Grace said with an openness and honesty that was easy to read on her face.

"I need to run down to my truck for a second. I've got a pair of bolt cutters in the box in the back. I'll have you out of these in a jiffy. You okay by yourself for a moment?"

"Of course," Grace said with a small laugh. "The sooner you go, the sooner I'll get out of these things." She lifted her hands, making the chains clink together loudly.

"You need to use the restroom before I go?" Logan asked, strangely reluctant to leave her side.

"No, thank you. I'd rather wait until these are off."

"Of course." He didn't move from his protective hover over her.

"Logan?" Grace asked, tilting her head in concern. "You okay?"

"Yeah. You're beautiful, Grace. The years have been good to you," he blurted out.

She felt herself blushing and bit her lip. "Thanks. You too."

He brought a hand up and smoothed a lock of hair behind her ear before bending down all the way to brush his lips over hers in a barely-there caress. "I'll be right back."

"Okay."

Grace watched as Logan stood up and strode out of the room. She pushed herself into a sitting position and brought a hand up to her lips. The last hour or so had been intense. She'd fallen asleep plotting her escape, and woken up to Logan saying he was there to get her out. She hadn't hesitated. Didn't care that her parents would be pissed. She was done with them. *Done*.

But the most vivid part of the night had been when Logan kissed her. One second they'd been sitting there staring at each other, and the next he was devouring her mouth. It didn't feel weird, or awkward, as it had the few times she'd kissed other men. It felt like coming home.

She could still feel his tongue in her mouth, dueling with hers, stroking nerve endings she didn't know she had. It was all she'd ever dreamed about, and more.

Grace had wanted Logan Anderson for so long, and the kiss they shared hinted at the intimacy she'd long fantasized about. Their kiss had fanned the flames of desire she'd kept tamped down from the moment she'd first met him in the tenth grade.

But now they were adults.

And sort of living together.

She'd never be able to keep him from finding out how much she wanted him.

"Got it." His triumphant voice coming from the front of the room made Grace jump a foot. She looked over the top of the sofa at him.

The place wasn't anything special. Most people who saw it would think the person who lived there was down on his luck, but Grace had a feeling that Logan simply didn't care about appearances. He dressed comfortably, didn't say anything he didn't mean, and was one of the most honest people she knew.

But he definitely wasn't neat. Grace could see empty dishes stacked up in the sink in the small kitchen. There was a box of cereal sitting on the counter, along with a loaf of bread, a jar of peanut butter, and two bags of potato chips. There was a small table off the kitchen that was piled high with unopened newspapers and mail, and a laptop sitting in the middle of the chaos. He obviously didn't eat at the table much.

She was sitting on a black suede couch, which still smelled somewhat new. A beat-up coffee table sat in front of her, also piled high with magazines, and the remote control to the television was across the room. There was a recliner at one end of the couch and a bookcase against the opposite wall, filled with books.

And the shoes. They were everywhere. Grace counted three pairs of sneakers, scuffed-up combat boots, hiking boots, and even some flip-flops strewn around the room. It looked like Logan had left them exactly where they'd landed when he took them off.

Her words came out without thought. "Don't you have a closet?" She swore she saw a blush move up Logan's face. He turned around sheepishly to look at the room through her eyes.

He shrugged. "Sorry. I'm a bit of a slob."

"I thought military guys were neat freaks."

"We are. When we're in. But the moment I got out, I decided that no one was going to tell me how I had to keep house. It looks messy, but I swear it's clean."

He bent down to pick up a pair of sneakers, but Grace stopped him. "It's fine. Seriously. I actually like it. It looks . . . lived in. If I'd ever dared leave something sitting around like this, I would've been in big trouble. Even at my own apartment, I feel like I have to pick up . . . just in case my mom ever stopped by."

Instead of feeling sorry for her, he felt a sort of kinship. Logan merely smiled and huffed out a laugh. "I felt that way for a long time. But I got over it. Which is why I guess it looks like this now."

They smiled at each other and Logan came over to sit next to her on the couch. "Ready?"

"Definitely." Grace held out her wrists.

Logan made quick work of the padlocks holding the chains to her wrists and helped her remove the cuffs. He frowned at the red marks they left behind.

"When I saw your wrist the other day, I wasn't sure what you wanted me to notice."

Grace rubbed her wrist, sighing in relief at the feeling of air getting to her skin again. "Yeah, I couldn't exactly stand up and tell you my mother was psycho and beg you to take me away."

"Why not?"

Grace looked up at his short question and stared at him for a beat. Why hadn't she? What would her mother have done? Yeah, her mother would've been pissed, just like she most likely was now. But if Grace had told Logan to take her away from the house, she could've prevented the insane dinner scene with the Grants. It was almost as if she'd still been trying to please the woman. "I should have," Grace told Logan angrily. She clenched her teeth and shook her head.

He pulled her into him and held on tight. Grace buried her nose into his neck and inhaled deeply. He smelled masculine and musky from the night's adventures . . . and she liked it.

Logan pulled back and tilted her chin up so he could see her eyes. "You want to talk about it?"

Grace thought about it for a half second, then shook her head. "Not right now. Maybe in the morning. I'm exhausted. I haven't been sleeping very well. Is that all right?"

"Of course, Smarty. Whatever you need. Come on. I'll show you where you can lie down." He helped her stand and kept his hand on the small of her back as he led her down a short hallway off the main living area and into a small guest room. There was a queen-size bed with a wooden chest at the foot of it. A small bookcase and a dresser rested against the opposite wall. There weren't any clothes strewn about, and the bed was made, but there were several boxes stacked against the wall, and she could see the closet was stuffed with odds and ends.

"I'm still figuring out where everything should go. It's not much, but believe me, it's much cleaner than my room is," Logan joked.

The last thing Grace wanted was to be alone, but she couldn't exactly tell him that she wanted to sleep in his room. They really didn't know each other that well, no matter their joint past, her current feelings, or that amazing kiss they'd shared.

"It's great. Thanks."

Logan nodded, then paused for a moment before taking a deep breath. "We'll talk more in the morning, but I just want to say, I'm sorry for how things turned out between us. I shouldn't have just let it go back then." He held up his hand when Grace opened her mouth. "Please, let me finish. With that said, things are different now. My eyes are open. I see you, Grace, and you're safe with me. I know it'll take time for us to get to where we might've been before, but please know I'm sincere when I tell you I *want* to get there."

God. He made her feel so many things. Anger because she realized she *was* upset that he'd given up on her so easily back then. He made her feel safe too . . . she had no doubt Logan would protect her. Anticipation as she wondered where their relationship might go from here. And desire. Oh yeah, now that she was older and wiser, she definitely wanted to experience all that was Logan Anderson in bed. Logan put his hand on her nape and pulled her into his chest. Grace sighed and wrapped her arms around him. It was amazing how good she felt when he did this.

"This isn't going to be easy," he warned. "I don't know what your parents want, but they've got power and influence. It's going to be hard to get people to see them as the monsters they obviously are."

Grace inhaled and relaxed further into Logan's embrace. She knew she should be worried about her parents, but she couldn't make herself care at the moment. She was warm, her belly was full for the first time in many days, and she was with Logan. The boy—no, man—she'd once thought she'd end up marrying.

"You still awake?"

"Mmmmm."

Logan chuckled lightly. "Okay, come on sleeping beauty." He steered her toward the small bathroom in the hallway outside the bedroom. "There's an extra toothbrush on the counter and I'll go grab a T-shirt for you to sleep in. I'm sure Felicity will be around tomorrow with your own clothes. We'll make do until then."

Grace nodded and let go of him reluctantly. She brushed her teeth and scrubbed her arms, wanting a shower, but wanting to sleep more. She changed into the huge T-shirt Logan brought her, smiling at the Army logo on the front.

When she finally wandered out of the bathroom, Logan was leaning against the wall waiting for her.

"Feel better?"

She shrugged, exhausted. "I don't know why I'm so tired. It's not like I've done a whole lot recently."

Logan's arm went around her waist and pulled her into his side as he walked them back to the guest bedroom. "It's probably a lot of things. Adrenaline wearing off, the fact that you know you're safe here, and you have some food in your stomach. You'll feel more like yourself in the morning."

Grace let him lead her back into the room, surprised to see the bedding had been pulled back. Logan had obviously gone out of his way to make her comfortable. She climbed onto the mattress and smiled when Logan tucked her in.

He sat next to her hip on the bed and leaned over her, his hands resting next to her arms. "I put your letters on the nightstand." Logan gestured to the small table next to the bed.

Grace glanced over and saw the letters she'd written to him, still tied up in their ribbon, lying safely next to her. She looked back up at Logan. "You want to read them?"

"Yes." She saw sincerity and eagerness in his eyes. He wanted to see what she'd written to him all those years ago as badly as she wanted to read what he'd said to her.

He continued as if he could read her mind, "And I want you to read the ones I wrote you. Although I have to warn you, the letters I sent toward the end aren't as nice as the ones in the beginning. I was . . . upset."

Grace wiggled until she had one arm free of the covers and put it on his arm. "It's okay. I understand. My mother told me she kept the last one you sent and recited it to me."

Logan winced, and she hurried to reassure him. "It's okay. Really. I understand. I was upset too. You'll see when you read mine."

"I'm sorry you had to hear it from her, though," Logan said, his eyes going soft as he gazed down at her. "I want you to know that I absolutely wrote to you. That I wasn't lying about wanting you to come and stay with me once I got to my first duty station."

"I believe you."

"You should know that the feelings I had for you back then haven't died, Smarty. I was upset when I never heard from you, I admit it, but it was because I knew I'd lost something precious." He brought his hand up and traced her eyebrow, then ran the backs of his fingers down her cheek. "We've lost so much, but Grace, we've also gotten a second chance. I'm not going to let anyone come between us again. If we decide we don't suit, then that's on us. No one else."

Grace understood and liked what he'd said. A lot. And told him so. "I like that." Her heart sped up when Logan leaned down to her. He brushed his lips over hers in a too-short caress before sitting up again.

"Good night, Grace. I'll see you in the morning. Sleep as long as you need."

"I'll be up early. My mother likes to be up and get her day started. She trained me well."

"She's not here now. You can sleep in," Logan said seriously.

Grace smiled at him. "I'll try, but don't be surprised if I'm up at five thirty. My body is used to it."

Logan mock-groaned and raised his eyes to the ceiling as if looking for divine intervention. "A morning person. Lord help me. That's the one thing I really don't miss about the Army." He brought his eyes back to hers and leaned down again, kissing her forehead this time.

"Thank you for coming to get me, Logan," Grace whispered.

"You're welcome, Smarty. Sleep well."

"You too."

Logan sighed and stood up. He didn't look back, but strode to the door, turning out the light on his way and leaving without another word. He closed the door most of the way, leaving it open a crack. Grace turned on her side and smiled. How he knew she couldn't be shut inside another room, especially since she hadn't known it until right that second, was beyond her. All it would take was her calling out his name, and she knew Logan would be at her side within seconds.

She hadn't thought she'd be able to sleep, but she'd underestimated her body's need to rejuvenate itself. Grace was asleep in minutes.

She never heard Logan push open the door an hour later.

She never knew he stood watching her sleep for several minutes.

She didn't hear him come over to the side of her bed or feel his hand brush over her head in a soft caress.

She didn't hear him place something on the bedside table next to her.

She especially never heard his soft whispered words as he bent over her.

"I'm sorry, Grace. Letters be damned, I should've come for you."

Chapter Seventeen

Grace woke up confused. It was still dark outside and she wasn't sure where she was. Sitting up quickly, it came back to her. All of it. Her parents severing her last hope of ever being a daughter they could be proud of. Being chained to her bed. Logan, his brothers, the food he'd gotten for her, his apartment.

Looking at the clock, Grace saw that it was 5:43 in the morning. She mentally shrugged. Even though she'd been tired, as she'd warned Logan, habits were hard to break. She threw the covers back, moved her legs to the side of the bed, and clicked on the small table lamp next to the bed. Squinting against the bright light, she didn't immediately understand what she was seeing, but as soon as her vision adjusted, she froze.

The letters she'd written to Logan were still where they'd been when she'd gone to sleep, but now there was a second stack next to them. She reached out a trembling hand to pick it up.

This pile of letters was wrapped up with a rubber band, unlike her batch, which was lovingly preserved with a ribbon. Grace looked down at the envelope on top of the stack.

It was addressed to her, and the return address was a military one. Her eyes filled with tears. Logan's writing was slanted and messy, as if he'd quickly dashed it off. She could imagine him trying to hurry and get it addressed so he didn't get in trouble with a drill sergeant.

But it was the garish words written in block letters across the bottom that made the tears in her eyes spill over.

RETURN TO SENDER

Grace recognized her mother's handwriting right away. It was one thing to know that her mother had purposely kept Logan's letters from her, but it was another to have the proof in her hands and see it for herself.

Grace swiveled her hips and plumped the pillows up behind her, leaning back against the headboard.

The postmark on the first letter was only a week after he'd left all those years ago. With hands that shook with emotion, Grace carefully pulled the first letter out of the stack, leaving the rubber band in place. She turned the precious envelope over in her hands. It hadn't been opened. Closing her eyes, Grace imagined Logan licking it closed and smiling at the thought of her reading it. It hurt. A lot. But it also felt good. He'd written. She kept thinking those two words. She couldn't help it.

Feeling excitement she hadn't felt in years, Grace turned the plain white envelope over and put one finger under the edge of the flap. She carefully opened the letter she should've received so long ago. The letter was short and to the point and sounded so much like Logan she couldn't help but smile.

> Grace,
> Thank you for coming to the bus station with me. I just started Basic yesterday and my drill sergeant is obviously related to the devil himself. :) I have a lot to tell you, but I wanted to keep my promise and get a

note off to you as soon as I could so you would have my address.

I can't wait to hear from you.

More later,

Logan

Grace finally gave in to the feelings inside her and sobbed. Great heaving sobs that came from the depths of her soul. His letter wasn't mushy, wasn't declaring his love for her, but he'd done as he'd promised. It made her chest ache thinking about all the lost time.

Ten minutes later, face blotchy from her tears, her nose running from her crying fit, Grace carefully put the letter back into the envelope and set it aside. She then reached for the next one. It was a bit longer than the first.

Grace,

I have a bit more time to write today. I know I haven't given my first letter time enough to get to you yet, but when I think about all that's happened in the last couple of days, there wasn't anyone I wanted to tell more than you.

Basic training is tough, but I love it . . . besides the being neat thing. I hate having to fold my clothes a certain way, and making my bed every day is just stupid since no one sees our bunks but us, and we fall into them exhausted at the end of the day.

Our daily schedule is very monotonous. We get up, do PT (physical training), then we eat. Then we work out more and go to some classes. Then we have lunch and get yelled at for being too slow, or too fast, or for not paying attention. (Our drill sergeants yell at us for anything and everything, even if they have to make it up.) We then usually do some sort of team-building crap, then more classes (shooting, hand-to-hand combat, Army values, etc.), then dinner and one more workout. Then we have to clean the barracks, even though the floors are already spotless.

It all seems pointless to me, but I get why. They need to break down what we might think being in the Army is all about, then bring us back up together, get us working as a team. I understand it, but it's still annoying. I'd much rather be sitting next to you in the library, Smarty, listening to you talk about dead presidents or something. :)

I wanted to let you know I was serious when I told you I wanted to see where a relationship between us could go. I should've asked you out this past year, but I knew I was leaving and that I'm not good enough for you. Not to mention, I wasn't 100 percent sure if you liked me or not. One day I'd think you were as into me as I was you, and the next you'd act distant. I should've just manned up and asked you out. Sorry. Being away from you and not being able to talk to you every day has really made it obvious (to me) how much I like you.

I like the way you smell, the way you're always so serious, the way you listen to me, and how you tried to take care of me when I came to school with a welt from my mom. I'm doing my best to make myself a better person. The kind of person you might want to be with. Joining the Army was a way to get out of Castle Rock, but I also knew that if we were ever to have a chance together, I'd need a career so I could take care of you.

That sounds corny as hell, and I probably would never have the guts to tell you in person, but it's easier to say in a letter.

Well, my fifteen minutes of free time is over, the DS is yelling at us, "Get your goat-smelling asses out front in ten minutes." (Not lying about that, it's a direct quote! Lol.) I'm going to put this in the mail this afternoon.

I can't wait to hear from you. I miss you.

Logan

And so it went. Grace devoured every word on every page of every letter. Eventually the tone of Logan's letters changed from eager anticipation of her letters to confusion about why he hadn't heard from her.

Grace-

It's been two months since I left and I'm worried about you. I know you keep returning my letters, but I don't know why.

Please, don't send this one back. I need to know that you're okay.

If you don't want me to write, just let me know. It might kill me, but I'll stop.

I hope that's not it. I want to see you. I long to hear from you. Please.

Logan

Eventually the letters lost their innocent and loving tone. Grace held the last letter in her hand and took a deep breath. She was almost afraid to open it, but knew she needed to. She unfolded the last letter and took a deep breath, bracing herself. But his words were not what she expected.

> Grace-
> Please. Please talk to me. Why are you doing this to us? I thought we had something good. I wanted you to come and live with me. I know I've been an asshole in the past, but I love you. God, that sounds pathetic when we haven't even made love, but I've thought of you and how you'd feel in my arms. I've dreamed about us waking up in the mornings and laughing together. You're all I can think about, and I'm worried sick about you. Are you all right? Are you sick? Is that why you haven't written? Just one letter. That's all I ask. Whatever I did, I'm sorry. Please, write me back and let me know you're okay.
> All my love,
> Logan

Grace had thought this letter would be full of accusations and angry words, instead his concern for her leaped off the page and into her heart. Even though every letter he'd written had been returned, unopened, he hadn't given up on her.

She looked at the postmark. Eleven months. He'd written to her for eleven months before he'd given up.

For the first time in a long time when Grace thought about her parents, she wasn't scared or worried about what they felt about her. But now she was angry. Pissed the hell off. How *dare* her mother meddle in her life the way she did. How dare she reduce Logan to begging and make him question her feelings for him. He'd said he loved her, and Grace hadn't had the chance to return his words. Or to reassure him. Or anything.

She carefully bundled the letters back together. Even if she was pissed, those letters meant the world to her. After placing them carefully back on the table next to her, she snatched up the letters she'd written to Logan and stalked out of the room.

Enough morning light was coming into the apartment that Grace could see where she was going. She stomped down the hall to Logan's room. She opened the door, not even considering she might be intruding on his privacy.

Her eyes on the lump in front of her, Grace walked over and sat heavily on the side of his bed.

The second her butt made contact with the mattress, Logan moved. He grabbed her around the waist and flipped her over his body until she lay on her back next to him. She kept hold of the bundle of letters she'd carried into the room, clutching them to her chest as Logan moved her. She gasped as he loomed over her. One hand was at her neck and the other held her arm over her head.

The second he realized who was under him, he immediately loosened his grip, but didn't let go of her altogether, and swore. "Fuck, Grace. Don't ever sneak up on me. Are you all right? Did I hurt you? Shit."

"I'm okay, Logan. Sorry. I didn't realize."

"Please. Don't startle me when I'm asleep. Ever. I could've hurt you."

"Is it because of your Army training?" she asked, looking up at him fretfully.

He ran a hand over his face, the sound of his five o'clock shadow loud against his palm. "Partly. And partly because my mom used to come into our rooms in the middle of the night and start hitting us for whatever made-up reason she had at the time."

"Damn. I'm sorry. I won't do it again." Grace rubbed her hand up and down his arm, trying to soothe him.

Logan tilted his head and asked, "What's wrong? Why are you here? Are you okay?"

She'd been scared for a moment at Logan's quick actions, but now she was pissed all over again. "My mother is a bitch," she declared as if he didn't already know it. "Seriously. I knew she wasn't mother of the year, but hiding your letters from me was horrible."

Logan's lips quirked up into a small smile before saying unnecessarily, "You read my letters."

"Yeah, I read them. She made you doubt yourself. She upset you. Dammit, she made you *beg*. I know I don't really know you, but the man I knew back then didn't beg. Here," Grace pressed the bundle of letters she'd been clutching into his chest. "Read mine. Now. Every one."

Logan covered her hand holding the letters to his chest with the hand that had been in her hair and leaned down into her, smiling tenderly. "Can I get up and shower and have a cup of coffee first?"

"No!" Grace shook her head. "You have to read them. Immediately."

"Grace—"

"It's not right that you didn't know. I wrote you every week. Every *week*, Logan. I—"

"Grace—" Her name was said more forcefully now, but she still ignored it.

"I couldn't wait to get out of Castle Rock and come be with you. I had the biggest crush on you in high school and was so excited because I thought you'd finally noticed me. It—"

Done trying to get through to her with words, Logan simply tilted her head up and silenced her with his mouth.

Grace froze for a moment, then melted into him. The kiss, which started out hard and rough to shut her up, changed in an instant to sweet and erotic. Their tongues danced and dueled.

The letters fell unnoticed to the bedside as they made out. Logan nibbled on Grace's lower lip, she sucked on his in return. When he licked the roof of her mouth, Grace gasped and moaned, moving her hands to the back of his head and tugging on his hair in her ecstasy.

Reluctantly, Logan pulled back, but he didn't go far.

Grace felt his weight all along her body, his obvious erection throbbing between her legs, his hands framing her face.

"You really are a morning person, aren't you?"

She nodded up at him, not sure whether to hang on to her anger or be embarrassed.

"I like it. Feel free to wake me up this way every morning," Logan told her as he rubbed his nose against hers.

"What? By getting pissed and then scaring you?"

"No. With your enthusiasm and passion. I don't like that you're angry, even if it's on my behalf. But I *do* like that you didn't hide it from me. No more secrets between us. Okay? I think we both have firsthand knowledge of the damage they can do."

"I agree." Grace hesitated, then blurted out impatiently, "Will you read my letters? Seeing what you wrote to me was heartbreaking and maddening at the same time," Grace told him honestly. "Reading your words in black and white brought home how much I let my parents control me as I tried to get their approval."

Logan was shaking his head, but Grace continued, "Yeah, I did. I *let* them control me. Maybe I could've broken free of them if I'd stopped caring what they thought about me like you did when you got away from your mom. Maybe not. But I didn't get the chance. *Now* is my chance. I want the air cleared between us, Logan. I wanted to be with you so badly back then. And when I finally accepted that you didn't feel the same way, it hurt, so I turned to what I was used to . . . namely letting my parents make all the decisions for me. Doing whatever I could to get them to show me a shred of affection. The last few years I've started breaking free in little ways. I want a clean slate between us, and I don't think I can do that unless you know what was in my heart back then."

"There will never be a clean slate, Grace," Logan said, then quickly followed it with, "No, don't take that the wrong way," when she wrinkled her brow in distress. "There can't be a clean slate, because we have a history. We were friends. Good friends. And I wanted more, but was too chicken to ask you out. I thought I'd have plenty of time, when I should've known better. Nothing is guaranteed in this life. I knew it, but ignored it like the stupid teenager I was."

He leaned down and kissed her forehead before continuing. "We have a history. One that was pretty darn amazing. Amazing enough that I told you I loved you in a letter when we hadn't ever done anything but brush our lips against each other." He ignored her blush and went on. "So no, there will never be a clean slate between us."

"Wow, um, okay," Grace said, staring up at him, stunned. "No clean slate. I'm okay with that."

"Good. Now, come on, Smarty, we have a lot to do today. Get showered. I'll make breakfast. I'll read your letters. We'll talk about this week with my brothers and figure out where we go from here. But, Grace, wherever it is, know that I'll be at your side. You've broken free of your parents' hold, and I'm not letting you go back."

"I don't want to go back."

"Good." Logan rolled off her and lay on his side next to her, his head propped up on his hand. "Now scoot, before I lose what little control I have and find out what you're wearing underneath my shirt."

Grace blushed, but did as he asked. She headed for his door before looking back. "Do you have bacon?"

"Am I a guy?"

She giggled. "I'd love to have a heaping plate of bacon. And scrambled eggs. And toast with a ton of butter and jelly."

"Then that's what you'll have. I take it that's not what you usually eat in the mornings?"

She made a face. "No. Usually dry toast, an egg-white omelet with spinach and goat cheese, or sometimes a small bowl of plain oatmeal."

Logan's face got hard for a moment before softening. "Go, Grace. Take as long a shower as you want. I'll make a breakfast fit for a queen. Your new life starts this morning."

"Awesome," she breathed, smiling widely at Logan as she turned once more to the door.

"And make sure the bacon is extra crispy," she called out when she was halfway down the hall.

Grace heard Logan's bark of laughter as she closed the bathroom door behind her.

Chapter Eighteen

Logan cooked an entire package of bacon and fried it up exactly to Grace's specifications. Crispy, but not burnt. He loved watching her enjoy her meal. She ate daintily, obviously a by-product of the way she was raised, but with a gusto that made him feel good.

They sat on the couch to eat since the table was covered in his papers, but Grace didn't seem to care. She smiled and laughed as she ate her meal, praising him for how delicious it was. The fact that she could still be lighthearted and sweet after everything she'd been through was a miracle. The more Logan thought about it, the more he realized that he was an extremely lucky man. The past ten years could've completely changed Grace's personality, but by some miracle, they hadn't.

They laughed at shared memories from high school, and Logan could feel the electricity between them, stronger and deeper than it had been back in the day. Every time their eyes met she blushed but didn't look away. They were building their relationship anew each time they made eye contact.

When they'd finished eating, Grace looked at the stack of her letters sitting on the coffee table and then casually informed Logan, "I'm a bit tired. I'm going to take a short nap while you read through my letters. Okay?"

"You don't have to go."

She shrugged. "You gave me privacy to read yours, it's the least I can do. Besides, I'm embarrassed. I was eighteen when I wrote those."

Logan stood and gathered her into his arms. He was getting used to her in his embrace. He liked it.

Pulling away, Logan looked into her eyes for a long time. She looked worried and shy at the same time. Logan let her off the hook, not wanting to make her any more uncomfortable than she already was. "I'll come get you when I'm done. Yeah?"

"Yeah. Sounds like a plan. You'll know where I'll be," she said with a saucy grin, leaning up and kissing him on his chin.

She walked away and Logan stared after her even after she disappeared down the hall, his thoughts all over the place. Relieved she was safe. Happy she was with him. And anticipating getting to know her better.

Logan went back to the couch and picked up the packet of letters. He slowly pulled the faded pink ribbon until the bow came undone. Unlike his letters, there were no postmarks to tell him which came first. He decided to start at the top, figuring Grace most likely kept them in order.

His name was on the front of the envelope, and her return address was penned neatly in the upper left-hand corner. Seeing her writing for the first time since high school, he recognized it and mentally kicked himself once more. Her flowery feminine writing was nothing like the 'RETURN TO SENDER' block script that was on every single one of his returned letters. One more mistake to put on his plate.

The letter wasn't sealed, and he pulled out the folded piece of paper carefully, not wanting to wrinkle it or do any sort of damage to it whatsoever. Grace's cursive filled the page, and even without reading a word, Logan knew her words were going to break his heart.

Logan,

I can't wait to get your first letter. I can't imagine all the interesting things that you're going through at Basic. I know it's hard. We talked about how you'd get yelled at and have to work out all the time, but I just know you're going to be great. You were born to be tough, and I'm so proud of you.

Logan took a deep breath and looked up at the ceiling for a moment to get control of his emotions. Damn, he hadn't even made it through the first letter and his chest already felt tight and the back of his throat burned with unshed tears.

He looked back down at the letter, cleared his throat, and continued reading. It went on and on about how she'd be starting classes that summer up in Denver, and how she really wanted to major in marketing, but her parents thought it would be better for her to go into office administration. She babbled on about the weather and other local gossip about people he'd long forgotten about. The last paragraphs of her letter struck him hard.

You're so lucky you got to get out of here. I know your mom was horrible to you and your brothers, and I'm so glad you were able to get away from her. My mother doesn't hit me, but she can be really mean sometimes, and she's never been satisfied with anything I've ever done. When you graduate from Basic and your other training, if you still want me to come out to wherever you are, I'd love to. I can continue my college classes anywhere. I'm sure the credits will transfer.

Logan, I've admired and looked up to you for years. You have to know that. While we might not have been boyfriend and girlfriend, I'd love to give us a shot.

Stay safe. Looking forward to your letters.

Grace

The letters got somewhat easier to read after that first one. There weren't as many emotional pleas for him to write her. They were more of a diary of her days. How her classes were going, how she hoped he was doing okay. They got shorter and shorter as time went on. Grace had more willpower than he did, though, because she'd written him for a year and a half after he'd left. He'd lasted less than a year.

Her last letter made him ashamed that he hadn't put aside his own hurt feelings and acted like the man he should've been.

Logan,

Today it's been eighteen months since you left. I honestly thought you were serious about wanting me to come be with you, but obviously I was the stupid one. My mother tells me all the time that I have no common sense, and I guess she's right.

I finished my first year of college, and when I got my final grades, I immediately thought of you and how you'd laugh that I got all *As* . . . except in Western Civilization. So much for being a smarty. Lol. Of course my mother wasn't amused and was so disappointed in me. She grounded me for two weeks. It wasn't so bad. I didn't have to eat dinner with my parents and have to deal with their disgusted stares.

I hope wherever you are, you're happy and safe. I see all the time on the news about soldiers being deployed, and I hope if you ever have to go overseas and fight that you'll come back safe and sound.

A guy in one of my classes asked me out last week and I told him no, but then got to thinking . . . why? Why not accept? Because I was waiting for you. I wanted my first real date to be with you. But something my father said to me tonight finally sank in. He told me to get myself together because you aren't coming back. You left Castle Rock and had no plans to ever come back. He told me I reminded you of all the bad memories you had here and that was why I'd never heard from you.

So tomorrow, I'm going to find that boy and tell him that I accept. I'm sorry we never had a chance to see what we might've had.

I hope the Army is all you wanted it to be and that your brothers are doing well. I miss the Logan I used to know, but then again, maybe he never existed in the first place.

Grace

Logan didn't know how much time had passed, but he folded up the last letter and put it back in the envelope. He stacked them all up and carefully retied the ribbon around the entire batch. Standing up, he put the bundle on the counter and made his way down the hall.

Without a word, he pushed open the guest room door. Grace was lying on her side with her back to the door. Logan padded over to the small bed and climbed on. He knew she was awake because she went stiff the second she felt him at her back.

Ignoring her body language, Logan curled into her and put an arm around her waist, pulling her until she was flush against him. He didn't say anything for several minutes, but sighed in relief when her arm moved and she grabbed his hand to interlock her fingers with his.

Logan finally broke the silence, saying quietly, "I wish I had been your first date."

"Me too."

"I fucked up."

"You didn't know."

"Doesn't matter. I *did* fuck up. I should've made the time to come home and see what was up. Why you were sending my letters back. But you should know, from this moment on, I'm making it my mission in life to make up for lost time."

Grace turned in his arms and Logan let her. When they were face-to-face, she looked at him with tears in her eyes. Her voice cracked when she said, "We're different people now than we were then, Logan. We might not even like each other anymore."

"I like you." Logan pulled her hips forward until they were nestled together. One hand dipped low on her ass, holding her to him, letting her feel how being near her affected him.

"You just want to have sex with me. It's a natural reaction. That happens to guys when they're around women," Grace told him stubbornly.

Logan shook his head in denial. "Let me guess, that's what your mother told you."

She looked up at him with big eyes. "My father."

"It's bullshit, Grace. Yes, I want you. I want to bury myself so far inside your body that you don't know where you end and I begin. But it's not because you're simply female. Give me a little more credit than that. It's because you're *you*. You're my first crush. The first person who saw the real me. I told you things back in high school that I haven't even told my brothers. We lost a lot of time because of my stupidity and your parents, and I'm not willing to give them even one more minute."

He watched as Grace blushed, but she didn't look away. The combination of her shyness and strength was so appealing to him, it made

Logan more determined than ever to see where things could go between them.

"Make no mistake. I want you, Grace Mason, but while you're living in my apartment, I'd like to take things slow. We can get to know each other again. This is not a "friends with benefits" arrangement. I won't take advantage of you. I want you to be 100 percent sure before we take that step."

"But you will make love to me . . . right?" she asked, lifting her eyebrows and pressing her hips harder into him as she teased.

He smiled back at her. "Oh yeah. There's nothing I've looked forward to more." He caressed her lower back and his smile died. "I like to touch you." Logan demonstrated by caressing Grace's ass with his hand. "I want to taste your luscious lips again."

He smiled as she licked them as if in anticipation of his touch.

"I want to touch you and have you touch me back. But until we figure out where we stand, we need to decide on our living arrangements. You can stay right here in my guest room, and we can get to know each other day by day. Or you can sleep in my bed with me at night, and I'll keep my hands, and other body parts, to myself until you say differently. The speed you want us to move is up to you. Having sex with me is not a requirement for you to be safe. Understand?"

"I think to start, it might be best if I stayed in here for a while," Grace said uncertainly, picking at an imaginary thread on his shirt.

Logan moved his hand from her ass to cover her fingers on his chest tenderly. "No problem, Smarty. This room is yours as long as you need it."

"I'm not a virgin," she blurted, looking at his forehead, not his eyes. He knew she was still uncomfortable with the conversation, but he admired she was still brave enough to bring it up.

"I'm not a virgin either," Logan told her seriously.

She giggled at his response, and the sound lightened his heart. "I didn't think you were," she told him, meeting his eyes for the first time.

"But I'm also not a manwhore. Believe it or not, I've only slept with five women. I know this isn't the kind of thing most couples talk about, but I feel as though I owe this to you."

"I'm . . . I'm not that thrilled hearing you talk about other women," Grace admitted reluctantly.

"And I'm not all that thrilled *telling* you about them. But hear me out?"

She took a deep breath, then nodded firmly.

"One was in high school. My junior year. I can't even remember her name now."

"Ruth," Grace volunteered immediately.

Logan flexed his arms and smiled wanly at the fact that Grace knew exactly who he was talking about. "I guess. Anyway, If I'm being honest, I was frustrated that I couldn't get up the courage to ask my tutor out, and figured even if I did, she'd say no because she was so far out of my league. So in a teenage-boy snit, I decided that if you didn't want to be with me, I might as well be with her."

Seeing the hurt look in Grace's eyes, which she tried to hide, Logan hurried on, wanting to make his point. "After I stopped writing you, I briefly dated three women, one right after the other. I was trying to get you out of my system. And I have to say, it didn't work. The last woman I slept with was three years ago. I hadn't been with anyone in a couple of years and decided that I needed to at least try to be in a relationship. It was what adults did. They dated, got married, had kids. She was a very nice woman, but after a while, I realized that I didn't trust her enough to tell her about myself.

"I broke up with her. The last I heard, she was married and had a child on the way. It's been three years for me, Grace. I haven't even been interested in sleeping with anyone in all that time. I took care of my own needs, if you know what I mean. But here I am, harder and more turned on lying fully clothed with you than I have been with any other woman I've ever been with."

Grace bit her lower lip and stared at him before asking disbelievingly. "Three years?"

"Yeah, Smarty. Three years. So this isn't just because I'm a guy and you're a girl. You're Grace. My Smarty. The woman I've wanted since I was seventeen. I'm not going to mess this up, at least I hope not. I want you to know that I want you for you, not because I need to get off. Got it?"

"Okay, but I've never . . ." she paused as if embarrassed, then hurried to finish her thought. "I didn't really like it."

"Did you come?" He knew what "it" she was talking about.

She blushed bright red, but answered, "No."

"Did they even try? Go down on you? Get you wet at all?"

"No on the oral sex. My first wasn't interested in anything but sticking his dick in me and getting off, and that was fine with me because it wasn't exactly comfortable. The others said they weren't comfortable with oral, and honestly, neither was I. And yeah, I've had a bit of foreplay and used lube, but the Earth didn't exactly move, if you know what I mean."

"So they weren't complete assholes then? Didn't hurt you?" Logan murmured before looking her in the eyes again.

"No," she said softly.

"Grace, I promise you here and now, whenever we get around to making love, you're gonna like it."

She smiled at him then, a teasing little grin that made his libido kick up a notch. "I will, huh?"

"Oh yeah."

"I want *you* to like it too," she insisted.

"Have no doubts on that score, Grace. I will."

"I've never gone down on a guy before."

Logan groaned, a new picture now in his head. Before it had been Grace lying under him looking up at him in wonder as he pushed inside her for the first time. Now it was Grace kneeling between his legs as she looked up at him with her big brown eyes before opening her mouth and taking him inside. She had no idea what her not-so-innocent words were doing to him. "At least I get *one* of your firsts. I'll teach you. Show you what I like. And you can tell me what feels good for you when it's my turn."

"You really want to do that with me?" she asked uncertainly, her brows wrinkling adorably.

"Oh yeah," Logan breathed. "I really want to do that with you." He kissed the tip of her nose. "And now we need to get up. I can't talk about this anymore without wanting to act on it, so please have some mercy on me." He smiled as he said it so she knew he was teasing . . . mostly.

"Kiss me?"

Logan moved his hands to cradle her face, his favorite way of holding her as they kissed. "That I can do. I hope you get used to my lips on yours, Grace, because I have a feeling I won't be able to stay away."

Logan leaned forward the inch or so it took for him to reach her and kissed her long, slowly, and sweetly. Showing her how much he treasured having her in his life again. She followed his lead, not changing the kiss into the passionate embrace they both knew was simmering below the surface, just waiting to explode.

She nipped and licked at him, just as he did to her. Finally, Logan pulled back and rested his forehead on hers. "Thank you for letting me see your letters. Thank you for not giving up on me, even if I let you down after only eleven months. And thank you for trusting me with your secrets. I know we still have things to discuss, but I appreciate your trust."

"Thank *you* for kidnapping me," she said immediately, poking him in the chest to emphasize her point.

"I should've done it nine years ago."

"Maybe." She lifted one shoulder in a half shrug. "But better late than never."

He laughed again and sat up, pulling Grace with him. "Come on, we need to get ready for company. You sure you want to do this today?"

"Yes. It's time. I need to come clean about my parents and how they've behaved toward me."

"Their reign of terror ends now," Logan told her, helping her stand up next to the bed.

"I hope so."

"It will. Come on, we'll watch TV and relax until everyone gets here. Are you nervous?"

"You'll be there?" she asked with a hopeful look in her eyes.

"Of course."

"Then, no, I'm not nervous," she said with a small shake of her head.

Logan had no idea how he'd gotten so lucky, but he wasn't going to blow it now. He didn't even know most of what she'd been through . . . but figured he would in a few hours. It didn't matter, he'd guard her tender heart from the world from here on out.

Chapter Nineteen

Grace looked around at her friends. They were waiting for her to start. Blake looked relaxed, sitting on one of the recliners next to the couch. He was leaning back and had one foot propped on his knee. But there was something about his too-relaxed stance that belied his irritation. He was pissed. But Grace appreciated him trying to bank it for her.

Cole, on the other hand, wasn't trying to hide his anger. He was pacing back and forth in front of the couch in agitation. Grace had told them that she'd been locked up in her room for the last week or so and given them an overview of her life inside the Mason mansion. She didn't know Cole that well, but she wasn't scared of him . . . exactly. He and Felicity were close friends, and she knew his bark usually was much worse than his bite. But she was thankful he was pissed at her parents and not at her.

Nathan was the wild card of the group. She'd always thought he was the soft-spoken Anderson brother, but looking at him now, she wasn't so sure. He was standing with one leg bent, his foot resting flat on the wall behind him, his arms crossed, fists clenched. When they were teenagers, Grace had watched him ignore taunts and teasing from their classmates, but the second a girl caught the attention of the bullies, he turned into a different kind of man and never hesitated to jump to her defense. It was obvious that he was outraged and pissed off at the way Grace had been treated by her parents. He was ready to do battle for her.

Grace was glad to see Felicity at the door. Logan had told her Felicity would be coming by, and she needed some girl time. When she'd heard what had happened to Grace, she insisted on joining the Anderson brothers and Cole.

Grace took one look at Felicity and fell into her arms. It was nice to have a friend who knew her almost as well as she knew herself there to talk to. She also appreciated that Felicity had brought over a suitcase full of clothes and things she'd need since she was going to be staying with Logan for a while.

Then there was Logan. Grace looked over at him. They were on his couch; she was sitting right next to him, almost in his lap, and Logan was holding her hand. Even though he'd had a bit more time to get used to the idea that her parents weren't good people, he was still highly agitated, as evidenced by the way he pressed his lips tightly together and fisted his free hand on his thigh.

She wanted to comfort him, but curling up on his lap and kissing him probably wasn't appropriate at the moment.

"What went on at the dinner with the Grants?" It was Logan who asked. Even though it had just happened, it seemed so inconsequential to everything else.

"They want me and Brad to get married and have a son they can steal from me and raise as their own." Grace laid it straight out, not beating around the bush.

"Jesus," Cole breathed.

"No fucking way," Nathan swore.

"That bitch," Felicity hissed from her perch on the edge of the coffee table.

Blake merely pressed his lips together tightly.

The only outward sign from Logan was the tightening of his fingers around hers. "Go on. How do they think that's gonna work? Did they invite the Grants over to talk about it?"

Grace appreciated his restraint. She knew he was upset, but he was keeping his cool so she could explain. "Yeah, pretty much. They paraded me downstairs and told me if I did anything to embarrass them, they'd lock me in the crawl space instead of my bedroom."

"How have they gotten away with locking you in your room for so long?" Blake asked. "Didn't the servants notice?"

Grace shrugged. "They get paid enough to look the other way. It's not like my parents are beating me or anything."

"Look at me, Grace," Logan ordered.

She did and saw he wore an intense look on his face. "It took me a long time to realize this, and Cole had to help point it out, but just because they aren't hitting you doesn't mean you haven't been abused. We've talked about this."

Grace shrugged self-consciously and glanced at her best friend. "Felicity said the same thing, but it's not the same as what happened to you and your brothers."

"You're right, it's not," Logan agreed. "But they sound to me like textbook abusers. They started out by controlling your behavior, convincing you they were doing it to protect you. They put unrealistic expectations on you and kept moving the finish line so you could never reach any of their goals. They've withheld their affection from you your entire life. Dangling it in front of you like you were a dog expected to please its master. They manipulated you so you don't trust your own judgment, substituting control for love. Not to mention that they constantly tell you you're stupid and no good. They monitor the money you spend and try to make you marry a man you don't want in order to have a baby for them."

Grace stared at Logan for the longest time. She was scared to say what she was thinking. When he laid it all out like that, she'd sound stupid if she argued with him. Besides, the last thing she wanted to do was point out her shortcomings, especially when it seemed like he wanted to finally be with her.

But Logan knew she was holding something back. "What is it? Tell me what you're thinking behind those beautiful brown eyes."

She didn't look away from him as she said softly, "I should've realized what they were doing and left just like you did. But I'm weak. I wanted them to love me. Why didn't I just leave?"

"You aren't weak, Grace. Not even close," Logan told her.

"I could've left. I could've walked out of my job a thousand times, but I didn't. I just kept going back every time they said they needed my help. They made me feel like they needed me. And that was the closest thing I could get to being loved by them. Even if it was a lie."

"Grace, look at me," Nathan said.

She turned her head to Logan's brother and bit her lip, worried about what he was going to say.

"Being weak would've been becoming like them. Manipulative and hard. Weak would've been believing everything they've told you over the years. Not bothering to write my brother. Not registering to take the college classes you want. Not making friends with Felicity because your parents didn't approve. For years, you've defied them in the only way you knew how. Sometimes being strong isn't about having the most muscles or talking back. Being strong is about standing up for what's right, even when it means you get hurt in the process."

She let go of Logan's hands, stood up, walked over to Nathan, and put her arms around his neck. She squeezed him hard and sighed in relief when she felt him return her embrace. She whispered in his ear, "Thank you."

She pulled away, not wanting to embarrass the sensitive man who she now understood a bit better. She looked shyly back at Logan.

"I'm in awe of you, Grace," he said, resting his forearms on his thighs and leaning toward her.

She shook her head in denial, "You shouldn't be."

Logan ignored her protest. "You've grown up in a battlefield, but you've stayed the same sweet person I met when I was sixteen. I swear, you don't ever have to go back or talk to them again. We'll do whatever it takes to keep them away from you."

"I've made so many mistakes in dealing with them, I don't want to make another."

Logan reassured her, "You're not alone anymore."

"I'll be there for you too," Felicity added, coming over to wrap an arm around her waist. "You've fought this fight for a long time by yourself. You're not alone anymore, girlfriend."

The other men added their assurances as well, and Grace smiled a small smile and looked around at her friends through the tears in her eyes. She had no idea what she'd done to get so lucky, to have such awesome people supporting her, but she was thankful for it.

Blake broke the heavy silence that followed. "What's your parents' plan with the Grants? How were they going to make Bradford marry you? Can you tell us more about the dinner?"

Grace nodded and went to sit back down next to Logan. She looked over at Blake. "The dinner started out like most of them do. Lots of small talk and some discussion about business. Since Alexis was there, the Grants tried to steer clear of a lot of the work stuff, though. They said something about how she wasn't really interested in the family business. Bradford might be an architect, but I think Alexis is still searching for what she wants to do with her life."

"Did the Grants seem upset about that?" Blake asked.

"Surprisingly, no. I remember thinking how great it was that she'd be able to do whatever she wanted. It was just one more thing to convince me that my parents had never acted like they truly loved me. They hadn't ever supported me unconditionally. The Grants were proud of their kids, no matter what they did.

"Anyway, talk turned to Bradford and me and how we were still single. My mother brought it up, said that we'd make a good couple. Everyone laughed, except for her. She insisted that she was serious and that it would be a good business decision to tie our families together. The Grants seemed confused at first, but when my mother started talking about how, if their two companies merged, they could be the biggest firm in Colorado, they finally realized she wasn't kidding."

Grace took a deep breath and rushed to get the rest of the story out. "It got really uncomfortable then, and we all moved to the sitting room. I didn't say anything, because of my father's earlier threats to cut their brake lines . . . I was freaking out, scared out of my mind not only for me, but now for the genuinely nice people sitting in front of me. I used to think that there was no way my parents would ever do anything like that—that all their threats were just empty talk—but considering what they'd done to me and what they'd said, I just wasn't sure any more.

"They argued back and forth, Mrs. Grant telling my mother that she'd never force her son to marry anyone he didn't want to marry, and then, my mother threatened them not-so-subtly by saying that if Bradford didn't marry me and produce a son that they might start losing business."

"She flat out said that?" Blake asked, sitting forward in his chair.

"Yeah. Needless to say, it didn't go over very well, and the Grants left soon thereafter."

"It'd be Margaret's word against theirs," Nathan warned his brother as if he knew what Blake was thinking.

"True, but now there are witnesses other than just Grace. By threatening the Grants, they've opened themselves up."

"My mother will deny it," Grace warned. "She'll say that everyone misunderstood her. It's what she does. She's good at manipulating people into believing what she wants."

Logan patted her hand. "Probably, but if five separate people say they heard her threaten the Grants, it's more believable. What else? After Brad and his family left, what happened?"

Grace looked up at Logan with huge eyes. "I went upstairs."

"I was watching, Grace," Logan said in a soft voice, trying not to spook her. "What did she say to you before you went to your room?"

She looked down at her lap rather than into the eyes of the strong people around her. "The usual. That I'll do what she wants, or I'll disappoint her and she'll hurt one of my friends."

"How does she think she can force you guys to marry?" Cole asked, perplexed. "This isn't medieval England. Forced marriages disappeared a long time ago."

Grace snorted. "They exist; you just don't know about them. You're right in that she wouldn't hold a knife to our throats and parade us in front of a judge, but she has other ways. Money talks and so do threats and bribes."

Her words hung in the air like a grenade falling in slow motion.

"What has she threatened you with?" Nathan asked in a hard voice next to her.

Grace shrugged. "What hasn't she?" She really didn't want to get into this, but her friends had come over to help her, and she'd already decided that she'd do anything she could to break free of her parents once and for all. If she embarrassed herself in the process, it was just a part of the painful process. "When locking me in my room didn't seem to be having the effect they wanted, she threatened to have me committed, Felicity killed, ruin your business, Cole, cut brake lines and have a car accident arranged to hurt one of you." Grace's words trailed off as she finally realized the effect her words were having on the others in the room.

If she thought her friends were angry before, it was nothing compared with how they felt now. Not liking that she made them that way and wanting to fix it, Grace hurried to backtrack. "But usually it was just things like giving me a bad review at work or telling me that I was stupid."

"Did she tell you to stay away from me back in high school? Threaten you with something?" Logan asked in a tight voice.

She refused to look at him, but nodded. "Yeah. Of course she did. She hated you and your family and couldn't stand that I even talked to you.

Logan lifted her chin and turned her face so she was looking at him. "What threats did she use to keep us apart?" he repeated in a gentle voice.

Grace gave in. It wasn't as if he didn't know already what horrible people her parents were. "One of her favorites, and most effective, was that she said she knew an officer in the Army who could deny your enlistment."

"Son of a bitch," Nathan swore in a low voice, but Grace ignored him and kept her eyes on Logan.

"You defied her and kept tutoring me," Logan said. It wasn't a question, but Grace nodded anyway. He went on. "But any time it seemed like we were getting too close, you pulled back. Put some distance between us. One day I'd think you liked me as more than a friend, then the next you'd be back to canceling our sessions and treating me like a buddy again. You were protecting me . . . and yourself."

"I was," Grace said a little belligerently. "Because it was one thing for her to make *me* feel like shit. I was used to it. But I didn't like her trying to make you look like a bad person when I knew you weren't. So I tried to do whatever I could so you would be willing to spend time with me, but not get too close, so she'd back off me a bit."

"You've been protecting your friends from your parents for a long time, haven't you, Grace?" Logan asked gently.

For the first time in her life, Grace admitted what she'd held close to her heart for as long as she could remember. "I tried. I'd heard rumors around town about what they were capable of and never wanted to take the chance they'd actually follow through with any of their threats."

Without a word, Logan pulled her into his arms.

Grace felt like the load she'd carried for so long suddenly didn't seem so heavy anymore. She knew just because she wasn't under her parents' control anymore didn't mean that she'd escaped their threats, but for just a minute, she wanted to pretend she was safe. That the people she cared about were safe. That she didn't have to bow to Margaret and Walter Mason's will to try so desperately to earn their love.

How long they sat on Logan's couch, Grace had no idea. No one said a word for the longest time. Finally, Grace sighed a huge sigh and sat up straight. "What now?"

"The first thing we gotta do is get a restraining order against your parents." At her look of horror, he ran his hand over the side of her hair, soothing her. "I know it's hard, but we need to do this by the book. They will not hurt you again, Grace. If they try, we need to have the cops involved."

"You'll help me?" Grace asked. "I've never done that before . . . I don't know what to do."

"Of course I will. Ace Security does this all the time. It's not like I was gonna drop you off at the police station and say, 'See ya later.'"

Grace smiled at his teasing. "Then what?"

"Then we wait," Logan said easily.

"Wait? For what?"

"For them to make their move. They're gonna hate that you aren't under their thumb anymore. I have no doubt they'll try to get to you, but you have to be strong. Do you hear me, Grace? Don't do anything stupid. Don't be one of those too-stupid-to-live heroines in books and movies. They think you're weak and that you still want their affection, so they're gonna try to manipulate you just like they've done your entire life. When that doesn't work, they're gonna threaten you, but don't listen to them. You come to me, or my brothers, or even Cole or Felicity, and tell us what they said. We'll bring it all to the cops so there's an official record of it. We're not stupid, we need the police. But even as civilians, we won't stand by and do nothing."

"But if they—"

"Grace," Logan interrupted sternly, putting his hands on either side of her face. "I'm not a teenager anymore. I spent a lot of time in the Army learning how to protect myself and those around me. Blake is good at what he does. When we're done here, he's going to reach out to the Grants and find some dirt on Margaret and Walter, and if we have to, we'll use it to keep them at bay. And Nathan? Look at him. Look how pissed he is on your behalf. You've got a champion for life in him. And not only them, but Felicity and Cole too. Your friends have your back and you can go to them whenever you need something."

"Damn straight," Felicity murmured.

"He's right," Cole said at the same time.

Logan continued, "And *I* can and will protect you. You've been doing it for others for so long, let me help you now. Let us all help you."

"You guys don't know them like I do."

"You're right," Logan agreed, "we don't. But I think we've all known people *like* them. People who will use anyone in any way to get what they want. I know they've got money and connections, but it doesn't matter. They aren't going to win."

"I don't want to marry Brad." The words spilled out without thought. She knew they came out of the blue, but she desperately wanted to make sure Logan knew that she didn't like Brad in that way.

He huffed out a short laugh. "I know you don't, Smarty."

"He's nice. Really nice. I like him. I have a feeling he's probably gay, which doesn't really have anything to do with anything. I think his parents know and don't care, which makes me like *them* too. But he doesn't deserve to be caught up in my parents' insane plan to get me pregnant with a boy they can steal and raise in their perverted world."

She looked around at her friends. "But if any of you get hurt because of something I did or didn't do, I wouldn't be able to forgive myself."

"First of all, anything that happens is on your parents. *Not* you," Logan said firmly, putting one finger under her chin and turning her head toward him. "They're responsible for their own actions. You're done taking that shit on yourself. Second of all, you're the most unselfish person I've ever known. Ever. And while I love that about you, it also worries me. I'm going to work on seeing if I can't get you to make demands of me."

"What?" Grace asked, horrified, partly because she couldn't ever imagine making any demands of Logan and partly because of what he might be implying in front of his brothers, Cole, and Felicity.

Logan grinned. "Yeah, and that right there is why I'm falling in love with you." He looked around at the others. "You guys good?"

Everyone nodded.

"Cool. We'll touch base tomorrow then." Logan's words were clearly a dismissal, which no one seemed to take offense to.

Felicity was the first to come over to Grace. She tugged her up and off the couch and gave her a long hug. "You need anything, you know my number. All you have to do is text or call and I'm here. Got it?"

"Got it," Grace told her best friend through watery eyes.

After another long hug, Felicity stood back and let Cole hug Grace. "Give me a yell if you have any questions or need anything," he said gruffly, stepping back. Grace nodded.

175

Next up was Nathan. He also put his arms around her, then merely stood back with his hands on her shoulders. After looking in her eyes for a moment, he nodded.

Then she was passed to Blake and engulfed in his embrace.

"I haven't been hugged so much in my entire life," Grace grouched good-naturedly, patting Blake on the back as she squeezed him.

"Get used to it. We like hugs," Blake told her with a grin.

"Find your own woman to hug," Logan complained from where he was standing next to Grace, tugging on her hand to bring her back to his side.

Everyone laughed, and they all made their way to the door. After more assurances that yes, Grace would call if she needed anything, the door finally shut behind them.

"Jeez, I didn't think they'd ever leave," Logan teased. Not letting go of her hand, he started back to the TV room. "Come on, this place is a pigsty. If I'm gonna have a roomie, I need to get my shit sorted. Help me?"

"Of course," Grace answered. "Although I have to say, it's much more comfortable sitting in your arms than cleaning."

Logan leaned down to her and she felt the hot air from his breath on her ear as he whispered. "I want nothing else than to sit on the couch all night with you in my arms, but that would be selfish of me."

"As if I care," Grace said with a wicked look in her eyes. It felt good to be able to say whatever she wanted without having to worry about what the other person might think or do. Logan was not Margaret or Walter Mason, and it felt good to just be herself.

Logan had a huge smile on his face and held out his hand. Grace smiled back shyly and put her hand in his. She followed as they headed to his cluttered table. She took a deep breath. She could certainly help him get organized . . . she *did* have a degree in office management, even if it wasn't what she wanted to do for the rest of her life.

She had no job.

Didn't really want to go back to her apartment in case her parents tried to get at her there.

But apparently, she had a friend named Logan.

And his brothers. And Felicity and Cole.

It was all she needed . . . for now.

Chapter Twenty

The weeks following Grace's dramatic rescue from her parents' house were actually pretty anticlimactic. Walter and Margaret Mason didn't jump out of any bushes demanding that Grace continue to work for them or insist she come over to their house and help with chores. She wasn't snatched off the street by thugs in black clothing. None of her friends went crashing over a mountainside because of their brake lines being cut. It was almost enough to have her lowering her guard . . . almost.

Grace finally truly understood what Logan had told her a few weeks ago . . . he was not the same person he was back in high school. He could more than take care of himself. His time in the Army had hardened him to some extent, but it had also given him the confidence to stand up to any bully . . . big or small. It was a comfort, and most definitely a turn-on.

Grace had spent a lot of time with his brothers, and saw that same confidence in them as well even though it manifested itself in different ways. Blake had a lot of the same mannerisms as Logan, which Grace figured was because he had also been in the Army, but his badassery was more below the surface. She had no doubt he could wipe the floor with anyone who crossed him, but he was more content to use his head before simply pounding someone who might look at him sideways.

But Nathan was the most intriguing of the three brothers. He was quiet and thoughtful, and seemed like a gentle soul, but Grace saw the same protective light in his eyes that she saw in Logan's. She figured all it would take were the right circumstances, or person, to bring his own brand of badassery to the forefront.

Her apartment was sitting empty, but she continued to pay the rent with the money she had saved up in the secret bank account in Denver, hoping at some point she'd be able to go back. In the meantime, however, she was enjoying living with Logan, even if it was only temporary.

She'd spent a lot of time with Felicity, who often came over to Logan's place. He understood that having some girl time would be good for her and frequently left them alone while he went to work or ran errands.

During one such visit, Grace decided to ask her friend something that had been bothering her. "Do you think Logan and his brothers will regret helping me?"

"What? Why would you say that? No. Hell no," Felicity responded, obviously shocked.

"It's just that . . . I know that I need their help. I need your help, but it's hard for me to let others fight my fight. It seems wrong," Grace admitted, biting her lip and fiddling with the remote control rather than looking at her friend.

"Grace," Felicity said firmly. "Here's a secret about guys . . . they like to help. They like to feel needed. You letting them do this for you is a good thing. First, they know what they're doing; and second, it makes them feel good to help a friend."

"I get depressed sometimes. Knowing my parents didn't really love me, were using me for whatever reason. Every other day I think that it'd just be easier on everyone if I left here for good. Moved away and started anew someplace where no one knows me or my parents."

Felicity scooted closer to Grace and put her arm around her shoulders. "Grace, you're my best friend. I don't know what I'd do without you. I can't really blame you for being sad about everything that's happened, but the bottom line is that your parents don't deserve to have you in their lives. And how you turned out as amazing as you did, I'll never know." Seeing that Grace still wouldn't look at her, Felicity hugged her closer and asked, "What else are you thinking?"

When Grace didn't say anything, Felicity pushed, "It's me. Felicity. Your best friend. The chick who convinced you to get a tattoo. You can tell me anything."

Grace nodded, as if shoring up her defenses, and turned to look at her friend. "Sometimes I feel like it'd just be easier if I just gave in and did what they wanted. Marry Bradford."

Felicity made a clucking sound in the back of her throat, and Grace hurried to finish. "But then I think about what they'd do to any child I might have, and how they'd surely be just as emotionally abusive to their grandchildren, and I realize that I can't do it. No matter how depressed I become or how hard it gets."

"I'm proud of you, Grace," Felicity said, resting her head on Grace's shoulder. "None of this is easy, but you're hanging in there and being really brave about it all."

"I don't feel brave most of the time," Grace countered.

"But you're not giving in, and you're moving forward. That's bravery."

The conversation had gone a long way toward making Grace feel better about everything. She wasn't using her friends to do her dirty work, and living with Logan was good. It was also proving to be harder than either of them had thought. Not because they discovered that they didn't like each other after all, but because they enjoyed each other's company more and more with each passing day.

Grace was still sleeping in the guest room, but every day that went by, she felt less and less like she needed or wanted to sleep separately from him. He'd done just as he said he'd do . . . left it up to her to determine how far and fast she wanted to take things. They spent almost all their time together when he was home. He didn't go into the Ace Security office much, only when Felicity visited. He said it was because Ace Security was just too close to Mason Architecture for his comfort, and because he wanted to be by her side as much as he could.

One day, after he'd come back from running some errands, Grace approached Logan. "I'm bored," she said bluntly. "I'm used to doing stuff all day. Working. Sitting around your house watching TV just isn't working for me. Can I please *do* something to help you? Maybe some of the paperwork for Ace Security or something?"

Logan looked surprised, but then he smiled. "That's a great idea. I don't think Nathan will let you touch any of the accounting stuff, it's kinda his baby, but I know Blake and I would love some help with emails and the website. We can't keep up with it. And besides, we just plain suck at it."

"I'd love to," Grace said gleefully, clapping her hands excitedly. "So, just let you know if there are any urgent messages from anyone needing security or something like that?"

"Exactly. The website itself is pretty static at the moment, we don't have many updates, but if you have any ideas to jazz it up or make it more user friendly, feel free to jot them down and I can discuss them with Nathan and Blake. If they agree, we could see about having you update it . . . if that's something you'd be up for."

"Oh, I'm up for it," Grace told him, eyes shining. "Thank you!"

"Don't thank me yet," Logan said. "You might find out it's more work than you bargained for. We're not exactly at the top of our game when it comes to organization and paperwork."

Grace hugged him. "I think you're selling yourself short, but thank you for letting me help. It'll help keep my mind off of everything else."

Evenings were Grace's favorite time of all. She used to hate them, but then again, she'd been dealing with trying to please both her parents. Now she and Logan hung out on his couch, watched TV, and talked. She learned a lot about Logan from spending time with him.

It's as if they were speed dating, except it felt comfortable rather than like their relationship was on fast-forward.

One night during dinner, Grace noted, "You know you eat really fast, don't you?"

"Yeah." Logan shrugged, not at all concerned. "It's a habit I learned growing up, and the Army certainly didn't help it any."

Grace looked at him with her brows furrowed. "You learned it growing up?"

"We were forced to eat at the dinner table every night, even though we all dreaded it. If I ate fast, my mom couldn't find an excuse to smack me, and I could leave and get out of her reach that much faster."

Grace stared at him, her fork halfway to her mouth.

"Grace? Is it gonna be a problem? I can try to slow down, but I've been shoveling my food into my mouth my entire life. I don't think it'll be easy to change."

"No!" Grace told him, appalled that he'd even think she cared about such things. "I was just thinking that I was forced by my parents to eat slowly and ladylike, no matter how hungry I was. Just like you were trained to eat fast." She shrugged a little self-consciously. "We have that in common."

"So we do. And, I think the way you eat is cute."

"Cute?" Grace wrinkled her nose. "It's not cute. It's polite. And annoying. I have to say, I'm a bit jealous of how you don't care about what others think of you when you're eating. Just once I'd love to be able to scarf down pizza or spaghetti and not have to worry about what I look like while I'm doing it."

"Tell you what," Logan told her with a grin, "if you teach me some of your fancy manners, and what the hell all the silverware is for, I'll make sure you have plenty of opportunities to stuff finger food in your mouth without having to worry about an audience judging you. Deal?"

"Deal."

They'd also spent a lot of time acting on their mutual attraction. The first few nights were awkward for both of them, but as the newness of living in the same apartment wore off, so did the barriers they'd both erected to protect themselves.

"You want to watch a movie?" Logan asked after they'd reviewed the morning's events together. Grace had told him about the upcoming jobs she'd booked for the company, and he'd informed her that her parents seemed to have completely forgotten about her . . . once again showing up for work on time and leaving right at five.

It was one in the afternoon. They'd had lunch and while they could always do some work, she had something else in mind. She shook her head. "I'm sick of TV. Would you . . ." she paused, not sure she should ask what she was thinking.

"Go on, will I what?" Logan encouraged.

"It's silly, but I saw you one day outside Ace Security and I've never—"

"Spit it out, woman." Logan smiled to let her know he was teasing.

Grace mock-glared at him, but secretly was thankful he'd made a joke out of her reticence. "Will you take me for a ride on your motorcycle? I've never been on one."

Logan eyed her up and down. "I'd love to. You'll need to go put on jeans and a long-sleeve shirt to protect your skin."

Grace nodded. "Yeah."

"Excellent. Then you're all set. You can wear my leather jacket, and I'll make sure Blake picks one up for you if you enjoy the ride and think you might want to do it again sometime."

"Buying me a jacket isn't necessary," Grace protested. "I'll be fine with the one Felicity brought for me."

"Grace, it's not just a matter of me wanting you to have one, it's for your safety and protection. I'd rather drive a nail in my eye than do anything to put you in danger. Trust me on this. A regular long-sleeve shirt or coat isn't safe enough. There's a safety reason behind the heavier leather jackets that motorcyclists wear. It helps protect us against the weather as well as guards against road rash if we take a fall."

"Oh, okay. I didn't realize. But, Logan, if I wear yours, then you won't have one. I don't want to put you in danger. Maybe this was a bad idea; we can do it some other time."

Logan walked over to where Grace was standing in the kitchen and loosely put his arms around her waist, hooking his fingers together at the small of her back and pulling her into him. Grace could feel his semi-hard cock against her belly and could smell the scent of his soap on his skin. The peppermint he'd eaten earlier wafted into her face as he spoke.

"I'm good. I've been doing this a long time. I know what I'm doing. I don't think we're gonna crash, but just in case, I'd prefer for you to be covered, rather than me."

"Then why didn't you just say that then?" she semi-teased.

He smiled and ran his finger down the tip of her nose. "Brat. Thank you for being concerned about me, though. It's been a long time since a woman has given a shit what I do."

"I give a shit."

He grinned wider. "I'm glad."

"And thanks in return for being concerned about me as well," Grace returned. "Not about how what I'm doing reflects on you, but about *me*."

The smile on Logan's face melted away and he looked down at her seriously. "Don't doubt that for one second. I want you to do what you want, when you want, because it's what pleases *you*. Don't ever *not* do something because you're worried about what I might think. No wait, I take that back. If it's something dangerous . . . like riding on a motorcycle without the proper clothing and safety equipment . . . then definitely think about how upset I'll be with you. But if it's taking the classes you want, or accepting a job in Denver with a top-five marketing firm, or what to eat and how to eat, then you should only think about what's best for you, and what will make you happy."

"*You* make me happy," Grace told him in a solemn tone, meeting his eyes head on.

"The same goes for me. I'm happier than I've been in a long time."

"Even though you've been stuck in your apartment with me?"

"*Because* I've been lucky enough to be holed up in my apartment with you. Now, go change. I can't wait to show you the world from a biker's perspective."

Five minutes later, wearing a pair of jeans and a long-sleeve baby-blue shirt, Grace turned her back to Logan and held out her arms, letting him help her into his way-too-big jacket.

She turned to face him and shrugged self-consciously. "It's huge on me."

Logan reached down and zipped it up as if she were a little kid. It could have felt patronizing, but instead, Grace felt protected. She ducked her head and inhaled the smell of leather and the man standing in front of her.

"What are you doing?"

Without looking up, Grace answered, "It smells like you. I love it."

"Grace . . . Jesus . . . you're killin' me."

She smiled, then gasped when Logan roughly pulled her on her tiptoes and covered her lips with his. The kiss was full of passion and Grace participated with gusto. Her hands found their way under his shirt as far as they could go, which unfortunately was only to the middle of his chest. She felt the coarse hair there and licked her lips in anticipation. He felt good under her hands.

Logan took advantage of her breathlessness and palmed one of her butt cheeks and pulled her hips harder into his own. The other hand went to the back of her head and held her to him as they kissed.

Grace shifted restlessly in his grasp and opened her mouth wider to him. Their tongues curled together. She moaned when Logan sucked on her tongue, causing goose bumps to race down her arms.

She pulled back, panting, and looked up at him, licking her lips and tasting peppermint. Neither moved for a long moment until Logan stated, "Ride first."

"First?" Grace asked in a daze. The last thing she wanted to do was leave. They'd made out almost every night since she'd moved in, and every night they'd gone a bit further. In the beginning, it was the brush of his hand over her breasts, then it was her head in his lap while his hand rested on her breastbone while his thumb and pinky caressed the slopes of her breasts.

She'd had him take off his shirt one night and had examined each of his tattoos, going so far as to run her lips and tongue over his ink, worshipping him, letting him know without words how much she liked the designs he'd chosen.

They'd been slowly but surely getting to know each other sexually, although both sensed that the time wasn't right to go all the way. Sometimes Grace pulled back, and other times it had been Logan, like last night when he'd reluctantly backed off after Grace had crawled on his lap and ground herself onto his rock-hard cock.

"Yeah, first," Logan said looking her in the eyes. "Ride first, then we'll come back here and see about the chemistry we've been flirting with for the last month or so . . . if that works for you."

Grace kept her hands where they were, and used her thumbs to rub up and down over the hair on his chest. "It definitely works for me, Logan. You've been so good about not rushing me. I want you. We don't have to go anywhere if you don't want to. We can go right back to your bedroom. I'm ready."

Logan closed his eyes as if in pain, but when he opened them again, Grace saw determination and relief.

"You wanted to ride on the back of my bike, so you're gonna ride on the back of my bike. I'll take you up into the mountains so you can really get a good feel for how being on a motorcycle makes everything seem more alive, more beautiful. Then we'll come back here, and if you're still willing, I'll make love to you like I've been dreaming about for the last ten years. You ready for that?"

"Yes." The look in her eyes spoke volumes.

Grinning, Logan untangled his fingers from her hair and ran his hand over her shoulder and down her arm to grab hold of her hand. He turned and led her out of the apartment, stopping to grab a canvas jacket and helmet hanging on the back of a chair. He locked the door on their way out. She followed him down the stairs to his motorcycle, which was parked under an overhang next to his truck.

He carefully buckled an extra helmet from his saddlebag under her chin, making sure it was tight, but not too tight. He shrugged on his own jacket then placed his helmet on his head. He took both her shoulders in his hands, leaned down and kissed her hard, then climbed onto the large motorcycle.

"Throw your foot over the seat and put it on one of the pegs . . . yeah, there. Good," he praised as Grace did as he asked. Keeping his hands on the handlebars he turned his head and ordered, "Lean when and where I lean, and trust me to keep you safe. Now, put your arms around me and hold on tight."

Grace swallowed hard and leaned forward, sliding her arms around Logan's waist and plastering her boobs against his back. When he inhaled at her touch, she smiled. This was going to be fun.

Chapter Twenty-One

The bike ride wasn't fun, it was amazing.

Grace felt like she was in a different world riding through the countryside surrounding Castle Rock on the back of Logan's bike. At first she'd been scared, seeing the pavement so close to their feet, hearing the noise of the wind and nothing else.

But the longer they rode, the more she got used to it. The wind on her face and in her ears made it seem like nothing could touch her. Feeling Logan's muscles bunching and flexing as he controlled the massive machine under them was reassuring.

Even watching the world go by was a different experience on the back of a motorcycle. She could smell the cows and horses when she passed by the fields and could somehow see every dip and sway of the land around her.

As they headed west toward the Front Range and climbed higher and higher, the air around them got cooler. Grace was glad for the heavy leather jacket Logan had made her wear and snuggled closer to him. Laying her head on his back, she watched the rocks and landscape of the mountainside pass by her eyes in a blurry cacophony of colors.

She felt free. Finally, free. Free of the shame her parents had heaped on her for years. Free of the guilt of never being good enough for them. Free to be her own person. To be who she wanted. Free to be *with* who she wanted.

And she wanted to be with Logan.

Every part of her body vibrated with the engine under her, reminding her how much she wanted Logan. There was nothing in her mind at the moment but her and Logan . . . and her ever-increasing desire for him accentuated by the strong engine between her legs.

Even though she was wearing jeans, the vibration of the motorcycle seemed to be centered right on her clit. No matter how she shifted on the seat, it wouldn't stop. By the time Logan pulled off at an overlook high in the mountains over Denver, she was more than ready to get off, in more ways than one.

Logan had simply smiled as if he knew exactly what she was feeling when he helped her step off the bike. He'd propped her up against the guardrail at the end of the pull-off and proceeded to make love to her mouth. He kissed her as if she was the most desirable thing he'd ever gotten his hands on. She'd been ten seconds or so away from a monster orgasm, helped along by Logan's palm rubbing her through her jeans and his lips caressing hers, when a car pulled into the overlook.

"Damn," Grace breathed. "I was so close. Is riding always like this?"

He smiled and kissed her forehead, then held her against his chest tenderly. "You get used to it."

Grace snorted. "I'm not sure that's true. I think women probably just tell their men that so they don't know exactly how horny they get every time they get on the bike with them."

Logan chuckled and ran a finger down her nose affectionately. "You like riding." It wasn't exactly a question.

"Yeah, I do. It makes me feel free. Like I don't have any worries or problems. The wind on my face, watching the dotted lines go by on the road beneath us . . . it's hard to explain."

"You're explaining perfectly," Logan told her. "I'm thrilled you enjoy it."

"I like it with you," Grace clarified. "I'm not sure I'd like it as much if I had to drive, or with anyone else."

Logan backed up and held out his hand. "Come on, time to get us home."

They'd settled back onto the bike, and Grace winced as she straddled the bike seat again. "It's going to be a miracle if I don't come before we get home," she mumbled, snuggling up against Logan's back.

She watched as Logan's eyes filled with lust . . . and something else she couldn't quite identify. "I'm going straight home and I'm not taking the scenic route."

"Awesome," Grace breathed. "Although I'm not sure it'll really help."

"Don't think about it," Logan suggested. "Look at the scenery as we pass by."

"Your motorcycle has a really strong engine, Logan," Grace teased, pouting.

He half turned in his seat and kissed her long and hard.

"And that's really not helping," Grace griped with a smile when he turned away to start up the motorcycle once again.

She didn't want them to get into a wreck, but she also loved the feel of Logan underneath her palms. Her hands wandered freely, but not into dangerous territory, while they made the drive back to Castle Rock. She wasn't really trying to torture him, was more trying to keep her mind away from the incessant throbbing between her legs, but at one point, Logan grasped her wandering hand as it got a little too close to his dick, and forced it back up to his belly, holding it flat against him, and still. He didn't say a word, not that she would've been able to hear him anyway, but she smiled into his shoulder when she realized that the vibration from the large machine under them was affecting him too.

They arrived back home and Logan didn't say a word. He helped her stand and kept his hand on her waist until he was sure her legs would hold her up. He unhooked his helmet, then hers, before pulling her into his side.

They walked side by side into his apartment and as soon as the door was shut, he dropped the helmets and went to work on the zipper of her too-big jacket. Logan pushed it off her shoulders and then shrugged off his own coat. Again not caring where they landed in the small entryway.

"Shoes, off."

Without looking, keeping her eyes on his, Grace brought one foot up to her hand and undid the lace. She repeated the motions with the other foot and toed off both sneakers. Logan did the same with his boots, tugging them off and not flinching when they made a loud thud as they fell to the floor. There was definitely something to be said about leaving one's shoes where they fell when you came home and took them off. Grace knew she'd never again see a pair of Logan's shoes lying haphazardly around the house and not think of this moment.

Without another word, Logan put one hand under her knees and the other behind her back and picked her up. She gasped, loving his show of strength, and grabbed hold of his neck as he strode down the hall.

Whenever she'd fantasized about making love with Logan, she'd imagined it would be dark outside and they'd have had a nice dinner, followed by making out on his couch, and then they'd make their way into his room and get it done.

But the reality was so far outside of what she'd thought would happen, so much better than anything she could've conjured up.

Grace held her breath as Logan carried her into his room. The late-afternoon sun shone brightly through the open curtains of the window, the golden rays warming the covers on his bed. The air smelled like Logan, she'd noticed that before, but now that she was in his arms, it was more potent.

She kept her eyes on his as he gently dropped her legs and she stood in front of him.

"Are you nervous?" he asked running his hands up and down her arms.

Grace shook her head. "No." Then changed her mind and nodded. "A little bit. I don't want to disappoint you."

"You won't," he told her with absolute conviction. "Nothing you could do would disappoint me. Do you trust me?"

"Yes." Grace could answer that question with 100 percent honesty. From the moment he showed up in her room to steal her away, she trusted him.

"I've waited for this moment for over ten years," he told her, running a fingertip over her lips, making her gasp. "I'm not going to rush this. I want to memorize every inch of your skin and learn what you like and what you don't."

"I like you. That's what I like," Grace told him impatiently. "I don't want to go slow. I'm afraid that if we don't hurry up and get naked that something's going to happen, and we'll have to stop."

Logan's lips twitched in a ghost of a smile, and he brought a hand up to tangle in her hair at the side of her head. "We have all night. My brothers won't expect me to check in until tomorrow morning. You talked to Felicity this morning, and any emails that come in this afternoon can wait or Nathan can get to them. It's just you and me and I'm not stopping. Not until we're both satisfied."

Grace licked her lips in anticipation, feeling herself growing wet merely from his words. "Make love to me, Logan. Please."

"With pleasure."

Logan took Grace's face in his hands and leaned down. He'd done it many times over the last few weeks, but this time was different. They both knew he wasn't going to stop with a kiss. He slanted his mouth over hers and took her mouth urgently.

Over the last month or so, they'd had plenty of time to get to know each other, and with every day that went by, Logan was more sure than ever that Grace was the woman meant for him. Even when they disagreed, they did it with respect. She never yelled and he never felt the need to get away from her for some space. They simply disagreed, talked it out, and went on as usual. It was refreshing and something that Logan hadn't ever had with a woman.

He found it extremely satisfying when he could break through that outer shell she showed to the world to find the sensitive woman underneath. He'd seen it more and more over these past weeks, and there was nothing more satisfying than to see that shell cracking when they made out. A brush of his hand over her nipple made her gasp, his fingers running over the skin at the small of her back caused goose bumps to race down her arms. And sucking on her earlobe never failed to make her squirm in his embrace. Her reaction to the powerful engine of his bike vibrating against her pussy while they'd been riding had exceeded his wildest dreams.

Grace Mason was one of the most passionate women he'd ever met, and learning what she liked, what kinds of touches made her lose it, was going to be fun. He had a feeling she would keep him on his toes and constantly surprise him. He was looking forward to bringing out her playfulness, snarkiness, compassion, and yes, passion.

Without losing eye contact, Logan pulled his shirt over his head, baring his chest to her. Again, without a word or looking away from her, he undid his belt and the button at his waist and pushed his jeans and boxers off. Standing in front of her completely naked, Logan waited.

Grace looked away from his face then, and he watched as her eyes trailed down his body. A blush rose up from her neck to her face, but she didn't stop her perusal of his body. Logan knew he was already hard for her, she'd felt how much he wanted her under her hands on the way home, and as she drank him in, he felt himself grow even harder. God. Even her eyes on him was sexy.

"You're . . . um . . . big," she told him hesitantly.

Logan wouldn't be a guy if her words didn't make him feel proud of his body. "Mmmm."

"Your tattoos are amazing. I mean, I know I've seen them before, but I was a bit . . . preoccupied at the time. What do they mean?"

The last thing he wanted to talk about was the ink on his body, but he was trying to go slowly and explaining the meaning of his tattoos would go a long way toward that goal.

He turned slightly, showing her his right side. "I've got my name, Blake's, and Nathan's inked here, inside the words 'Brothers Forever.' On my back, behind my left shoulder I have the Army crest. Then, as you can see, there's a bunch of random tribal designs on my right upper arm." He shrugged. "They don't really mean anything to me. I was young and dumb and wanted to be cool." He smiled, then got serious. "I'm not really addicted to adding more ink to my body, but there is one more piece I want done." He reached out and put one hand behind Grace's neck, caressing the tattoo he couldn't see, but knew was there, with his thumb.

She shivered at his touch, putting her palms on his warm chest and asked, "What's that?"

"It's going to go right here on my forearm." Logan turned his left arm over, showing her the tan skin, unblemished by any kind of ink. "It's going to be two birds, flying free. Pink. And if I can swing it, they'll each be carrying letters in their talons. I want the bundled letters in that same ink you used to get yours done . . . so only we know they're there. That's gonna be ours and ours alone."

"Pink?" she whispered, squeezing his sides unconsciously. "That isn't very macho."

"Don't care. It'll remind me of you every time I see it. Your femininity. Your beauty. How you've found the courage and strength to fly out of your cage and find out who you are." He could tell his words moved her as she breathed out a shaky breath.

"Logan," Grace whispered in an awed voice.

"Lift your arms."

She did, no longer wanting to talk about tattoos, and Logan slowly but steadily stripped the long sleeve T-shirt from her. He loved when she wore his shirts. She'd been sleeping in them from the first night she'd been in his apartment, but peeling her out of her close-fitting tee was sexy as hell. He almost preferred the experience to her wearing his own baggy shirts . . . almost.

Grace's hair fell around her shoulders as he whisked it over her head and dropped it absently behind him.

She moved her hands behind her back and quickly unsnapped the cream bra she'd been wearing and dropped it to the floor.

Logan had felt her tits before, but seeing them up close and personal with nothing covering them was absolutely amazing. He couldn't take his eyes from her chest. She was full and round, and she had large areolas that surrounded nipples that were puckering even as he watched. Her breaths were coming short and hard, causing her breasts to rise and fall. Her nipples were pulled taut and sticking out as if begging for his touch.

Keeping his voice low, Logan said, "A pink bird. Right here on the inside curve of your breast. By your heart. That would look so fucking amazing."

Not able to resist, Logan brought a hand up to her chest. Using only his index finger, he touched the area where he could practically see the ink he'd mentally designed. She didn't speak, but her breathing quickened. When her nipple beaded even more next to his fingertip, he smiled and moved his hand so it circled the eager bud begging for his touch. It tightened even further, something he didn't think was possible.

"Feel good?" He knew he didn't need to ask, but loved the way Grace's lips parted and she nodded at him with heavy-lidded eyes.

Logan's mouth watered with the need to taste her, but he held back. He was enjoying unwrapping her little by little. He had plenty of time to lick her from head to toe. He moved his finger to her other nipple, treating it to the same reverent touch, satisfied when it too tightened immediately.

"Damn, your skin is so beautiful. Unblemished." He went on, describing the tattoo he wanted to see on her skin. "Not a big bird.

Small, petite. Right here, where I can see it when I'm sucking these beautiful tits, see it flutter as your breath hitches . . . yeah, like that . . . and it can fly as you sit on top of me, riding me."

"Logan," she protested huskily.

"Would you do that for me?"

"Yes. I'd do anything you asked." Logan felt his dick twitch and a bit of pre-come oozed out the slit at the top at her response.

He sucked in a breath as he felt Grace's fingers tracing his own nipples. "God," he moaned and moved his hand down to his cock, squeezing the base as he throbbed in his hand. If just the thought of her inking her skin and the touch of her hand on his nipples made him want to come, he was in big trouble. It'd been years since he'd made love to a woman, and his dick was practically begging him to take her. To sink into the hot, wet depths of her body.

He grabbed her hands and pulled them away from his body, smiling at the pout on her face.

"I wanted to touch too."

"I'll give you all the time you want . . . later."

"That's not fair."

"Believe me, Grace. I want your hands, and lips, on every inch of my skin, but later. If you so much as breathed on my cock right now, I'd immediately come. And while that image is one that I've dreamed about, it's important to me to make sure you enjoy our first time. Can you give me that?"

"But I want you to enjoy it too," she told him as she took a step into him, biting her lip as his cock brushed against her belly.

"Oh, Smarty, I will," Logan told her without a shred of doubt in his voice, "but men have a harder time coming more than once in a short period of time, while women have the ability to come several times . . . as long as their man knows what he's doing."

"And you know what you're doing?" she said, one side of her mouth tipping up in a teasing half-grin as she put her hands on his waist.

He tickled her sides gently in retaliation and laughed as she squirmed, her tits bouncing with her movements. "Yeah, brat, I know what I'm doing. I might not be the most experienced man out there, but making you come in my arms is something I won't fail at."

Grace didn't answer, but moved her hands to her own pants. Logan immediately brushed them away. "Let me."

He made quick work of the button and zipper at her waist and pushed her jeans down her legs. She was left standing in front of him in nothing but a plain white pair of panties. And it was the hottest thing he'd ever seen in his life.

"Damn, Grace," he breathed. Logan couldn't have expanded on his thoughts if his life depended on it.

"They're not sexy or anything," she told him, obviously self-conscious, and went to push them off.

He halted her again simply by reaching out, grabbing her wrists, and holding her still. Logan licked his lips in anticipation.

"I disagree. On you, they're the sexiest thing I've ever seen in my life." Logan let go of her hands and knelt in front of her, licking his lips and inhaling deeply. He felt her hands rest on his shoulders, but couldn't tear his eyes away from the white cotton covering her. He swallowed hard, ignoring his erection, which was pulsing in need.

He brought his eyes up to hers. Grace was looking down at him, biting her lip. Her tits looked even more amazing from this vantage point. Losing his train of thought, one of Logan's hands actually inched upward toward one of her breasts before he remembered what he had set out to do.

"May I?" he asked politely, canting his head toward her hips, asking for permission to remove her panties.

"Yes. Please," she breathed out.

Logan grinned and brought his attention back down. He put his palms against her sides and slowly, ever so slowly, inched her panties down, making sure his fingers slid under the elastic. He moved slowly, but didn't stop, pushing the white cotton over her hips and down her legs until the underwear puddled at her feet.

The curls at the juncture of her thighs were trimmed short, leaving a strip of hair above her folds, but everything else was bare.

Logan ran his hands up her inner thighs and watched her shift under his intimate touch. He skipped over her folds, stretching out the moment, and ran his thumbs over the silky skin on either side of the strip of hair. He brushed against her once, then twice.

"Logan, touch me," she begged.

"I am," he told her seriously.

"You know what I mean."

Logan looked up at that. "Easy, Grace. We only get one first time together and I'm memorizing everything about you. How you smell, how you shift under my fingers, how you look, where you're the most sensitive . . . I have so much to learn. I'm going to be here awhile."

"Damn," Grace breathed and looked up at the ceiling. She still held onto his shoulders and Logan could feel her short nails digging into his skin. He focused on the skin under his fingertips as he caressed her tenderly.

"I would love to see you get another tattoo here," he brushed his thumb over her hip. "A bird on your hip, just like the one on the back of your neck and the one I'm getting on my arm. I want to see you covered in birds, representing the freedom you have to do whatever you want. But under your clothes, where only I can see them. A proper woman on the surface, who flies free with the right incentive. With my fingers. And lips."

Grace made a sound, but it was more a groan than an actual word.

Logan felt the vibrations against his hands and abruptly stood, throwing the comforter back, exposing the sheets underneath. "Come here, Smarty. Lie back on the bed."

She did as he asked without hesitation, scooting up onto the mattress and turning so her head rested on a pillow and her torso was in the sunlight coming through the window. Logan crawled up next to her, straddled her thighs, and rested his elbows on either side of her, next to her rib cage, bringing his hands up to her chest. Now he was face-to-face with her gorgeous tits and could use both his hands and his mouth if he wanted. He looked up at her.

"Okay?"

Grace nodded. "Oh, yeah. It's more than okay. It's absolutely fantastic."

Using the same light touch he'd used before, Logan used his fingers to make circles around her nipples. They peaked and tightened, showing him once more how sensitive she was. How in the world any of the idiots she'd been with hadn't been able to get her off was beyond him. If he wasn't mistaken, his light touches already had her squirming.

The wetness between her thighs hadn't gone unnoticed either . . . and he hadn't even touched her yet. She was already more than ready for him. But he wanted her dripping, so wet he'd slide right inside her tight body without giving her even a twinge of discomfort. He wanted only pleasure for his Smarty tonight.

He moved to engulf her nipple in his mouth. He didn't start out slow and easy, but bit down somewhat roughly and sucked at the same time he wrapped his tongue around the stiff peak.

"Ungh," she moaned and arched her back into his touch instead of pulling away from him.

Logan smiled even as he kept his mouth on her. He moved his other hand until it was under her back and pressed upward, urging her to arch farther into him. He loved seeing Grace out of control and lost in what he was doing to her. A light sheen of sweat had already broken out on her body, causing it to glisten in the sunlight.

Moving his mouth to her other breast, he gave her other nipple the same treatment. Laving it with his tongue, nibbling and sucking, eliciting the same reaction out of her. Suddenly needing to *see* the first orgasm he gave her, not just feel it, Logan moved down her body until he was lying between her legs. He buried his nose in the crease between her folds and her right leg and inhaled deeply. She was musky, and he could smell some sort of flowery body wash. She was delicious.

She tried to close her legs, but couldn't because his shoulders were in the way.

"Easy, Grace."

"But it's so . . . intimate."

"You're right," he agreed. "It is. That's why I want it. You trust me, right?"

"Yeah, of course I do."

"Then stop worrying about what you think I want to do and relax and enjoy me loving you."

She gave him a small nod. Then asked, "And you'll let me do the same to you?"

"Oh yeah," he breathed out. "Not only *let*, but I'll *beg* you to do it."

"Awesome," she said with a smile, and slowly let her legs fall open, granting him access.

"Awesome," he echoed, turning his attention back to her folds and licking his lips in anticipation.

Logan leaned down, and using the point of his tongue, licked her from bottom to top, catching the drop of excitement that had slipped out of her and spreading it up to her clit. He didn't linger, but licked his lips when he pulled away.

Holy shit, she tasted good. He hadn't really been that enamored with giving oral sex in the past, but realized that loving the person you were with made all the difference. Logan stared down at the most beautiful pussy he'd ever seen. Maybe it was because it was his, maybe it was because he'd spent the last month and a half getting to know the woman attached to it, but whatever the reason, Logan knew he would never, not in a thousand years, get tired of looking at, licking, and touching her wet folds.

Seeing Grace squirm lightly under him, soaking wet, reminded Logan of a fantasy he'd had about her. He caressed her clit with one finger, slow and gentle. Not rushing, taking his time, watching the hood around her clit slowly draw back as it hardened. His plan was to drive her crazy with only one finger while she got more and more turned on, until she wouldn't be able to hold back her orgasm.

"Spread your legs more, Grace," he ordered in a gruff voice. He hoped like hell it was possible. He had a feeling that because the woman lying under him trusted him so, anything was possible, especially after how turned on she'd gotten on the back of his bike. "Grab hold of your knees and pull them back for me."

"Logan . . ." Grace began, unsure and obviously out of her element with his request.

"You're so sensitive, Grace. This is gonna be amazing, for both of us. I'm not going to hurt you, and you can stop me at any time." He looked her in the eyes as she stared nervously down at him.

Without a word, she made her decision and reached her hands down to hold her knees open for him.

Logan knew he should probably wait and do this later, once they'd gotten to know each other sexually a bit better, but he wanted to give this to her. Let her feel this pleasure between her knees this way. Slow and gentle. His gift to her as a woman.

Placing his left hand on her inner thigh, holding her open to him, he ran the thumb of his other hand up her dripping folds, gathering up her juices as he went. Then he lightly circled her clit with his thumb. Rubbing and massaging the bundle of nerves slowly and deliberately.

Grace let herself relax into his touch.

Logan shifted, using his other hand to pull the hood back from her pink pearl so he could caress it more directly. He alternated between rubbing her clit, and running his thumb alongside it, learning what Grace's body liked best.

He could see her clench her muscles as he brought her closer and closer to the edge. He didn't rush, he didn't press down harshly, he kept his touch light and methodical. Logan could see just how good it felt by the amount of juices escaping her hot channel. Every so often he'd catch some of her come on his thumb and smear it upward to help lubricate his touch on her clit.

"Logan, God . . . I can't . . . that feels . . . yeah . . ."

Her words were disjointed and almost incoherent. Logan loved every one. The next time a drop of her come escaped, he leaned down and caught it with his tongue. She was so sexy, and he wanted to sink inside her more than he wanted his next breath.

But he was patient. He wanted to see her come with only his light touch on her clit. He kept up the steady pressure and rhythmic caress, but added his praise as her inner muscles squeezed.

"You have no idea how beautiful this is, Grace. You're perfect. So responsive to my touch. You're gonna come like this, with just my finger on you. You'll come so hard you're gonna soak my sheets. You'll be so hot and wet when I sink inside, you're gonna burn me alive. Are you close, Grace? Do you want to come?"

"Please, yes. Faster . . ."

"No. Slow and easy. Let it build. Fuck, this is amazing. I can see you clenching. You feel empty? You want me inside?"

"Yes! Please, Logan. I need more. Harder and you inside me."

"And you'll get me."

"Now, please. I'm so empty."

Logan could see her muscles desperately searching for more pressure inside her passage. He wanted to ease a finger inside her, feel how tight she was, but wanted her to come this way more. Wanted her to experience this, to fully let herself go, for it to be about her, not about him this first time.

Grace's legs began to tremble, and she tried to close her legs as her orgasm neared. Logan rested his elbow on her thigh and held the other open with his free hand. His thumb never stopped its slow relentless caress of her clit.

"That's it, Grace. You're almost there. Close your eyes, let yourself go."

She did as he suggested, arching her spine and groaning as she dipped her head back. Logan watched her open body as it readied itself for the orgasm that had been slowly building up within her. He increased the speed of his thumb slightly, but not the pressure. He circled her bud faster and faster, watching, fascinated, as her ass squeezed shut while every muscle in her body bore down in preparation for her climax.

He hadn't expected it, but the moment she went over the edge, she pushed upward, opening her legs even wider than they'd been and yelled his name.

Grabbing a condom from his bedside table, Logan covered himself and knelt between Grace's legs, loving the fact that she still trembled with aftershocks even after he'd removed his hand.

"Grace?"

She opened her eyes then and met his gaze. For the first time since they'd come into his bedroom, he didn't see anything but pure desire in her eyes. "Take it off," Grace demanded.

"What?"

"The condom. Take it off. I want to feel you."

"Grace—"

She interrupted him. "You told me you hadn't had sex in years. Me either. I'm clean. Please. I want to feel you, I need *you*, just you this first time. Please."

"Are you sure?" Logan asked urgently, his eyes boring into hers. He was an asshole for even considering it, he knew that. It was his responsibility to protect her, and at the moment he knew she was too far gone with passion to really be thinking coherently. The last thing he wanted was for her to regret *anything* about their first time together.

"Absolutely."

Logan waited a beat, and saw no hesitation in her eyes. "God, you're amazing." Logan quickly stripped off the rubber and dropped it on the floor, not caring where it landed. He took hold of himself and winced at how ready to explode he was. He gave her one more chance. "You're sure?"

"I'm sure. Make love to me, Logan."

"Grace," he groaned, easing the tip of his erection just inside her slick folds. He felt her clench against him, trying to pull him inside, and his hand came up to brace himself over her once again.

"You're so warm," she said reaching up with both hands to grab hold of his arms.

He ground his teeth together and pushed in another inch. Dear God in heaven, he wasn't going to last. He'd had an erection for the last fifteen minutes, and it hadn't waned one bit during all that time. It wanted one thing and one thing only . . . to be inside Grace Mason.

Logan pushed in farther, groaning as she squeezed him. "God, Smarty, relax. Let me in."

"I can't help it, you feel so good," she told him, not taking her eyes away from his.

Sweat beaded on both their brows as he slowly took what should've been his for years.

Logan licked his lips and pushed the rest of the way inside her, feeling his balls flush up against her ass. She shifted in his embrace and he gained another few millimeters.

"Shit, Grace, I can't . . . you . . ."

She smiled. "I see you're the speechless one now."

Logan opened his mouth to respond to her sass, but gasped instead when she used her inner muscles to squeeze him as hard as she could. "Fuck, yeah. Jesus, Grace. You have no idea how amazing this feels. It's like a thousand warm pulsing fingers brushing against my cock."

He eased back, then pushed back in, not wanting to leave the hot cavern of her body. Being inside her was one of the best feelings he'd ever had. Ever.

He pulled out, then pushed in again. Then did it again, all while cognizant of Grace watching his face intently. Logan had no words for what he was feeling, and didn't even try to talk. Her body was soaked, and he slid in and out easily. Wanting to feel her squeeze his dick in the midst of her orgasm, Logan moved a hand down to where they were joined, and found her clit once again.

Instead of being gentle and methodical, as he'd been the first time he'd made her come, Logan roughly strummed her bundle of nerves while pumping in and out of her.

"Oh, God, Logan. Damn, I . . . yes, right there," she moaned shoving her hips up into his thrusts and against his thumb.

He finally found his voice. "I can't hold off. You're too damn sexy and feel too good. I want to feel you come around my dick, Grace." He sped up the movements of his thumb. "Come on me, Smarty. That's it . . . I can feel it. Let go, give it to me once more."

Grace screeched and lifted her hips into his once more, and exploded for the second time.

Logan felt her hot release against the sensitive skin of his dick and sped up his thrusts, pushing through the spasming folds of her pussy until he felt his own come surging up from his balls and out his dick. He thrust inside her roughly and held still as he emptied himself inside the sexy, sated woman beneath him.

Logan shuddered through his orgasm, his eyes closed, letting the euphoria race through his body along with his release.

"Holy cow," Grace whispered, making Logan grin even though he hadn't quite recovered yet.

He fell onto her, catching himself so he didn't squish her, then rolled over until she was lying on top of him, making sure to keep their hips glued together. Grace propped herself up gently onto his chest, peering down at him. They were both still breathing hard, and their bodies were slicked with sweat.

"I've never felt anything like that in my life," Logan told her honestly, bringing his hand to the nape of her neck and rubbing his thumb against her tattoo.

"Me either," she agreed breathlessly.

"Thank you."

"You're welcome?"

He smiled at her in amusement. "Yeah. Thank you for giving yourself to me and trusting me. It was everything I dreamed it would be and more."

"Really?"

"Really. You enjoyed it?" Logan asked, his eyebrows raised.

"I can't believe you even have to ask me that. It was amazing. You were amazing. *We* were amazing." Grace told him without a trace of guile in her voice. "I had no idea sex could be like that. Is it normally?"

"No," Logan answered definitely. "At least not for me. And I don't think sex could ever be like that for you again with anyone else."

She huffed out a laugh. "Only *you* can make that happen, huh?"

"Exactly." He grinned devilishly at her.

"Then I'd better keep you around."

"Yup. For at least another eighty years or so."

"You think you can get it up when you're a hundred and eight?"

"If you're in my life, yeah, I think I'd have a pretty good shot."

Grace laid her head down on his shoulder and relaxed comfortably into him. "I know we need to shower, but I don't think I can move."

"Then don't. The shower can wait."

"Don't we need to . . . uh . . . clean up?"

Logan wrapped his arms around Grace and held her to him, making sure she didn't move. "Eventually."

"Well, wake me up when you're ready."

"I will," Logan whispered. He felt himself finally slip out of her body as the blood finally left his cock. They both groaned but didn't move.

Logan held Grace as they both dozed, and for the first time since she moved in, he didn't think about her situation, her parents, or the danger she might be in. He simply soaked her in, thankful as all fuck he'd gotten a second chance to be with her.

Chapter Twenty-Two

It was eleven in the morning and Logan had gone to Denver to meet with a man who wanted a security guard. It wasn't the type of thing that Ace Security did, but the man had been so insistent that Logan had finally agreed to at least meet with him.

Ever since the first afternoon when Grace had made love with Logan, it seemed as though their relationship was on fast-forward. They made love almost every day, and she felt as comfortable around him as if she'd been with him her entire life. As a bonus, she felt calmer when Logan was around, and less worried about what she should and shouldn't be doing.

There were times when she found herself falling back on old habits, like going along with something Logan said even when she didn't agree or want to do it, but luckily, most of the time he noticed and called her on it. He encouraged her to be herself. To say what she liked and act on it, and perhaps more importantly, to say what she didn't like and not do it to please him or anyone else . . . and not be afraid to speak up about it.

It was around the time she thought he'd be heading back to Castle Rock, so Grace didn't even think twice when a knock came at the door. Figuring it was probably Felicity, she looked through the peephole and almost choked when she saw her father standing on the other side of the door.

Immediately panicking, Grace quickly stepped backward, almost tripping over her own feet in her haste to get away from him.

"Grace. I know you're there, I heard you at the door. Please talk to me," her father pleaded.

Her breaths came hard and fast, and she closed her eyes and tried to keep herself from hyperventilating. "What do you want?" she asked in a cold, hard voice when she could speak normally once again.

"Just to talk to you. I know I don't deserve it, and you don't trust me, but all I'm asking is for you to hear me out."

"Why should I?" Grace's hands trembled. They'd all been waiting so long for something to happen, but she still wasn't prepared. And it figured that Logan wasn't here with her when her father made his move.

"I've left your mother."

That was the last thing she expected to hear. "What?"

"Left her. When you left, it opened the door for me too. Your mother has been blackmailing me her entire life. But when you weren't around for her to hold over my head, it allowed me to get out as well. I had stayed with her because she had always threatened to hurt you if I left."

Grace's head spun. "What are you saying? That you stayed all those years to protect me?"

"Yes. That's exactly what I'm telling you," her father said in a sad voice. "Every time Margaret sensed I'd reached my limit or that I was upset with how she was treating you, she told me that she'd make your life even more of a living hell if I didn't do as she asked."

"So, when I was twelve, and you told me I was fat and could only drink chicken broth for a week, Mother made you do that," Grace said sarcastically.

"Yes."

"And when you laughed in my face when I tripped and fell into the coffee table and had to get three stitches in my head, that was all Mother too I suppose?" she pushed.

"You don't understand," her father pleaded. "I hated it. I hated what I was being forced to do to you. But you know about the cameras in the house. If I didn't, she'd know, and then you'd pay for it."

"It wasn't too long ago that you handcuffed me to my bed and told me I had to shit in a bucket," Grace railed, unconvinced.

"Remember when I was hospitalized when you were around seven or eight?"

Grace rolled her eyes at the abrupt change of subject, but said, "Yeah."

"It was right after you came home with a picture you'd drawn in school. It was of you and me, remember?"

She did. They'd been assigned to draw their family. Grace had been upset at her mother for not letting her eat breakfast that morning and had drawn a picture of her and her father instead. They were standing in front of a restaurant. He'd taken her there, just the two of them, the week before. "I remember."

"You came home and showed it to me and were so happy about it. I put it on the fridge. Your mother was gone that night. She had a meeting up in Denver with a builder."

"The picture was gone the next day," Grace remembered out loud.

"Yeah. Margaret wasn't happy with me . . ." His voice trailed off.

"Why? What'd she do?"

"She pushed me, and I fell and hit my head on the corner of the fireplace in the study. A blood vessel broke in my head and started bleeding. I almost died."

"What?" Grace blurted. "That's not true! There's no way."

"Grace, it is. You were at school, and she said she wanted to talk to me about something. When I entered the study, she told me I was a sorry excuse for a man and that it was all my fault you weren't a boy. She shoved me as hard as she could. I can still remember the look of rage on her face as I fell."

Grace had no idea what to say. None. It didn't matter, because her father continued without waiting for her to comment.

"She called 911 and told the EMTs that I'd tripped and fallen. Put on quite the show too. But the bottom line was that she thought I was getting too close to my daughter."

Her father sounded sincere and sad, and his voice held a caring tone that Grace hadn't heard since her childhood. Grace's chest hurt. She was so confused. She almost couldn't remember any good times with her parents. Either of them.

Her father continued. "When she came to me and told me the plan for you to marry Bradford, I didn't want to go along with it, but she'd shown me time and time again that she was ruthless . . . she told me what she'd do to *you* if I didn't go along with it."

"You guys locked me in my room," Grace said with a hint of acid in her voice. "It seems like she did what she said she would anyway . . . and you went right along with it."

"I didn't want to," Walter said sadly. "I didn't want to do any of it. Please, Grace. Open the door. Let me talk to you face-to-face. I want to prove to you that I'm telling the truth."

"I don't think so," Grace said uneasily.

"I've got the hospital records with me, you can see the date on them, and you'll know that I'm not lying. I really did almost die. I was afraid for my life if I didn't do what she wanted me to do. She's lost her mind in the last few years. She's never been this bad before. I'm not living at the house anymore. I moved out. I figure you don't ever want to step foot in there again . . . and I can't blame you. I have no desire to see that place ever again either."

"I'm not going to open this door. If I agree to meet with you, and that's a big if, it's going to be somewhere else. Somewhere public," Grace told her father sternly.

"Where?" her father asked immediately. "Name it and I'm there."

Grace thought quickly. Her father allowing *her* to choose made it seem even more likely that he was telling the truth. "Rock Hard Gym."

"It's right across from the firm. If your mother saw us together, or any of the spies she has at the office did, they'd tell her in a second and we'd be screwed."

He had a point. "Fine. How about Ace Security? It's still downtown, but not as close to the firm."

"Great. How about in thirty minutes?"

"No." Grace knew that wouldn't give Logan enough time to get back into town. She wasn't going to be one of those dumb heroines that she sometimes read about in romance books. "Two thirty."

"Okay, that'll work." Her father paused for a moment, then spoke again. "Thank you, Grace. You have no idea what this means to me."

Grace didn't say anything else, but crept forward to look out the peephole and watch her father's back as he walked away from Logan's door. Her heart was beating hard in her chest, and she felt slightly nauseous. She didn't want to be deceived, but her father had sounded so earnest, and for some reason she wanted to trust him. She certainly believed her mother could be as coldhearted as he'd said. Her mother was usually the one who berated her, who doled out most of her punishments, and who harped on the fact that she wasn't a boy her entire life. Yes, her father had participated, but he never seemed as angry as her mother.

Grace walked to the kitchen counter, picked up her phone, and pressed Logan's contact button. She waited impatiently for him to answer.

"Hey, Smarty. What's up?"

"My father stopped by." Grace didn't beat around the bush when she heard Logan's greeting. "I didn't open the door, but he said a lot of stuff, and I'm 80 percent sure he was telling the truth, but the bottom line is that he wants to meet with me. Face-to-face."

"That motherfucker was at my place? Shit. You don't go meet him. No way. Not without me."

"Of course not," Grace agreed immediately. "I'd never willingly put myself in danger by going to meet him alone. I have no desire to end up chained to my bed again."

"What did he say? Exactly?" Logan's words were clipped and controlled, and Grace could tell that he was not a happy man.

"Are you done with your meeting?"

"I am now."

"Oh, I didn't mean to—"

"Grace, you're way more important to me than anyone or anything else I'm doing. I have most of the information I need from this guy, and his situation isn't dire. It can wait. Yours can't. Now, what did your father say?"

God, Grace loved this man. "He said lots of stuff. Mother has been making him do what she wanted him to do by using threats against me. He said that he never wanted to do anything that he did to me, but Mother made him."

"And you believed him?" Logan asked incredulously.

"I know, it sounds crazy. But Logan, he said that Mother shoved him and made him fall into the fireplace when I was younger and caused a brain bleed. I remember him being in the hospital for about a week around the time he said it happened. And Mother was especially upset with him. When he came home from the hospital, he was different toward me. I didn't understand why at the time, but it makes sense now. My mother told him that if he didn't treat me the way she wanted him to, that she'd hurt me next."

"Are you fucking kidding me?"

"Unfortunately, no."

"What time?" Logan clipped.

"I told him two thirty at Ace Security. I figured that would give you time to get back and go with me."

"That should work. It's twelve now. I have one more thing I have to do before I head home. No matter what, you don't leave until you hear from me and know that I'm on my way. If you're early, you drive around until it's exactly two thirty. I'd come home and pick you up, but I don't think I'll make it before the meet time."

"I like that," Grace said softly.

"What?"

"Home. You'd come *home* to pick me up."

Logan's voice dropped to the rumbly growl he used when he was making love to her. "Wherever you are is home to me, Smarty. It could be a crappy apartment, a mansion in Beverly Hills, or a hole in the side of a mountain."

"Logan . . ." she whispered, then cleared her throat and got herself together. "Okay. I'll wait until you call, then I'll head out. Thank you."

"For what?"

"For agreeing to meet him with me. For not calling me crazy."

"For the record, I *do* think you're crazy, but it doesn't matter. You're an adult who can make decisions on her own, I can't make them for you. But I sure as hell can be by your side when you execute them. If anything goes wrong, call Nathan or Blake. Hell, even Cole. Okay? Nathan should be at the office when you get there, but call him anyway if you even feel one second of unease about anything."

"Okay. I'll talk to you soon. Be safe."

"Always. Later."

Grace clicked off the phone and held it to her chest. She closed her eyes and sent a thankful prayer upward once more that she'd been able to reconnect with Logan. He treated her as an adult, didn't belittle her, and made her feel as if she could do anything. She'd do whatever it took to keep Logan in her life. He was worth whatever she had to sacrifice in order to have him by her side. She was one lucky woman, and she knew it.

Glancing at her watch, Grace saw that she had about two hours before she'd need to leave. There were Ace Security emails to go through, financial aid forms to fill out for her classes, which started in the fall, and other things she could be doing, but the only thing she felt up to at the moment was pacing. And trying to think back through her life. Was her father telling the truth? And if not, what was he planning?

Chapter Twenty-Three

Grace looked nervously at her watch. It was two-thirty. Logan had called and let her know he was on the highway and would meet her at his office around two fifteen. She'd taken his truck, since he'd taken his motorcycle up to Denver, and had pulled into the public parking lot at the opposite end of the block, away from her parents' architectural firm.

She didn't want to just aimlessly drive around waiting for Logan to text her and let her know he'd arrived, but now that he was almost twenty minutes late, she was nervous.

A knock at her window startled her so badly, she shrieked in fright. She turned and saw her father standing next to the truck door. He shrugged apologetically and motioned for her to get out.

Grace looked around and didn't see anyone else suspicious nearby. She grabbed her purse and stepped out of the truck.

"Hey."

"Hi. Thank you for agreeing to meet me. I appreciate you giving me a second chance."

Grace looked at her father with hard eyes. "I'm just here to hear your side of the story. Don't think this is the beginning of a loving relationship with me. It's about twenty-seven years too late for that."

"I know, but I wouldn't be able to sleep at night knowing you thought I was a horrible person like your mother." Her father stepped away from her, giving her some room. "You ready to go?"

Grace opened her mouth to speak, but didn't get any words out before a large arm wrapped around her chest and another clamped over her face. She wanted to scream, to make some noise to bring some attention to what was happening, but couldn't open her mouth at all. The grip over it was too strong. She breathed in sharply and smelled something pungently sweet. She met her father's eyes and saw his concerned facial expression had morphed into one of pure evil.

It was the last thing she saw before losing consciousness.

"Dammit," Logan swore. "I can't get ahold of Grace." He'd called his brother as soon as he'd been able to, but he knew in his gut, it was too late.

"What the hell is going on?" Blake asked, picking up on Logan's mood.

"I don't know, but I have a really bad feeling. Grace called and said her father came by the apartment and wanted to talk to her, but she refused to open the door. She said he told her that her mother had been holding her safety over his head their entire lives and that he'd finally left her."

"And she believed him?" Blake asked incredulously.

"Yeah, he told her one heck of a convincing story. She agreed to meet him but called me so I could go with her."

"So again, what the hell happened?"

"I called before I left Denver. I had to stop in and see Dad's lawyer about his will. It wasn't anything important and nothing the lawyer couldn't have told me over the phone. It was a giant waste of my fuck-ing time."

"Where are you now?" Blake asked.

"That's the thing. Some asshole ran me off the road before I could get out of here."

"Fuck, you okay?"

"Yeah, but the fucker took off. I'm stuck here for the time being. Not only did I have to talk to the cops, my bike is out of commission. I tried to call Grace to tell her to postpone the meet with her father, but she's not picking up," Logan told his brother.

"They were going to the office to meet? Did you call Nathan?"

"Yeah, I did, but no one is answering in the office. I was supposed to be there twenty minutes ago, but was dealing with the bullshit here."

"I'm already on my way to the office. I'll try Nathan again and see what's up when I get there. You'll be able to get home? Or do I need to send Cole or Felicity up there to get you?"

"I'm getting the bike towed and renting a car. I don't have a good feeling about this. Call me when you have eyes on Grace, yeah?"

"Of course."

"Good. I'll be waiting. Thanks, bro."

"No thanks necessary. Later," Blake said and hung up.

Logan clicked off his phone and paced. The tow truck should be arriving any moment, but it wasn't fast enough for him to get back to Castle Rock any time soon.

The car that had hit him had been a piece of shit. It was a beat-up silver hatchback with a faded piece of paper in the back window instead of a license plate. Logan had been riding along minding his own business, his thoughts on Grace and the upcoming meeting with her father, when the other car ran a red light. It would've killed him if he hadn't reacted as quickly as he had.

Logan thanked his military training for that. He'd learned to trust his instincts, and before his brain had processed what was happening, his muscles had automatically turned away from the oncoming car, causing him to sideswipe the vehicle next to him and narrowly miss being crushed by the asshole driving the hatchback.

He'd hit his head pretty hard when he'd been thrown over the hood of the Mustang next to him, but the helmet and leather jacket kept Logan from being hurt more seriously. The man in the car who had run the light had immediately backed up and taken off down a nearby street. It had all happened in the blink of an eye, and made Logan wonder if he'd been purposely targeted.

Twenty minutes later, Logan's phone rang. The tow truck had just pulled up to a garage with his bike. He held up a finger to the mechanic, who was waiting to speak to him, and answered his phone.

"Hey Blake, you get her?"

"She's not here, bro. She was driving your truck?"

"Fuck. Yeah. I told her to drive around if she got there early, and the last I heard from her was a message telling me she was leaving the condo. You're sure she's not at the office? Is Nathan there?"

"I'm sure. Nathan was inside the office the whole time, but he had his headphones in and didn't hear the phone ring and never saw Grace."

Logan's head hurt, and he wanted to punch something. "The downtown cameras?"

Obviously having already thought about that, Blake answered, "Yes. We're on it. If she was here, we should be able to find her. What's your ETA?"

"Probably at least another hour. I need to talk to the mechanic then convince someone to take me to the nearest rental center. Damn damn *damn*. What about her parents? Anyone know where they are?"

"Let us watch the tapes first. If we need to get the cops involved, we will. Drive safely, Logan. The last thing Grace needs is you getting hurt. Well, more hurt."

"Later." Logan clicked off the phone without another word and immediately headed over to the mechanic who was eyeing his motorcycle. At the moment, he didn't give a shit about the hunk of metal, no matter how many good memories he had with Grace on the back of it. He only wanted to get to Castle Rock and find her.

Fifty-four minutes later, driving a rental car, Logan pulled into Ace Security's parking lot. He hadn't heard from Blake since before he left Denver and wasn't sure what that meant.

Logan jogged to the office and saw Nathan sitting at a computer and Blake leaning over his shoulder, both concentrating on the screen in front of them.

"She was here," Blake told his brother without bothering with a greeting, simply getting to the point. "She pulled up in your truck right on time. Unfortunately, the camera is on the driver's side of the truck."

"They take her?" Logan asked.

"Yeah."

"Who?"

"Her father for sure. We're trying to get a good shot of the other person," Blake bit out.

"Margaret?"

"No, it wasn't her. Another man." It was Nathan who spoke that time. "The part with her on it is only about forty-five seconds long because the camera was sweeping the lot. It doesn't look like she was here long before they got to her," he told his brother, rewinding the video to where Grace pulled into the lot.

Logan watched the screen intently, trying to catch anything important that would help them find her. She pulled into a spot and fiddled with her phone. Her father walked up to the truck door from out of the frame and knocked on the window. He motioned for her to get out. She did, and they exchanged a greeting. Through the windows of the truck, Logan saw another man come up behind Grace and cover her face with a cloth. She slumped into the man's arms and Walter opened the back door of Logan's truck. The man not-so-gently shoved Grace onto the backseat. He then climbed into the truck, keeping his head down, and drove off.

"Any other angles?" Logan barked out.

"No, but I pulled up the footage from fifteen minutes before she arrived to right after that asshole drove off with her," Nathan explained. "I'm not sure where the other man came from, because I didn't see him pull in driving another car at all. And here you can see her father enter the lot, and no one is in the car with him."

"Nathan, you'll stay here in case you find anything else?" Logan asked, his mind already moving to what he needed to do next.

"Of course."

"I've called the cops," Blake told the others. "Because of the restraining order against her parents she took out a month ago, they're taking her disappearance more seriously than they might've otherwise, but they're still being cautious. They reminded me that Grace is an adult and she's only been missing for less than an hour."

"You coming with me to their house?"

"Wouldn't miss it," Blake informed his brother.

"Nathan, let us know if you find anything," Logan ordered.

"On it." And he was. He'd already turned to the screen and was leaning forward, scanning the grainy black-and-white footage as if it held the meaning of life.

Logan fisted his hands as he and Blake quickly walked back outside. It was time to confront Mrs. Mason again. She wasn't going to get away with whatever she'd done with Grace. He'd search that damn house from top to bottom if he had to. If she had Grace stashed away somewhere, he'd find her.

Logan hammered on the Masons' front door thirteen minutes later, Blake standing at his side. "She's a piece of work," Logan warned his brother. "She acts demure and classy, but underneath, she's all viper."

"I got your back, bro."

The door opened and James stood there, looking as "butlery" as ever. "Mr. Anderson and Mr. Anderson," he said with a nod to each of the furious men standing on the doorstep. "There's no need to pound the door. I apologize for the time it took me to get to it. I'm not as young as I used to be."

"Where's Grace?"

"Miss Grace?" the old man answered, surprised. "She does not live here."

"Where. Is. She?" Logan repeated, his voice lower and meaner than it'd been the first time he'd asked.

"There's no need to browbeat my staff, Logan," a feminine voice chided to their right.

Logan and Blake turned their heads to see Margaret Mason looking calm, cool, and composed.

"Thank you, James. You may go."

"Ma'am." The old butler bowed, walked down a long hallway, and disappeared.

"Do come in," Grace's mother said with a hint of sarcasm. "Please, let's not stand in the entryway. It's so gauche. We can talk in the sitting room." She gestured toward a door off the entryway.

"Where's Grace? And don't bullshit us. We know you know what happened to her," Logan demanded, not moving toward the room she'd gestured to.

She sighed in disgust before replying, "I have no idea what you're referring to. If I'm not mistaken, *you* were the one who trespassed onto my property and kidnapped her in the first place."

"I don't think you want to play the kidnapping card," Blake drawled. "You won't win that battle."

"This isn't a battle, young man. Not at all. But you don't seem to understand that Grace is confused. She's always been a bit . . . touched . . . if you know what I mean." Margaret tapped her head. "We have done our best with her, but she's always had too much of an imagination. Whatever story she's concocted and got you to believe, believe me, it's all in her head. Her father and I have tried to help her . . . giving her a wonderful job and making sure she got the help she needed, but when she's off her meds . . ." Her voice trailed off.

Logan snorted, not buying Margaret's crap for a second. "Bullshit. You're insane. Grace hasn't lied about one thing that ever happened under your roof. You're a bully and too used to getting your way. You came between us once, but you won't ever again. I'll ask one more time. Where. Is. She?"

Margaret smirked and her exterior shield cracked just a bit. "I did what was best for Grace. She's always been too good for the likes of you, Logan Anderson. You should be thanking me. What kind of life would you have given her . . . moving every couple of years, living on some horrible Army base, wondering if you'd get deployed and killed, leaving her alone?"

"You don't know anything about me or the life I could've given Grace," Logan bit out.

"My point is that you're trash. All of you Andersons. There was no way I was going to let my daughter get involved with you."

"What the fuck did you do to her?" Logan bit out once more, any patience he might've had now gone.

"I'm sure I don't know what you're talking about."

Her chin went up and Logan recognized the futility of any further questions. He wanted to strangle the older woman, not only for bad-mouthing his brothers, but for refusing to tell him anything about Grace.

"We've got your husband on tape present at her abduction," Blake informed Margaret. "The police know and are looking for him. I have no doubt when he's faced with spending the rest of his life bending over for the perverts in prison, he'll tell the cops everything they want to know . . . including throwing you under the bus. Especially if it means he gets to make a deal."

"I'm sure whatever you *think* you saw was taken out of context. We just want what's best for our only daughter. But it's obvious you think we're hiding her. You're free to search my home, if that's what you want to do. She's not here. Where were *you*, Logan, when she was supposedly being abducted? Shouldn't you have been with her? I wouldn't be surprised if she's glad to come back home where she's safe and protected from the likes of you."

Blake put his hand on Logan's chest, preventing him from doing something stupid. "We'll take you up on your kind offer to search your home. Don't bother to show us around, I'm sure we'll be able to find our way on our own," Blake told Grace's mother in an overly polite tone.

"As you wish," Margaret said with a wave of her hand, inviting them to investigate her home, a small, gloating smile on her face.

Logan and Blake spent the next forty minutes searching the Mason mansion from end to end . . . without finding any sign of Grace. They looked behind every door, tapped on every wall looking for hidden rooms, and searched under every bed. She simply wasn't there.

Defeated, but determined not to give Margaret an ounce of satisfaction, Logan informed her, "The next time we see you, it'll be as you're being placed in the back of a police car. We know you're behind this. Mark my words, you'll pay for every second of grief you've given your daughter over the years."

"I hope you have a nice day too," she fired back, not in the least cowed by Logan's words. "I'll be sure when Grace comes home to tell her you stopped by and made a scene."

Blake pulled Logan out of the house with a firm grasp around his arm. As soon as the heavy door shut behind them, Logan swore long and hard.

"Fuck, Blake. Where is she? What did they do to her?"

"We're gonna find her, Logan. If it's any consolation, I don't think her mother wants to hurt her. She just wants to control her."

"It's not any consolation, bro. Not one fucking bit," Logan told his brother in a defeated tone.

They quickly climbed back into Blake's black Mustang and sped down the lane. "I don't think you can believe anything either of her parents have ever told her," Blake tried to reassure his brother. "I think they're more talk than anything else."

"What if they're not?"

"Then you'll take Grace into your arms and tell her that you love her and that everything will be all right no matter what they've done to her."

Logan whirled his head around to stare at his brother.

Blake saw his look of disbelief and shrugged. "What? You've loved Grace Mason since you were sixteen years old. You might never have said anything about it, but I know you."

Logan didn't confirm or deny his brother's words. Instead he simply stated, "I can't lose her."

"And you won't. Nathan is going to find something else on those tapes we can use that will lead us to her. I've already called the cops. Cole and Felicity will do everything *they* can. We'll find her, because the alternative is unacceptable."

Logan didn't want to smile, but he couldn't help it. Blake was hell-bent and determined to find and save Grace, and he knew it was because *he* cared about her too, and he had no problem with that. The more allies Grace had, the better.

"But I'll tell you something else," Blake said without looking at his brother as he drove back to their office. "Not that you didn't already know this, but Margaret Mason is a bad seed. She's poison. Everyone she comes in contact with is covered in her filth. Every other word that comes out of her mouth is a lie. I can't believe someone as sweet as

Grace is related to her. It's a miracle she is as good of a person as she is with her mother as an example."

"What's our next step?" Logan asked, unable to think about anything other than what Grace might be going through right this second, and how every minute that went by was one minute that she could be suffering.

"We'll go back to the office to see if Nathan found anything else worth noting on the videos. Then we'll see if the cops have picked up her father yet."

Logan ran his hand through his hair and remembered back to earlier that morning when he'd last seen Grace. After some great morning sex, they'd taken a long shower together and made breakfast after they'd gotten dressed.

Right before he'd left to go to Denver, Grace had been laughing with him over something silly she'd seen online. He'd never felt so comfortable with a woman before. It didn't matter if they were making love, eating supper, or sitting around doing nothing.

The relationship was everything he'd dreamed it'd be when he was a teenager . . . and more. He couldn't lose her now.

"Step on it, Blake. The sooner this ends, the better."

Chapter Twenty-Four

"Hello?"

"Collect call from Brad. Will you accept the charges?" the automated voice droned.

"What the hell? Brad? Of course I will," Alexis said in confusion.

"Hold for the connection," the robotic voice intoned.

"Alexis?" Brad asked.

"Yeah, it's me. What's going on? Where are you calling from?"

"Listen. I'm in trouble. I need help."

"Anything. Where are you?" Alexis asked again.

"I think I'm at the Imperial Hotel in Denver," Brad told his sister.

"You *think*?" Alexis asked in disbelief.

"Yeah. I need you to call Ace Security down in Castle Rock for me. Tell them that Grace is in trouble and needs their help."

"Grace Mason? Brad, you're freaking me out. After that disastrous dinner, I thought we all agreed not to have anything to do with the Masons ever again."

"We did, but plans have changed."

"What's going on, Brad?"

"Alexis, *please*. Call Ace Security. I'll give you a number and you can tell whoever answers to call me back."

"I want to help," she said, her voice shaking.

"No. I don't want you involved."

"But I *am* involved. *You* called *me*," Alexis protested.

"Only because I don't have their number. Please, Sis," Brad begged. "This is important. I need you to do it right now."

"Should I call Mom and Dad?"

"No! Look, Grace told me the last time I talked with her, about a month ago, that she was dating one of the Anderson brothers. I don't remember which one."

"You talked to Grace?"

"Yeah. She called me to check to make sure I was okay."

"That was nice of her."

"I know. I didn't expect it either. She didn't say much, just that she didn't agree with her mother and that she didn't want to marry me. That she was doing her best to make sure her parents didn't bother me again."

"Okay. I'll do it. For you. But I swear to God, if Grace Mason or any of her family does anything to fuck with you, they'll have to deal with me."

"Thanks, I appreciate it. Now, get some paper to write this number down. Hurry."

"Okay . . . hang on . . . all right, I'm ready."

Brad gave her the phone number of the hotel and the room number.

"I can be there in twenty minutes," she told him.

"No. Please, Alexis. Don't," he begged. "I don't want you anywhere near here."

"I don't like this."

"Me either, but I promise that I'm safe right now. Okay?"

"Fine," Alexis huffed. "But I expect a full report as soon as possible."

"Deal. Now call, and don't quit until you get hold of one of the Andersons."

"I won't. I love you, Brad."

"I love you too, Sis. I'll talk to you later. Thank you for this."

"We're family. Talk to you soon."

~

"Ace Security," Nathan growled into the phone when it rang.

"It's about time someone answered. Jeez, I've been calling you guys for like, hours. Is this one of the Anderson brothers?"

"Yes. And this is an emergency-only line," Nathan lied, irritated at the attitude of the person on the other end of the line.

"No shit, why do you think I'm calling?" Alexis said grouchily. "Look, my brother, Bradford Grant, called me and told me to get in touch with you guys. He said to tell you that Grace Mason is in trouble and needs your help. I have a phone number where you can call him to find out more details. He wouldn't tell me anything."

"Logan!" Nathan bellowed, not bothering to cover the phone with his hand.

"Ow, jeez. That hurt. Warn a girl, would ya?" Alexis grumbled.

"I'm putting you on speaker. Repeat what you just told me," Nathan ordered.

"My name is Alexis Grant. I got a call from my brother, Brad, and he wanted me to call you guys and let you know that Grace is in trouble. I have no idea what's going on, but he sounded freaked out, which isn't like him at all. He gave me a phone number so you could call him."

"What is it?" Logan demanded immediately.

"I want to know what's going on," Alexis said firmly.

"If you don't give me the number right this second, I'll—"

Logan's words were suddenly broken off, followed by the sound of a scuffle.

"Hello?"

"Alexis, right?"

"Yeah."

"I'm Blake. And my brother Logan is extremely concerned about his girlfriend. Grace has been missing since early this afternoon. He's had a trying day, and whatever game you're playing isn't sitting well with him. The number? Please?"

"I'm sorry. I'm not trying to be obnoxious. I'm just worried about Brad. He sounded really upset when he called me. He said he's in room four sixty-two at the Imperial."

"Thank you," Logan said in what sounded like a sincere voice as he wrote down the number Alexis gave him.

"I don't know what's going on, but if the Masons are involved, it can't be good. They aren't high on my list of favorite people right now," Alexis said.

"We heard they wanted to force a marriage between your brother and Grace," Logan commented bitterly.

"Yeah. Mrs. Mason pretty much threatened to ruin my family if Brad didn't agree."

"How?"

"They said they'd let it leak that Brad is gay. Which is just dumb, because everyone already knows it . . . and doesn't care. The designs he comes up with speak for themselves."

"He's gay?" Logan asked.

"Yeah. You didn't know? He's been out since high school."

"Could be her parents don't know it," Nathan said.

"And if they did, it might ruin all their plans," Blake agreed.

"We need to find out what they're up to," Logan stated.

"You two call Brad on your way to the hotel," Nathan said, "I'll stay here and see what else I can dig up on them. I'm not as good with computers as Blake is, but you might need him."

"Hey!" Alexis blurted.

"Oh, shit. Yeah, we appreciate you calling us," Logan said in a rush. "We'll make sure Brad is okay."

"Wait, I—"

Logan didn't wait to find out what else Alexis had to say. He was grateful to her for calling, but he needed to get moving. All that mattered was Grace, and it looked like they had a lead. He immediately picked up the phone and started dialing. He wanted to get going, to start heading up to Denver, but he wanted to make sure that's where Grace really was before he went off half-cocked.

The phone rang only once.

"Hello?"

"This is Logan Anderson. Is this Bradford?"

"Thank God. Yeah."

"Where are you?"

"The Imperial Hotel in downtown Denver, room four sixty-two."

"Grace is there with you?"

"Yes."

Logan covered the speaker of his cell and told his brothers, "Bradford says she's at the Imperial in Denver. Keep us informed at what you find, Nate. We're going." At his nod, Logan and Blake headed outside to the car.

"What's going on? Is she all right? Can I talk to her?" Logan asked Brad.

"She seems to be."

"What the fuck does that mean?" Logan bit out.

"She's sleeping, or something, right now. And I'd rather she stay that way until you get here."

Blake started the car and Logan put the call on speaker so his brother could listen in. "Explain."

"First, you should know, I had nothing to do with any of this. I came to the hotel for a client meeting that turned out to be a setup of some sort. I came up to the room for the meeting, and as soon as I opened the door, I was yanked in and punched in the face. Then someone grabbed me from behind and stuck a needle in my arm. I don't remember anything after that."

"Where does Grace fit into all this?" Logan asked impatiently.

"I only woke up a bit ago. I feel like I've been sucking on cotton balls, and I've got a hell of a headache. I went to get up off the bed and realized someone was next to me. I was horrified to realize it was Grace."

"Fuck. Is she okay? Dammit, let me talk to her," Logan demanded impatiently.

"I told you, she's unconscious, but breathing normally as far as I can tell," Brad hurried to reassure Logan. "But, shit, man, we were both naked."

"Motherfucker. When I get my hands on her parents, they're gonna wish they were dead," Logan said, his voice rough with the fury he was holding in check.

"She's covered up now," Brad hurried to reassure Logan. "I drank a bunch of water and took a shower to try to shake off the rest of whatever they drugged me with. Her clothes are all here, and I'll give them to her, along with lots of water when she wakes up. My cell and wallet aren't here, and I can't find hers either. But . . . there's something else . . ." His voice trailed off as if he didn't want to continue.

"What else?" Logan snapped.

"There was an envelope on the dresser. Propped up against the mirror where I couldn't miss it."

"What was in the envelope?" Blake asked, obviously trying to move the story forward and knowing Logan was about to lose his shit.

"Photos," Brad said.

"Fuck," Blake swore. "How bad?"

"Bad. I was out, man. I don't remember *any* of it. They must've given me some serious shit because otherwise there's no way they could've posed me the way they did without me being aware of it."

"Jesus," Logan said under his breath.

"At some point another man apparently joined us and we were all posed to look like we were a consenting trio instead of two unconscious victims. I have no idea if these are all of them or not. I'll say this, though, if these are ever leaked, both our reputations are shot, which I'm assuming was the point."

"Pull over," Logan told his brother suddenly.

Blake didn't hesitate but did as Logan demanded.

"Everything okay?" Brad asked on the other end of the line, not able to see what was happening.

Blake watched as his brother opened the car door, took two steps, and threw up on the side of the highway. "No," he told Brad. "Everything is not okay. Quickly, before my brother gets back in the car. Do you think Grace was raped?"

"I don't know. As soon as I realized she wasn't wearing any clothes, I pulled the sheet up to cover her and went to the bathroom to change."

"You're there with her now, right?" Blake asked urgently.

"Yeah."

"Don't leave her."

"I wouldn't dream of it," Brad said. "I was waiting for you guys to call back. I've locked the bolt on the door and put on the security lock. I'll keep watch over her until you get here. It's why I had Alexis call you in the first place."

Logan wiped the back of his hand over his mouth and got back in the car. He nodded at his brother to continue driving. The thought of his Grace being unconscious and being manipulated and photographed without her knowledge or permission . . . not to mention some third man being involved . . . disgusted him beyond measure. Not about Grace, never that, but what might've happened to her.

"We're about thirty minutes out. Twenty if we can get away with it."

"Thank you for calling us. We'll be there as soon as we can. Keep my girl safe," Logan implored Brad.

"I will."

Logan clicked off his cell and looked over at Blake. For the first time since he'd gotten out of the Army, he felt like Rose Anderson's son. He wanted to kill someone and see them suffer. He supposed he was more like his mother than he'd thought.

"Don't," Blake warned.

"Don't what?"

"Don't even think about it. If you lose it and do something stupid to either of her parents, or whoever else was in that room, then Grace will lose you for the second time in her life. She *needs* you. Keep your shit together."

"They touched her, Blake," Logan said in a hard, cold voice.

"Yeah, but she's alive, and will be in your arms soon. They could've killed her and hidden her body in the mountains, and you never would've found her. You know it as well as I do. This isn't what we wanted to happen, but it's better than the alternative. Hold. It. Together."

Logan dipped his chin in a short, tight nod. Blake was right. It sucked, but he was right. The last seven hours or so had been the worst in his life. Even worse than the months he'd spent waiting to hear from Grace when he'd joined the Army. He couldn't lose sight of the fact that he now knew where Grace was and that she was alive and breathing. They'd deal with everything else later.

"You think they'll try to blackmail the Grants with the pictures?" Logan asked, trying to figure out what the hell Margaret and Walter had planned, and how they thought they'd get away with it.

"Yeah. If Brad says the pictures are bad, then they must be bad."

"We need to shut them down."

"Agreed," Blake responded.

"Got any ideas?"

"Some."

"Want to share?" Logan asked his brother. Sometimes talking with Blake was like pulling teeth. He'd always been that way, even when they were young.

"I'm thinking if blackmail is their way of getting what they want, this is probably not the first time they've used the tactic."

Logan caught the gleam in his brother's eyes as he continued.

"I would bet everything we own that there are others out there."

"We need to find them," Logan said.

"Yup."

"Think you and Nathan can do it?"

"Fuck yeah. After you get Grace and bring her home, I'm thinking a visit to the Masons' house is in order. We need to talk to the help. Then maybe some ex-employees of the Mason Architectural Firm. We'll get them, Logan. I swear to God. We'll take them down the same way they wanted to take Grace and the Grants down. Their blackmailing days are over."

"They better be. I don't want this hanging over Grace's head for the rest of her life. I've never wanted anyone dead more than I want Grace's parents wiped off the face of the planet. Not even Mom. And that's saying something."

Blake nodded in agreement. "We'll uncover all their secrets. I swear on Dad's grave, Logan, we will."

"Good. Now, how about we find out how quickly this hunk of junk can get us to Denver?"

Logan didn't say much else as they raced north, his thoughts only on Grace and if she was okay.

Chapter Twenty-Five

As soon as Brad opened the door to room four sixty-two, Logan surged in.

"Thank God you're here. She's just now coming around," Brad told Logan as he brushed past.

Seeing Grace vulnerable and groggy on the hotel bed made Logan both breathe a sigh of relief and grit his teeth together in fury. He went to her and gathered her into his arms. "Hey. I've got you. You're okay, Grace."

"Logan?"

"Yeah, Smarty. It's me."

"Where are we? My head is killing me."

"It's a long story. Just relax. I'm here and you're safe."

"Can I have a glass of water?"

"I was dying of thirst when I woke up too. Here," Brad said, holding out a plastic cup filled with water.

Logan didn't even look at the other man, keeping his eyes on Grace. Her face was pale, and she was squinting as if the light hurt her head, but she recognized him and seemed to be okay. It was enough for the moment. He took the cup from Brad and held it to Grace's lips. "Here you go. Don't drink too fast."

She ignored his warning and gulped the water down as if she hadn't had anything to drink in days rather than hours. "More," she demanded, holding the cup out.

A feminine chuckle sounded from the doorway, and all three men whirled toward the sound, ready for battle.

"I've never seen Grace Mason act with so little decorum," Alexis drawled. "I like it. Makes her seem more human and less like a robot."

"What the hell are you doing here, Alexis?" Brad demanded of his little sister.

"I'm worried about you, that's what," she shot back, hands on her hips. "You wouldn't tell me anything, and these guys wouldn't either. So I decided to see for myself that you really were all right. Excuse me for caring."

"Damn. Get in here and keep your voice down," Blake ordered, grabbing the slight woman by the arm and pulling her into the room. "Where did you come from?"

"I was waiting around the corner. I heard you guys come up, and I snuck in behind you. You were too concerned about getting to Grace and didn't pay attention to the door. Probably not something you should repeat."

"Ah, shit. Blake, I forgot to ask you earlier to get in touch with Alexis to see what she could tell us. Regardless, it's obvious you're losing your touch," Logan said with a smile, finding something humorous for the first time in way too long that day. "A five-foot-nothing woman got the drop on you."

"Fuck off," Blake told his brother without heat.

"Yeah, fuck off," Alexis repeated, looking pissed, her hands on her hips as she glared at Blake. "For your information, I'm studying to be a private investigator. I can sneak up on people with the best of them."

Blake rolled his eyes. "Spare me from wanna-be badasses."

"Here's another cup of water," Brad told Logan, interrupting the spat between Blake and his sister to hold out the freshly filled cup.

Logan held it out to Grace and helped her sit up farther on the bed, making sure to keep her covered by the sheet as he did so. Once again, she guzzled it down, burping loudly when she'd drained the entire thing.

"Oh, excuse me."

Alexis chuckled at the completely unladylike sound coming from Grace, but sobered quickly when no one else even cracked a smile.

"Better?" Logan asked her.

Grace nodded and closed her eyes again, leaning against his chest as she might if they were sitting at home in their bed.

"Grace, I need you to wake up and talk to me."

"Mmmm."

"Grace!" Logan called her name sharply.

"What?"

"Where are you?"

"Huh?" She opened her eyes and looked around.

Logan saw the second she realized they weren't at his apartment. She stiffened in his arms and asked, "What is your brother doing here? And Brad?"

"Me too!" Alexis piped up from the doorway.

Grace looked up at Logan. "What's going on?"

"What do you remember?"

"Nothing really, I—" She stopped suddenly and her eyes widened. "My father! I went to meet him. You weren't there yet, but I was waiting for you. He knocked on my window. I got out and . . . that's it."

With each word out of her mouth, she seemed to become more coherent. "I remember him smirking at me. He was lying about it all, wasn't he?"

"Looks that way," Logan told her, compassion easy to hear in his voice.

"Where are we?"

"The Imperial Hotel in Denver."

"Why are Brad and Alexis here?"

"Look at me, Grace," Logan told her, putting a hand on either side of her head and lifting her chin so she had no choice but to look at him. "Are you okay? Do you hurt anywhere?"

One of the things he liked about Grace was that she was always very deliberate. She thought before she acted and before she talked. She did the same thing now. Logan watched as she flexed her legs, shifted under his hold, and moved both arms.

"No. I'm okay."

"You sure? Come on, let me help you stand." Logan turned to Brad, Blake, and Alexis. "Turn around."

All three did as he requested without protest.

Grace scooted off the bed and stood, just then realizing that she wasn't wearing any clothes.

"Why am I naked?" she whispered, the panic easy to see on her expressive face. "Logan?"

"In a second. Tell me. And really think about it. Do you hurt anywhere?"

She shook her head quickly that time. "No. I'm just stiff and my head hurts, but otherwise no. What aren't you saying?"

"Come on, let me help you get dressed." Logan scooped up the clothes that Brad had folded and put on a nearby chair. He held her elbow as Grace shuffled to the bathroom, the sheet wrapped tightly around her.

"We'll be right out," he told the others, closing the door behind them and turning on the bathroom fan to give them some privacy.

He positioned her so her back was to the large mirror on the wall. "Let me see, Grace. Let go of the sheet."

She clung to the cotton for a moment, staring up at Logan. Finally, she let it drop and held her arms out to her sides. Her eyes filled up with tears, but she stood still, letting Logan examine her.

Logan put his hands on her waist and smoothed them down over her hips. She didn't wince or pull away from his touch. There were a few red marks on her breasts and stomach, but nothing that screamed that she'd been manhandled too badly. "Turn around, sweetie."

She did so, without a word, her eyes watching him in the mirror.

Her skin was smooth and pale, and Logan saw only a few more light bruises on her hips and the back of her thighs. He knelt down and turned her around to face him again. He looked up. "Okay?"

Proving that she was pretty darn smart, Grace bit her lip and asked softly, "Was I raped?"

Logan shook his head quickly. "I don't think so. Not if you don't hurt down here. We'll get you to a doctor and find out for sure, though." Logan stood, taking her hands in his.

"What happened to me?" she asked in a trembling voice.

"Come on, get dressed, and we'll go out and talk with the others."

"You're scaring me, Logan."

He couldn't hold back from taking Grace into his arms any longer. He enfolded her naked body into his arms and simply held her, rocking her back and forth, his heart slowing down for the first time since he'd learned she was missing. She was whole and relatively unscathed in his arms. Nothing else mattered at the moment. He whispered in her ear how much he loved her while caressing her back with his hands.

She shuddered a few times, but settled under his touch. Finally, she eased back. "I'm okay."

"I love you, Grace. I've never been so scared in all my life when I learned that you were gone. You're the most important thing in my life. I hate that we lost so many years, but I'm going to make those years up to you now."

"Logan, I—"

He put his finger on her lips. "Not now. Think about it. We've got things we need to discuss, and we need to figure this thing out with your parents. But no matter what, remember that I love you. I think I've *always* loved you."

Logan leaned down and kissed her on the forehead before reaching for her panties on the counter. He held them out, helping Grace step into them, pulling them up around her hips. He then held out her jeans and helped her get dressed, one leg at a time. She put her arms into the straps of her bra and he turned her and fastened it behind her, then held her shirt out for her.

She didn't need help getting dressed. She'd been doing it on her own for around twenty-five years, but Logan needed the connection with her, and she needed to feel cared for. There was no telling what the mystery men had done to her, and *could've* done to her, while she'd been unconscious with whatever drugs they'd given her and Brad.

They walked back out into the room and found Blake, Brad, and Alexis all waiting. Logan didn't care that they'd taken longer than they probably should've. Grace needed the time, and he needed to tell her how he felt about her.

He led her to the edge of the bed and sat down next to her.

"I looked at the pictures, Logan," Blake told him, "Brad was right. They're bad."

"Pictures?" Grace asked, tilting her head. "Oh shit."

Logan sighed then took her hands in his. "Yeah. Apparently your parents' plan is to blackmail the Grants and Brad into marrying you. They drugged you both and took compromising pictures."

"What? Every time I think they can't sink any lower, they do." Grace said incredulously. "Brad? Are you okay?"

"Yeah. I woke up before you, probably because I weigh more than you do and the drugs wore off faster. I was . . . um . . . naked too. There was an envelope on the dresser with the pictures in it. I called Alexis, and she called Logan and his brother."

Grace's eyes locked on the envelope in Blake's hand. She sucked her lips together nervously. "I want to see them," she said firmly.

"I don't think—"

Grace cut Logan off abruptly. "Do you remember anything?" she asked Brad.

He shook his head. "No. I was as out of it as you were."

"Give them to me." She held out her hand impatiently.

Blake looked at Logan, as if asking permission.

"Don't look at him. They're of me and Brad. I don't have to have permission from anyone to look at pictures of myself," Grace fumed. Her words probably would've held a bit more weight if she wasn't shaking like a leaf and her hand wasn't visibly trembling as she held it out in front of her.

Logan nodded at his brother, and Blake handed the envelope to Grace. Logan kept his eyes and hands on Grace, wishing he could spare her this, but knowing he couldn't. Once again he was proud as he could be of her. It would've been easy for her to let him and his brothers take care of the situation, but she refused. He knew she didn't think she was a strong person, that letting her parents manipulate her for years while desperately wanting their affection meant she was weak. But the fact that she was still the same beautiful person inside as well as out gave credence to her strength.

Grace pulled out the pictures and gasped in shock and outrage when she saw the first one. She would've dropped them, but Logan put his hand under hers to steady her.

Grace's hand shook as she looked through picture after picture of her and Brad, each one increasingly graphic and disgusting. A few included a man she'd never seen before, and it looked like they were having a ménage à trois. Grace closed her eyes and took a deep breath, trying to compose herself.

Logan plucked the pictures out of her hands and was surprised she let him. Grace turned and threw herself into Brad's arms and exclaimed, "I'm so sorry. God. My parents are such assholes. I'm sorry."

The other man looked shocked for a moment, then immediately curled his arms around her. "It's okay, Grace."

"It's *not* okay!" She whirled to face Logan. "What are we doing about this? Seriously. It's one thing to tie me up and try to force me to have a baby they can steal and raise to be an asshole. But it's another thing altogether to bring *other* people into their fucked-up world."

"Calm down, Grace," Logan said evenly.

"Calm down? You saw those pictures! How can you tell me to calm down? My parents are going to embarrass Brad and his family. That's totally not okay."

"Grace—"

"No! Seriously. How are we going to stop them? Am I ever going to be free of them? Am I going to have to look over my shoulder for the rest of my life wondering what they have in store for me next? Is Brad?"

"Grace. Look at me." Logan stood up in front of Grace, put his hands on her shoulders, and waited until she met his eyes. "They aren't going to get away with this. Everything went way too smoothly. This can't be the first time they've used blackmail to get something they want." He could see the wheels turning in her mind, and went on. "Maybe someone at work, or one of the servants?"

Grace closed her eyes and massaged her temples. "Yeah. I could probably give you some names of people you could talk to."

"Later," Logan said firmly. "I need to get you to the hospital, then home."

"I'm scared to go back there," Grace said in a soft voice, pleading with Logan with her eyes. "I know it's your place, but what if they come after me again?"

"You can stay at my apartment here in Denver," Alexis volunteered immediately. "I can go home and talk to my mom and dad with Brad. No one will think to look for you at my place."

"Grace?" Logan asked. "It's up to you. Whatever makes you feel the most comfortable is what we'll do."

She nodded and bit her lip as she thought about their options. "Okay. Thanks, Alexis. I . . . I know you probably think I'm a bitch, and this is really going above and beyond, but I appreciate it."

"I don't think you're a bitch. I don't know you well enough," Alexis told Grace, "but you've gone a long way toward redeeming any bad feelings I might've had after that horrible dinner."

The two women smiled at each other.

Logan turned to his brother. "Blake, I'll get in touch tomorrow with you and Nathan. I'll probably stop in and talk with the Grants, and see if we can't come up with a strategy to outmaneuver the Masons together. We'll need to come up with a statement if they do go ahead with publicizing the pictures before making their asinine demands of the Grants."

"Grace? You okay?" Blake asked, surprising Logan.

She blinked, as if not sure why he asked. "Yeah, I'm okay."

The other man came over and hugged Grace tightly. "I'm glad. You scared us. My brother cares an awful lot about you. Stick close to him, yeah?"

"No need to tell me. I'd already planned to," Grace reassured Blake.

"Good."

"Brad, you need a ride?" Alexis asked.

"No. My car should still be here," her brother told her with a shrug. "They took my phone, but my keys were still in the pocket of my slacks."

"What about you, Blake? You're going to need a ride back to Castle Rock if you let Logan take your car," Alexis told him.

"Damn. I hadn't thought that far ahead. You could go with your brother and let me borrow your car," Blake said, a hopeful grin on his face.

Alexis laughed. "As if. No one drives my Mercedes but me. I can give you a ride . . . but it's late . . . and I still need to talk to my parents with Brad. You can come too. You have a place I can crash for the night when we get to Castle Rock?"

Logan's brother eyed the younger woman. "How old are you?"

"Why? Afraid I'm not old enough for you?"

"You look like you're about fifteen."

"Fuck off. I'm twenty-five. Plenty old enough for you, old man. You got a place for me to stay, or what?"

"Yeah, I've got a spare room," Blake said reluctantly.

"Good. Then I can come and help you and your other brother figure out what the hell is going on and what we're gonna do about it."

"Why?" Blake's question was short and harsh.

The younger woman put her hands on her hips. "Because. He's my brother, it's my family's reputation on the line, and I can help."

"You? I doubt it."

Logan inwardly winced. Even *he* knew better than to blatantly bait a woman like his brother just did with Alexis.

Her eyes narrowed and her nostrils flared out in annoyance.

"We're gonna get going. Alexis," Logan interrupted before the other woman went off on Blake. "What's your address so I can put it in my phone? Anything we need to know about your place? Security guards who need to know us, alarms, anything?" Relieved he'd diverted her attention, Logan listened as Alexis gave them the ins and outs of her building as well as the alarm code and keys to her apartment. She said she'd call the doorman and tell him that they were on their way and that they'd be staying in her apartment for the foreseeable future.

Ignoring the "discussion" that resumed between Alexis and Blake when they went to leave, Logan took Grace's hand in his and led her out of the hotel to the elevator.

She paused and when they were in the elevator, she wrapped her arms around Logan's waist and held on. Neither of them said a word as the doors opened and they walked out into the lobby, arms around each other. They were both quiet as they got into Blake's car and pulled out into the still night.

The trip to the emergency room was surprisingly quick. For once, there weren't that many people waiting, and when the triage nurse heard that Grace might have been violated, she quickly got them a private room.

Much to his relief, and Grace's if the unclenching of her fists was any indication, a female doctor came in not too much after the nurse left. Grace explained, in brief, the situation, and the doctor took a blood sample that could be analyzed later for sexually transmitted diseases and to try to identify exactly what drug was used on her and Brad. She then did a quick exam, including swabbing for any DNA that might have been left behind if Grace had been violated. After the exam the doctor told Grace that, in her professional experience, she didn't think Grace had been raped, but because she'd been unconscious during the attack, the lack of any physical damage didn't necessarily mean anything.

Grace nodded and thanked her, obviously not happy with what the doctor said, and a few tears leaked out of her eyes. Logan had been beside her throughout the entire exam and now tenderly wiped away her tears and held her close to his heart, trying to show her with his actions how much he loved her.

They left an hour after they'd arrived, both relieved the exam was over. They hadn't said much while they were at the hospital and kept silent even as they nodded at the doorman and made their way up to Alexis's apartment. It wasn't until the door shut behind them, when they were safe inside, that Logan broke the silence.

"Shower?"

"God, yes," Grace breathed.

"Solo? Or would you mind if I joined you?"

"You. Please."

The shower wasn't erotic; it was more cathartic. While Logan always appreciated Grace's body, he only wanted to take care of her now. Show her how much she meant to him. How thankful he was that she was all right. He soaped up her body and made sure to scrub her thoroughly, but carefully. When he was satisfied she was squeaky clean from head to toe, Logan shut off the water and dried her carefully.

He drew the T-shirt he'd been wearing over Grace's head, needing to see her in her usual sleeping attire, and smiled as it engulfed her frame. He put his boxers back on and led them to the guest room.

Even after everything that had happened, maybe because of what had happened, Logan felt closer to Grace than he ever had before. She'd been through hell, but she was all right, and hadn't shied away from his need to be near her, to touch her, to reassure himself that she truly was okay. She crawled into the bed and waited for him to follow. Logan lay on his back and sighed in contentment as Grace snuggled into his side and threw one arm and a leg over his body, getting as close to him as she could.

"Are you . . . upset about the pictures?" she asked after a while in a soft voice.

"Yes, but probably not for the reasons you think."

Grace lifted her head and looked at him expectantly.

"I'm upset because they violated you. Oh, they might not have done anything to you sexually, but they took away your will. They touched you without your knowledge or permission."

"Do you think we'll find anything that will make my parents stop? Make them forget about me and move on with their lives?"

"Yes." Logan's answer was immediate and heartfelt. "Absolutely. My brothers and I have made it our personal mission to take them down. We're going to make sure they never hurt you again, Grace."

She put her head back down on Logan's shoulder. "I love you. I've loved you forever, it seems. Sometimes I'm afraid you're going to get tired of my parents constantly coming between us and decide it's just too much work."

"Not gonna happen, Grace. I know all about parents who aren't June and Ward Cleaver."

"If it becomes too much—"

"Never. Grace, we love each other. Period. I love *you*, not your parents. We're gonna deal with this and move on with our lives. Got it?"

Logan could feel her smile against his shoulder. He knew he'd spend the rest of his life making sure she could laugh with him.

"Got it. Yes, sir. Whatever you say."

"That's better. Now, get some sleep. I have a feeling we're gonna be very busy for the next couple of days."

"I love you."

"I love you too, Grace. Now sleep."

Logan lay awake long after Grace fell into a deep, healing sleep, realizing he'd been extremely lucky. He not only had gotten a second chance with Grace, but today he'd gotten a third one. He vowed then and there that he wouldn't risk her safety again. He wasn't going to lose her. No matter what.

Chapter Twenty-Six

The next week was a whirlwind of investigations as Ace Security worked with the Castle Rock police, then the FBI. Every morsel of information Nathan and Blake dug up was one more nail in the Masons' coffin. Every day, Logan drove down to Castle Rock and worked with his brothers, and surprisingly, Alexis, to dig into the Masons' hidden life.

Blake had been reluctant to involve Brad's sister at first, but she'd proven to be remarkably good at getting people to open up to her. Probably because she looked way younger than she was, and therefore totally nonthreatening. She was also really good at figuring out how to persuade each person to talk. She'd been able to get two of the women who worked in the Mason household to confess that they'd tried to quit years ago, but Margaret had refused to let them go. They knew too much about what happened behind the closed doors of the mansion, so she basically threatened their families to make sure they stayed.

They also discovered what kind of people Margaret and Walter met with during odd hours. The kind of people who were paid in cash, under the table. Nathan also found current employees at Mason Architectural Firm who told him about questionable business practices the Masons used to win bids on projects and safety steps they'd skipped when they were involved in an actual build.

They'd also found the third man who'd been in the pictures with Grace and Brad. The tattoos on his body were put into a database of known criminals, and they'd gotten a hit. He was a gang member in Denver, with several prior convictions on his rap sheet. Having no loyalty to either of the Masons, he hadn't hesitated to tell the cops how he'd been hired, exactly how much he'd been paid to participate in the blackmail scheme, and that neither Bradford nor Grace had been raped while they'd been unconscious.

The strongest lead, and the one that interested the FBI the most, was from the Masons' accountant. Nathan had convinced the man that it was only a matter of time before Walter and Margaret turned against him and set him up to take the fall for the company and their illegal activities. The man agreed to talk to the FBI in exchange for immunity.

Grace was more than happy to stay in Denver when Logan was working, hiding out in Alexis's apartment. She was in constant contact with him via texts and frequent phone calls, both of them needing the reassurance that the other was all right. Logan had bought her another new cell phone and brought her clothes from his place. Felicity had visited a few times, helping Grace pass the time and making her feel more normal with every visit. Neither Logan nor Grace particularly enjoyed not being at their own place, but at the moment, living at Alexis's apartment was the safest, and smartest, thing to do.

The Grants said they would fully cooperate with the investigation and allowed Ace Security to install hidden cameras and recorders at their home and office in case the Masons came to them with the photos. They agreed not to press charges until after the investigation was complete. The noose was quickly closing around Grace's parents, whether they knew it or not.

Five days after she'd been kidnapped, Logan was cuddling Grace on Alexis's huge couch. "How are you holding up?" he asked her gently.

"I just . . . it's so hard to believe," Grace told him honestly. "With everything that has happened, it makes me wonder if I *ever* really knew them. Do you think they loved me at all? Even a little bit?"

"I'm not sure they *know* how to love," Logan told her gently. "I mean, how anyone can *not* love their own child is beyond me. And I've been there. I know exactly what you're going through."

Grace nodded, understanding. "I think I stayed with them because they gave me small glimpses of the love I wanted so badly."

"I'm sorry I didn't realize what you were going through back then," Logan told her. "I figured because your family had money, a big house, and servants, that you had to have a perfect life."

"Money doesn't equal happiness."

"I understand that now," Logan told her.

"What if . . ." her voice trailed off.

"What if, what?" Logan urged her to continue.

Her voice lowered until he could barely hear her. "What if . . . do you think since I'm their daughter that I could end up being like—"

"No. Absolutely not. Grace, you're one of the most kindhearted people I've ever met in my life. You care about stray dogs and cats, and I've seen you happily snuggle up to children who you didn't even know. Margaret and Walter Mason might have created you, but despite all the odds being against you, you've become a beautiful, loving, caring, sensitive human being. You're twenty-eight. I think if you were going to turn out to be a raving lunatic, you would've seen some inkling of it by now. Are you afraid that because I'm Rose Anderson's son that one day I'm going to start beating on you?"

"No!" Grace told him emphatically, raising up on her elbows to glare down at him for even voicing the thought.

"Then why do you think you might suddenly turn into your mother?"

"Oh. I guess you have a point."

"Yeah. I do. How about we make a deal?" Logan asked, his eyes tender and soft as he looked down at Grace.

"What kind of deal?"

"Let's put our parents and everything they've done to us in the past. What's done is done, and we can't change it. Me and you are the future. Together we can put the pain of the past behind us so we can embrace the promise of what tomorrow holds. Yeah?"

Grace brought a hand up and wrapped it around the back of his neck, stroking him with her fingers. "I'd like that."

"Me too. I love you, Grace. We were meant to be with each other. I have no doubt."

She looked into his eyes, not shying away from direct eye contact. "Make love to me?"

"With pleasure."

He smoothed his hands up from her hips, taking the T-shirt she was wearing up with him and froze.

His eyes whipped up to hers, and he said in an awed voice, "When did you get this?"

"Two days ago when you went down to Castle Rock to help Blake with that escort job, Felicity and I went."

Logan leaned forward and ran his nose lightly over the new tattoo on her inner left breast, exactly where he'd told her he'd love to see it someday. "Does it hurt?"

"It's a little sore."

"It's beautiful."

"Well, it'll be more beautiful when it heals. I chose pink because, after you suggested it, I couldn't get the image out of my mind."

Logan ran a finger over the small bird in flight now inked on her skin, smiling as goose bumps rose on her torso and her nipples peaked at his touch. "I'm making an appointment for the first day I have off to get my own tattoo. I can't believe you beat me to it."

She smiled down at him in happiness.

Logan had a sudden thought, and he gave her an evil grin. "Was this the *only* tattoo you got the other day?"

Grace didn't respond, simply returned his smile with a flirty one of her own.

Logan got off her and leaned backward, taking Grace with him until she straddled his lap on the couch. He took her head in his hands and held her close to him and asked seriously, "You're okay with this? No weird feelings about what happened or about making love with me?"

"I'm sure. I feel safe with you, Logan. When we're together I feel strong, in control. Being with you is like riding on the back of your bike. I'm free. Free to do what feels good, to be myself."

He crushed his mouth to hers. They writhed in each other's arms, desperate for the other. Before she'd been kidnapped, they'd made love almost every day, but since then, he'd been holding off, unsure of how she'd feel about being intimate.

Grace arched away from him, her head thrown back, and her hands resting on his knees. Logan took his time, sucking and nibbling on each breast, worshipping her new tattoo with his eyes and his fingers. She squirmed in his lap, obviously loving what he was doing to her.

Grace moaned and moved a hand to the back of his head, pushing him harder into her. "Logan, please. Fuck me."

Knowing they'd never make it to the guest room, Logan reached between them and undid his jeans with one hand, not letting go of the nipple he was torturing with his mouth. It took a bit of maneuvering, but finally his cock sprang free from its confines.

He hooked his index finger in the gusset of Grace's pink cotton panties, pulling it to the side, exposing her glistening folds and urged her upward.

"You fuck *me*, Grace. Go on, take what you want. What we both need."

And she did.

It was as if his words set her free. She reached down and grabbed hold of his dick, wrapping her hand around it and caressing it from root to tip, then back down, smearing his pre-come along his length.

Then she grabbed the base and held him steady as she notched the purple-mushroomed head to herself and slammed down on him in one quick motion.

Logan didn't know where her moan started and his ended. All he knew was the tight, wet feel of her pussy contracting around his hard length felt so good, it was almost painful. He'd been afraid that she wasn't ready for him, but he shouldn't have been.

She was dripping, and as she pulled up then pushed down on him, Logan felt her juices coating his cock and dripping onto his balls. This wasn't going to be a nice, polite coupling. It was going to be a raunchy, messy fuck. And it was perfect.

Grace rode him as if her life depended on it. Her hands rested on his shoulders for balance, her head was thrown back and she moved both up and down and forward and backward on his lap, making sure her clit came into maximum contact with his cock on every downstroke.

He might've felt used if it wasn't for the nonstop praise and love coming from her mouth.

"Logan. God, you feel so good. I love you so much. I had no idea it could be this good. Fuck, yeah."

Logan was breathing as hard as she was but didn't even notice. His hands were clamped onto her hips, encouraging her to move faster on him. He leaned forward, biting the side of her tit next to the bird tattoo as it bounced up and down along with her movements. It really did look as if the bird was taking flight, just as he'd fantasized.

Logan finally drew back when he felt Grace's thighs begin to tremble. He knew her orgasm was close. Logan looked down at where they were connected, and moved his right hand to her clit, pushing her panties to the side and seeing the tattoo on her hip for the first time. These birds were smaller than the one on the side of her breast, but their impact on him was no less potent. There were two tiny birds on her left hip in black ink. Their wings were open as if in flight, and their beaks were open as if they were singing.

"The one on the right represents you and the one on the left is me," Grace said breathlessly, seeing where his eyes were. "It looks like they're singing until you use a black light, then you can see what they're holding in their mouths. Mine is holding an L and yours is holding a G."

"Fuck me," Logan breathed. "They're beautiful. *You're* beautiful. And mine. Come for me, Smarty," he encouraged, using his thumb to flick over Grace's clit.

Logan kept his thumb on her clit as she screamed out her release, undulating on his lap, her orgasm forcing his own. He held himself still inside her as both their bodies twitched.

She jerked in his arms once more as his thumb swiped over the sensitive bundle of nerves a last time, then collapsed onto his chest, breathing hard, as if she'd run a five-minute mile. Logan buried his nose in her neck, her hair covering his face, making him feel as though they were the only two people on the planet.

"I love you, Smarty. Will you marry me?" Logan hadn't planned the words, but he realized at that moment that he wanted nothing more than for her to become Grace Anderson. Ace would've been proud to have Grace as a daughter-in-law, and Logan knew his brothers would embrace having her as a sister.

Grace rolled her head back and looked up at him with a sated, almost drugged look. She bit her lip as her eyes filled with tears. She took a deep breath and nodded. "There's *nothing* I want more than to spend the rest of my life with you, Logan."

They both smiled and their lips met in a gentle, life-affirming kiss. There were still a lot of unknowns in their lives, but those could be worked out. The most important thing was that they loved each other.

Love overcomes evil.

Every time.

Chapter Twenty-Seven

One morning, weeks after she'd been kidnapped, Logan received a phone call. Grace heard only his side of the conversation, but it sounded like something was finally happening in the case.

"Hello? Hey, what's up? Really? This morning? Where? That's good. I'll see what she thinks. Appreciate the heads-up. Later."

"Who was that?" Grace asked eagerly as soon as he hung up. "Something's happening?"

Logan came over and sat on the small couch next to her, putting his hand on the nape of her neck, his thumb caressing her tattoo as he often did. He told her, "The arrest warrants were signed today. The police will be going to pick up your parents for kidnapping, extortion, blackmail, and several other charges stemming from their shoddy business practices."

Grace breathed a sigh of relief and clutched his biceps. "So it's over?"

"Yeah, Smarty. It's over."

"We can go home?"

A huge smile broke out on Logan's face. "We can go home," he confirmed.

Grace threw herself into Logan's arms and hugged him as tightly as she could. "Thank God. I don't mind staying up here in Denver, but I can't wait to get back into a real home."

"I'm not sure I'd call my condo a 'real home,' Smarty."

"You know what I mean," Grace said, pulling back and looking at him.

"Yeah, but I've been thinking about it. You deserve a home that's better than a cheap condo. What would you say to going house hunting with me?"

Her eyes sparkled with joy. "Really?"

"Really."

"Yes! Of course, yes!"

"Before you get too excited, I need to ask you a question. It's about today," Logan told her gently.

Grace's enthusiasm ebbed, but she still said lightly, "Shoot."

"Do you want to be there when your parents are arrested? I don't mean *right* there, but from a safe distance. Do you want to see it go down?"

Grace bit her lip in indecision. One part of her never wanted to see either of her parents again. They'd caused her enough heartache to last a lifetime. But on the other hand, seeing them arrested might bring her some closure. "Where would I be, and how is it going to happen?" she asked quietly.

"The police and FBI will be going to their house this morning. If it goes as planned, it'll be fast and easy. I don't really see your parents as the type to engage in a shoot-out, but there's always a possibility they'll resist arrest, especially considering how many years they're looking at behind bars.

"As for where you would be . . . with me. Blake's gotten to know one of the lead detectives on the case, and he said we could sit in his car while it went down. We'd be far enough away to be safe, but close enough that you could still see what was happening."

"You'd be with me?" Grace asked, eyes wide, seeking confirmation.

"Of course," Logan told her with conviction. "I wouldn't leave your side."

"Then yes. I want to see the moment they realize that what they've done has consequences. They've lived their entire lives doing whatever they want without anyone saying or doing anything about it. And if someone *did* manage to try to stop them, they just threatened them in some way. So yeah, I'm ready to move on to the next phase of our life together."

"If at any point you get uncomfortable and want to leave, all you have to do is say the word. Got it?"

Grace nodded. "Got it." She paused, then grinned, "Can we stop and talk to a real estate agent afterward?"

Logan put his head back and roared with laughter before hugging Grace to him once more. "I love that you can go from talking about watching your parents get arrested for making your life a living hell to wanting to get the rest of your life started without even blinking."

"How much time do we have before it goes down?" Grace asked, her head still tucked into Logan's neck, running her hands down his back and into the sweats he was wearing.

He groaned and pulled back. "Time enough for a quick shower."

"We should conserve water," Grace said playfully, moving one hand around to the front of his pants. He immediately grew hard under her intimate caress.

"Oh yeah, we need to do our part for the environment," Logan choked out.

Grace gave him one last caress and stood, taking off her T-shirt as she did. "Last one in is a rotten egg." She threw her shirt at him and speed-walked toward the bathroom, laughing.

Two and a half hours later, Grace watched as her parents were led out of their house in handcuffs to the waiting squad cars and reflected on the last few months. How she'd gone from feeling totally alone and depressed to feeling completely free. And loved.

Logan sat next to her, his arm around her waist, his chin resting on her shoulder as they watched the spectacle in front of them. Grace could feel his warmth all along her back and side, and even though she could see the hate and bitterness in both Margaret's and Walter's eyes, it didn't affect her at all.

She felt nothing toward the people who'd raised her.

All her feelings were wrapped up in the man behind her and the windfalls he'd brought into her life.

Turning away from the view of an officer putting his hand on top of her mother's head as she went to sit in the backseat of a squad car like the criminal she was, Grace looked up at Logan. "I think we need a house with at least four bedrooms."

"Four bedrooms, huh?" Logan asked with a small smile. "Any particular reason?"

"I hope you want kids," Grace whispered, kissing the skin under his ear.

"I want kids," Logan confirmed, then shifted until his mouth was over hers.

They sat in the backseat of a Castle Rock Police detective's car and didn't even notice when Margaret and Walter Mason were driven away to spend what would probably end up being the rest of their lives behind bars.

Chapter Twenty-Eight

The Denver Post

The sensational three-month trial of Margaret Mason, CEO of Mason Architectural Firm, and a leading member of the Castle Rock community, came to a conclusion late last night with the jury finding her guilty of all charges, including extortion, blackmail, and kidnapping. Her husband, Walter Mason, had been found guilty last month of the same crimes.

Many experts agree that the testimony that sealed her fate came from her daughter, Grace, who detailed years of emotional and mental abuse at the hands of her parents.

The sentencing will take place next week, where the judge is expected to give Margaret Mason the harshest penalty possible . . . up to twenty years to life with no possibility of parole.

Turn to page four for an exclusive interview with Brian and Betty Grant.

"Are you sure you want to do this?" Logan asked Grace for what seemed like the millionth time as they neared the county jail in Denver where her mother was being held before the sentencing hearing.

"I'm sure. I need to. I want her to know that as hard as she tried to keep us apart, everything she did since I was sixteen was for naught." She held up her hand and the diamond resting on her ring finger glittered in the sunlight. "This is going to upset her so badly, I can't wait."

"I never knew you had this evil side," Logan told her, grabbing her hand and kissing his ring on her finger.

"And I have one more surprise for her as well."

One of Logan's eyebrows lifted in question.

"You'll see. Trust me."

"Of course. Come on, let's get this over with. I have the rest of the afternoon off, and I can think of much better things to do to pass the time."

"I thought you had to go to Pueblo for a thing."

Logan shrugged, and a smirk cracked over his face. "Blake and Alexis are taking care of it for me."

"What's with them anyway?" Grace asked.

"No clue. I thought Blake was gonna choke her there for a while, but as it turns out, she's actually pretty helpful. He took her on as a sort-of intern, and so far, it's working out."

"Are they . . . together?"

"Blake and Alexis?" Logan asked as if horrified. "No. She's *so* not his type."

"I wasn't your type either."

"Wrong. You were always perfect for me," he retorted and kissed her quickly. "The bottom line is that we have the afternoon free. So let's go rub your mother's nose in how happy we are, then get on with living that happy life. Yeah?"

They walked hand in hand into the jail, signed in, went through the metal detectors. Then they were led to a room that looked like a stereotypical visiting room in a prison. Plexiglas separated the visitor from the prisoner and there was a phone hanging on either side of the partition.

Grace was a bit nervous about the meeting, but having Logan at her side gave her the strength she needed to not take anything her mother said to heart. Logan agreed to let Grace take the lead. He said as long as her mother didn't try to emotionally manipulate her, he'd let her have her say. But the second she said something hurtful to her daughter, he'd take over and they'd be done.

That was fine with Grace.

Margaret Mason was led into the small room by a large, muscular guard. She looked awful, at least twenty years older. Without her fancy clothes and makeup, her true age and her ugly soul were easy to see. The guard removed her shackles and pointed to the cubicle where she was to sit. As if she was at a grand party, her mother strutted over to the chair and sat with all the decorum of sitting at a fancy dining table. She reached for the phone and Grace did the same.

"Grace, how nice of you to come and see your poor mother after all this time. Still slumming it, I see."

The barb didn't even faze Grace; she'd known it was coming. "Mother. I hope you're enjoying your stay."

Margaret glared at her daughter through the Plexiglas. "Was there something you wanted?"

"Yes. I wanted to tell you that you failed. You tried so hard to keep me and Logan apart, but it didn't work. We were meant to be together, and you can't mess with something like that. It doesn't matter that you hid his letters from me. It doesn't matter that you tried to make me emotionally crippled. You didn't. And I win."

Her mother scowled, then leaned forward and hissed, "I knew from the moment I found out I was pregnant that you'd end up ruining my life. I should've killed you before you ever took your first breath. You were never good enough to have the Mason name. Never."

Grace held up her left hand, making sure her mother saw the huge diamond that rested on her ring finger. "All I ever wanted was for you to be proud of me, Mother. I lived for the times when you would smile or say something nice. And you knew it. You manipulated me and kept me tied to you and Father with your emotional games. No decent and sane person does that to their child. I don't understand it and I never will. But I don't care anymore. I have Logan, his brothers, Felicity, and Cole to stand by my side, and I'm happy. For the first time in my life, I'm truly happy. Next week when the judge sentences you, we'll be getting married. All your scheming and threats were for nothing. I'm going to be Mrs. Grace Anderson, and there's absolutely nothing you and Father can do about it."

Mrs. Mason turned bright red as she listened to her daughter.

"Oh, and one more thing you should know." Grace turned to Logan and put her hand on his cheek. She spoke to him, knowing her mother could still hear her. "I'm pregnant."

Logan's eyes lit up. Grace leaned up and kissed him. A long, slow, carnal kiss that would've embarrassed her if she cared one whit what her mother thought of her anymore.

She pulled back, kept her hand on Logan's face, and turned to her mother again. "It's a boy. Actually two. We're having twins."

The look of absolute fury that came over Margaret Mason's face was priceless. She slammed down the phone and stood up abruptly, knocking over the chair behind her. Grace caught a glimpse of the guard hurrying to her side to grab her arm before Grace felt Logan's hand firmly under her chin, pulling her face back to his.

"You're serious? You aren't just saying that to piss off your mother?"

"I'm serious. I'm sorry you heard about it this way, but I just found out yesterday. I didn't mean to keep it from you, but I wanted to be sure. Since multiples run in your family, I can't say I'm too surprised by the results of the ultrasound. In about six and a half months, you're going to be a father."

"Fuck, I love you." Logan kissed, then pulled her into his chest, squeezing her hard.

Grace laughed and wiggled in his grip. "Come on, let's get out of here. I believe you said you had the afternoon off?"

Margaret Mason already forgotten, Logan didn't answer and merely pulled her up from the chair, hung up the phone that Grace had dropped when he'd hugged her, and headed for the door.

Grace couldn't stop smiling as Logan walked impatiently toward his truck, her hand tucked firmly in his. When they left the jail and headed west instead of south to Castle Rock, she asked, "Where are we going?"

"The Four Seasons. There's no way I'll last the thirty minutes it'll take to get home to Castle Rock with you sitting next to me and my babies inside you. I have to have you or I'll lose my mind."

"Really?" Grace squeaked in a high-pitched, excited tone. "I've never been there before!"

Logan chuckled. "You sound more excited about seeing the fancy hotel than getting naked with me."

At his words, her nipples peaked. Even after all this time and every-thing they'd done together, he could still arouse her with mere words. And the thought of what Logan could, and would, do to her, made her squirm in her seat and her nipples ache.

She figured it was the pregnancy, but her breasts had become extremely sensitive. Another side effect was that she was horny as hell and needed Logan more than ever. So checking into a hotel for a few hours of hot, kinky sex was *more* than all right with her.

"Oh, I'm excited about staying at the Four Seasons, but if it was a contest, you'd win hands down every time." She picked up Logan's hand and kissed the two large pink birds on his forearm. He'd had them inked just like he'd said he would. But he'd done more than just inked the two birds. He'd had the artist add an entire tree around the birds in the special ink. And in the trunk of the tree, right below the two pink birds, was a heart with their initials inside. It was beautiful, and all theirs.

"I love you, Logan Anderson. If given the chance to live my life over again, I wouldn't change one thing. I'd go through it all again, every bit of it, if it meant I ended up right here, with you."

Logan looked over at her, and she saw the love shining in his eyes. For her. He put his hand over her slightly swollen belly and said in a reverent voice, "I dreamed I'd someday find a woman who loved me for who I am and maybe have a family, but I never, ever thought I'd have a second chance with you. You've made me the happiest man alive, Smarty."

"Shut up and drive, Logan. You need to take care of your horny wife."

"Yes, ma'am." He kept his hand on her stomach, smiling as Grace put her own hand on top of his and intertwined their fingers. "I fucking love you so much, Grace. Thank you for forgiving me. Thank you for believing in me. Thank you for giving me a second chance."

Four hours later, as Grace was soaking in the large Jacuzzi tub, Logan picked up his phone and dialed his brother.

"Blake here."

"Hey, it's Logan."

"What's up? How'd the visit go?"

"Grace told me she's pregnant with my twin sons."

"Holy shit," Blake breathed. "Seriously?"

"Yes."

"Congratulations. Fuck, that's awesome. Where are you?" Blake asked.

"Not home. We'll be staying the night up here in Denver tonight. Tomorrow we have an appointment with her doctor so I can see the ultrasound and hear my sons' heartbeats for the first time."

"Got it. Have fun with your fiancée," Blake told his brother happily.

"I always do." They both chuckled, then Logan said, "I'll be in the office tomorrow, but not until later."

"Grace too?"

"Yeah. She's already learned so much from her marketing classes and wants to redo our website completely and put up a Facebook page. She muttered something about pixels and web traffic and targeted ads. It all went over my head, but if it makes her happy and helps the business, I'm all for it."

"You're a lucky son of a bitch, bro. I'm extremely happy for you."

"Thanks. Your time is coming."

"Oh no. No matchmaking. Just because you found your high school crush, and it all worked out, doesn't mean we all want to be tied down."

"Whatever."

"What does that mean?"

"Nothing. I'll see you tomorrow, yeah?"

"Fine. Later."

Logan hung up the phone and smiled thinking about the mother-to-be waiting for him to join her in the tub. Grace had mentioned something about trying wall sex before she got too big for him to pick up.

He strode toward the bathroom, shedding the towel around his waist as he went. Standing in the doorway, looking down at the most beautiful woman he'd ever seen, Logan thanked God for the goodness in his life. Lord knew he didn't really deserve it, but he wasn't looking a gift horse in the mouth. His life couldn't be better, and he would hold on to their happiness with everything he had.

~

"Was that Logan?" Alexis asked from the desk across from Blake.

"Yeah. He and Grace are spending the night up in Denver tonight. They'll be in tomorrow."

"Cool. Hey, I was looking over the notes from her parents' case and something's bothering me."

Blake looked over at Alexis. He hadn't really thought he'd like her much. She was a couple of years younger than him, for one thing, and he usually went for older, more experienced chicks, but Alexis had grown on him. She was smart, she'd picked up the basics of being an investigator really quickly, and she certainly wasn't hard on the eyes.

It was difficult to admit, considering his initial reluctance about her involvement with the Mason case, but he enjoyed spending time with her.

Realizing she was looking at him expectantly, he said, "What's that?"

"The gang member that the Masons hired to take those awful pictures with Grace and my brother . . ." her voice trailed off uncertainly.

"What about him?" Blake asked.

"The gang he's with, the Inca Boyz . . . I'm thinking this gang is bad news. I know that's not exactly a revelation. They've been on the Denver PD's radar for years. But with their leader, Donovan, behind bars for what he did to Brad and Grace, at least for a few months, maybe we can look more into these guys and see what else they've been up to."

"You don't think we have enough on our plates with the security escorts and investigations? It's been both a blessing and a curse that Ace Security has gotten so much media attention after Grace's ordeal. I'm not sure we have the time to look into a gang up in Denver just for the fun of it," Blake told Alexis, "especially when the Denver Gang Task Force hasn't found what they need to bring it down."

When she opened her mouth to argue with him, he held up his hand to stop her. "With that being said . . . I agree. It doesn't sit well with me either that Margaret was able to so easily get in contact with them and hire them to do her dirty work. Who knows how many other Margarets are out there hiring them."

"So . . . I can look into them?" Alexis asked. Then added, "Discreetly, of course."

Blake nodded. "Yeah. *Discreetly*, Alexis. The last thing we need is them getting wind that you're looking into their shit and deciding to come after you."

"They'll never know. Cross my heart," Alexis swore, using her finger to draw an imaginary *X* across her chest.

Acknowledgments

Thank you to Maria Gomez at Montlake for your encouragement and belief in me . . . even before you read a word of my story. I appreciate your support and am thrilled for the opportunity to take this journey.

Another huge thank-you to all my readers. Seriously, I couldn't write nearly as many stories without your support. Thank you for letting me write damsel-in-distress stories . . . my way.

And I would be remiss if I didn't give a shout-out to my family. From my dad, who had my very first story hardback bound years before I thought I'd give this whole "author thing" a try, to my mom, who buys all my books . . . even if she can't stand the hero and thinks he's a male chauvinist pig, and of course, to Mr. Stoker—without his support I couldn't do any of this. Thank you.

About the Author

 Susan Stoker is a *New York Times*, *USA Today*, and *Wall Street Journal* bestselling author whose series include Badge of Honor: Texas Heroes, SEAL of Protection, and Delta Force Heroes. Married to a retired Army noncommissioned officer, Stoker has lived all over the country— from Missouri to California to Colorado—and currently lives under the big skies of Texas. A true believer in the happily ever after, Stoker enjoys writing novels in which romance turns to love.

To learn more about the author and her work, visit her website, www.stokeraces.com, or find her on Facebook at www.facebook.com/authorsusanstoker.

Connect with Susan Online:

SUSAN'S FACEBOOK PROFILE AND PAGE:

www.facebook.com/authorsstoker

www.facebook.com/authorsusanstoker

FOLLOW SUSAN ON TWITTER:

www.twitter.com/Susan_Stoker

FIND SUSAN'S BOOKS ON GOODREADS

www.goodreads.com/SusanStoker

EMAIL:

Susan@StokerAces.com

WEBSITE:

www.StokerAces.com